Dear Diary,

Honestly, if  *es any more successf* ... *new staff. I'm not* ... *ed we'd be this popula* ... *though. Our teenage aide, Amy Tidwell, has been showing up for work late and seems so tired all the time. Alexandra and I think Hannah should talk to her about this, since they're so close. Amy's such a great girl, and wonderful with the kids, so I don't want to lose her. Especially not with our numbers growing.*

We just had two more children sign up—little Becca and her brother, Noah. Actually, it was a favor to Alexandra's cousin Brad. Somehow he's become involved with their guardian, Danielle O'Malley.

Now, there's a combination—a hunky cowboy and a beautiful, high-flying ad executive. It sounds crazy, but Alexandra says the two of them are meant for each other. She's just worried that after what Brad's ex-fiancée did to him, he's become wary of women, and Danielle has to be in shock at finding herself with a ready-made family overnight.

They're both so good with kids, though, and you don't have to look too close to see they're falling in love. I sure hope they don't pass up what seems like a real chance at happiness. After all, love doesn't come along every day.

Till tomorrow, Katherine

KATE HOFFMANN

began reading romance fiction in 1979 when she picked up a Kathleen Woodiwiss novel. She was immediately hooked, and read the book from cover to cover in one very long night. Nearly ten years later, after a history of interesting jobs in teaching, retail, nonprofit work and advertising, Kate decided to try writing a romance of her own. Her first book was published in 1993 by Harlequin Temptation. Since then, Kate has written more than thirty books for Harlequin, including Temptation and Duets novels, continuity series and anthologies. Kate lives in a picturesque village in southeastern Wisconsin in a cozy little house with three cats and a computer. When she's not writing, she enjoys gardening, golfing and genealogy.

FORRESTER SQUARE
LEGACIES . LIES . LOVE .

KATE HOFFMANN
ALL SHE NEEDED

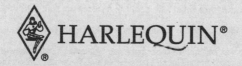

HARLEQUIN®

TORONTO • NEW YORK • LONDON
AMSTERDAM • PARIS • SYDNEY • HAMBURG
STOCKHOLM • ATHENS • TOKYO • MILAN • MADRID
PRAGUE • WARSAW • BUDAPEST • AUCKLAND

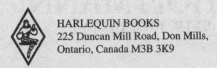

HARLEQUIN BOOKS
225 Duncan Mill Road, Don Mills,
Ontario, Canada M3B 3K9

ISBN 0-373-61270-2

ALL SHE NEEDED

Kate Hoffmann is acknowledged as the author of this work.

Copyright © 2003 by Harlequin Books S.A.

Visit us at www.eHarlequin.com

Printed in U.S.A.

Dear Reader,

Welcome to Forrester Square—or my little corner of it! It's been great fun to participate in this project. Most readers know me from my Harlequin Temptation novels, but writing for a continuity series like FORRESTER SQUARE gives me a chance to write a different kind of story and to travel to a new spot on the map, Seattle.

In *All She Needed*, Danielle O'Malley gets just that— the unexpected arrival of three children. Oh, yes, and a handsome cowboy named Brad Cullen. Kids and a cowboy—not my usual cast of characters, but I was curious to see what happened once I put them together on the pages of a manuscript. So I started writing, and Danielle's ready-made family began to come together. And a focused and determined businesswoman learned some important lessons about life and love.

I hope you enjoy reading *All She Needed* as much as I enjoyed writing it. And to learn more about all my releases from Harlequin, visit my Web site at www.katehoffmann.com.

Happy reading!

Kate Hoffmann

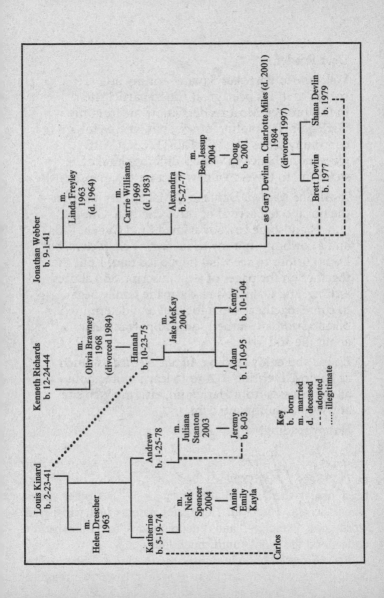

Kenneth Richards
b. 12-24-44

Jonathan Webber
b. 9-1-41

m.
Linda Freyley
1963
(d. 1964)

m.
Carrie Williams
1969
(d. 1983)

Alexandra
b. 5-27-77

m.
Ben Jessup
2004

Doug
b. 2001

as Gary Devlin m. Charlotte Miles (d. 2001)
1984
(divorced 1997)

Brett Devlin
b. 1977

Shana Devlin
b. 1979

m.
Olivia Brawney
1968
(divorced 1984)

Hannah
b. 10-23-75

m.
Jake McKay
2004

Adam
b. 1-10-95

Kenny
b. 10-1-04

Louis Kinard
b. 2-23-41

m.
Helen Drescher
1963

Andrew
b. 1-25-78

m.
Juliana
Stanton
2003

Jeremy
b. 8-03

Katherine
b. 5-19-74

m.
Nick
Spencer
2004

Annie   Emily   Kayla

Carlos

Key
b. born
m. married
d. deceased
- - - adopted
...... illegitimate

PROLOGUE

"DANI, DANI, sittin' on her fanny, she's so ugly, she'll never catch a manny."

A few more voices joined in the chorus until the sound of the chant filled Danielle O'Malley's ears. Anger bubbled up inside of her, obliterating the initial hurt she felt at their taunts. She had experienced cruelty before but had thought it might finally stop once she got to junior high.

It had been like this for her for as long as she could remember. Shuffled from foster home to foster home, she'd always struggled to fit in, and this school hadn't been any different. It didn't help that her clothes were a bit ragged or that she never had the benefit of a stylish haircut. Most of the foster parents she'd been placed with had enough to do to keep food on the table and shoes on her feet. Jewelled barrettes and cool clothes just weren't in the budget.

Though she'd once tried to be optimistic, she'd learned to lower her expectations. She just wasn't one of the lucky ones. She'd been taken from her single mother when she was six, and placed in foster care. Dani couldn't remember much of her life with Marly O'Malley, only that there had been times when her mother was happy and other times when she was very sad. Her foster parents had whispered words like "suicide" and "depression," but Dani hadn't understood the words until much later.

She did remember one thing from that time. She remembered crying when the social worker told her that her mother had died. It had been the last time she'd shed tears in front of another human being. Tears were a sign of weakness, and even at the young age of six, Dani knew she couldn't allow anyone to see how vulnerable she really was. She was on her own and she had to put on a tough front.

"Dani, Dani, sittin' on her fanny, she's so ugly, she'll never find a manny."

Dani clenched her fingers into a fist. With a low growl, she scrambled to her feet and launched herself at the instigator of the teasing. Ashley Kaplin's face showed a flicker of shock the moment before Dani's fist connected with her pert little nose. They both tumbled onto the dusty playground in a flurry of flailing arms and kicking legs. Dani was able to land a few more good punches before the playground aide dragged her off Ashley.

Dried grass clung to Ashley's hair, and her perfect outfit was now marked with dirt. A tickle of blood ran from her nose to her pouty mouth. Dani felt a surge of satisfaction that she'd been able to draw blood. Maybe now, Ashley and her gang would think twice before they teased Dani O'Malley.

"What do you two think you're doing?" the aide demanded. "This is no way for young ladies to act!"

"She just attacked me for no reason," Ashley whined, forcing a few tears to trickle down her cheeks. "I was just standing here, minding my own business, and she jumped on top of me." She flipped her blond hair over her shoulder. "She's jealous of me because I wear nice clothes and have pretty things."

"It's true," one of Ashley's cronies piped in. "We weren't doing anything and she just punched her."

The aide glanced down at Dani. "What do you have to say for yourself?"

Dani tipped her chin up defiantly and leveled her gaze at

Ashley. But she refused to make excuses. "I hit her. Three times. And I'll hit her again if she comes near me," she warned. "I'll beat the living crap out of her."

The aide grabbed Dani's arm and drew her along to the playground fence, to the spot where all the rowdies and outcasts were banished. "Sit here until recess is over. And after the bell rings, I want you to report to Mrs. Lang's office. She'll decide your punishment."

Dani refused to do as she was told. Instead, she stood, her fingers wrapped in the chainlink, her expression defiant. The aide shook her head and walked away. The instant she was alone, Dani felt tears push at the corners of her eyes. She'd thought maybe this time it would be different. Maybe this time, she'd fit in. Biting the inside of her bottom lip, she focused on the pain, willing the tears away.

"I'm glad you punched her."

Glancing to her left, Dani saw a frail-looking girl sitting on the ground just a few feet away, her knees tucked up beneath her plaid pleated skirt. She smiled, revealing a mouth full of braces.

"I've dreamed about decking her," the girl continued, brushing her dark bangs out of her eyes. "She can be such a snot. And all those girls do whatever she says. I'm pretty sure they share a brain, because not one of them thinks for themselves." She pushed to her feet, the effort causing a flush to rise to her cheeks. "I'm Evie Marshall."

She held out her hand and Dani wasn't sure what to do. Was she expected to shake it? "I'm Dani. Danielle O'Malley."

"I know. You sit next to me in history and math."

Dani hadn't remembered her. "I—I didn't—"

"Notice? The story of my life," Evie joked, the two spots of color in her cheeks blazing against her too-pale complexion. "I could walk down the halls of Walker Junior High stark naked and no one would notice."

"That's not true," Dani said. "I'd notice. And I'm sure Ashley would have a few things to say."

"Oh, she doesn't tease me," Evie said.

Dani felt her defenses rise again. "Why? Are you her friend or something?"

Evie shook her head, her wispy hair falling back into her eyes. "They don't tease me because I'm sick. Or at least I was sick."

"What was wrong with you?"

"I had cancer. A tumor in my brain." She tipped her head down and pointed to a scar that ran across the top of her head. "Everyone is supposed to be nice to me, but they mostly just ignore me."

"I wish they'd ignore me," Dani muttered, kicking her heel back against the chainlink fence.

Evie glanced up at her through her ragged bangs. "No you don't. It's terrible to be ignored. I just wish I had one friend. Then it wouldn't be so bad to come to school."

"You don't have any friends?"

"Everyone is afraid I'm going to die on them so they stay away. Or maybe they think cancer is contagious."

Dani sighed and pushed at a pebble with the toe of her scuffed loafer. She wanted someone to confide in so bad, but it was hard to know whom to trust. She swallowed hard and forced a smile. Maybe she could trust Evie Marshall. After all, they shared at least one thing in common. "I don't have any friends, either," Dani admitted. "Not that I need any. I'm always moving, so it's not worth making friends anyway."

"Why do you move?" Evie asked.

"I'm a foster kid. Usually they ask to have me sent somewhere else. I heard my social worker talking once. She said

I have a lot of attachment issues. I figure if I don't let anyone like me, then it won't be so hard when I have to leave.''

"Why don't you live with your folks?''

"I don't know my dad. And my mom died a few years ago.''

"So you're like an orphan.'' Evie nodded, as if she understood. "We could be friends,'' she said softly. "I mean, if you want to. I'll try not to like you too much if you try not to think that I'm going to die.''

Dani's heart leapt. A friend! No one had ever offered to be her friend before. And even though Evie was a little sickly, she dressed nicely and her hair was fixed pretty. It was obvious her parents cared about her. Dani's excitement faded. A girl like Evie could never be her friend. They were from different worlds. Sooner or later she'd realize the kind of girl Dani was. She'd been called all sorts of names, most of them a lot worse than what Ashley Kaplin could dream up. "I don't know,'' she muttered. "I'm not really looking for any friends right now.''

Evie's hopeful expression fell and disappointment filled her eyes. "I understand,'' she said. She drew a ragged breath. "I'm not going to die. My doctors say I'm in remission.''

Dani instantly regretted her refusal. Evie needed a friend a lot more than she did. Maybe she ought to give it a try. After all, what did she have to lose? As long as she didn't depend on Evie, then everything would be all right. When it came time to leave, she could say goodbye without any regrets. "I guess if you really want to be friends, we could. That is, until you find someone else who wants to be your friend.''

"I would never, ever do that,'' Evie said, her brown eyes wide and honest. "I'm not like Ashley. She changes friends like she changes those stupid hair ribbons she wears. She has a different best friend every day. You and me will always be best friends—forever and ever.''

Though Dani wanted to believe Evie, she knew better. No one stayed friends forever. Something always happened. But now that she had a friend, maybe she could work a little harder at pleasing her foster parents. She'd try not to be so prickly. And she'd offer to help around the house. And maybe, she'd even put a little more effort into her school work.

Portland might not be such a bad place to live after all.

CHAPTER ONE

"QUEEN ANNE HILL," Danielle O'Malley shouted to the driver on the other side of the Plexiglas partition. "Olympic Place. And step on it. I'm in a hurry."

She settled back and watched the familiar scenery fly by as the cab headed from Sea-Tac into Seattle. The day had started out sunny and warm in L.A., where she'd been on a business trip for the past two weeks. After a short client meeting, she'd cabbed it out to the airport and things had gone downhill from there. Her first flight had been canceled. She rebooked on a second flight, but got bumped at the last minute. By the time she boarded, she'd been in the airport for five hours. She was ready for a long bath and a good night's sleep.

Unfortunately, sleep would have to wait. She'd scheduled a Friday-night business dinner with a potential client, thinking she'd have the entire afternoon to get ready.

Nabbing Jason Wentland as a client would certainly be a coup, Dani mused. In fact, she'd taken to calling him her "six-million-dollar-man"—that's what his account was worth. If she could lure Wentland Software over to Bennett Marks Advertising, she was almost certain she'd be offered a vice presidency by the end of the year. A vice presidency and the financial security that came with it would finally make her happy—or would it?

Dani leaned her head back and closed her eyes. She'd been on her own since she'd turned eighteen. The foster care system didn't provide for a college education, so she'd worked her way through a business program at the University of Oregon, at the same time cultivating a totally new life.

She'd studied fashion magazines and business manuals, saved her pennies for expensive clothes and exclusive hairstylists, and learned to exude wealth and success. She'd put her childhood far behind her and projected a brand new facade. Not one of her acquaintances, personal or professional, knew the whole truth about her past—except for Evie Marshall.

Evie had always believed Dani would make a success of herself. In truth, Evie had been the only one who'd had faith, and Dani had done her best to prove her right. When Dani wondered where the money would come from for her tuition, Evie would magically appear with a check, drawn from the inheritance her elderly parents had left her. And when Dani finally had the chance to repay her, Evie had refused to take the money. "That's what best friends are for," she'd said. "Someday, maybe I'll need a favor."

Evie needed more than a favor right now. Since they'd graduated from high school, the two of them had moved in different directions. Evie had married her high school sweetheart, John Gregory, and promptly produced three adorable children, while Dani had chosen college and career over a happy family life. She'd been determined to make as much money as she could, as fast as she could. Security—that's all Dani wanted. The knowledge that she would never be dependent on another person the way she'd been forced to be when she was a child.

Dani had been lucky in her career, lucky for the first time in her life. But Evie wasn't faring as well. There was a time when Dani had envied everything that Evie had—her pretty clothes, her comfortable home, her doting parents, even her illness, which had made her a teacher's pet. But now it seemed as though their fortunes had shifted. Five years ago, Evie's elderly parents had passed away, her mother just six months after her father. Two years ago, Evie's husband had been killed in a car crash. And a year ago, Evie's cancer had returned.

Just last month Dani had driven to Portland to see her best friend, to reassure herself that Evie would make it through the chemo and radiation. As always, Evie chose to look at things positively. She promised Dani that she was going to beat the cancer the same way she had when she was eleven, and Dani believed her. She couldn't face the fact that she might lose Evie. Evie had become the sister she'd never had, the mother who watched over her and the friend who was always there.

Dani rubbed her fingertips against her temples, trying to ease the tension. She'd call Evie first thing tomorrow and catch up. Right now, she had business obligations to occupy her thoughts and couldn't afford to be distracted by personal matters. Tonight, she had to keep her mind fixed squarely on Jason Wentland.

At least a million of Wentland's advertising budget would end up in her agency's coffers if she could manage to land the account. But there was an upside to not getting the account. If she didn't convince Wentland to sign on the dotted line, Dani had other plans for her "six-million-dollar man."

Jason Wentland was wealthy, well-educated and obsessed with his work...exactly the kind of man she found attractive. In addition, he was sophisticated and worldly, fitting perfectly into the world she'd created for herself. From the first time they met, there had been an unspoken attraction between them, an attraction strong enough to promise a wonderfully passionate affair. And an affair was all it would be, for Dani knew better than to depend on love.

Shrugging out of her jacket, she tossed it on the seat beside her, then opened her briefcase. She'd put all her notes on her Palm Pilot, and she now carefully reviewed the pitch she make. After that, she decided what she'd wear and how she'd fix her hair. And then she made a plan for how she'd reply to Jason's seductive smiles and flirty remarks, wondering how difficult it would be to avoid tumbling into bed with him. By the time the cab pulled up in front of her building, she'd regained a small measure of her energy.

Dani paid the cab driver and he dropped her bags beside her at the curb. With a groan, she hefted two weeks' worth of designer business suits and Italian shoes through the courtyard to the front door of her building. But when she reached into her purse for her keys, she couldn't seem to find them. With a soft curse, she pushed the button for the manager's apartment. Louie would let her in—he was always there in a pinch.

But the buzzer went unanswered. Dani set her bags down and frantically began to search through the numerous pockets on the outside of her tote. When her keys didn't turn up there, she opened the bag and started pulling her belongings out. "I know I put them in here," she muttered, tossing aside lacy lingerie and toiletries. This was all she needed. Her schedule was tight enough as it was.

She felt a drop of rain on her face and looked up at the sky. As it did so regularly in Seattle, the wind suddenly freshened and the skies opened up. Rain spattered on the concrete steps. A tiny gust caught a pair of her silk panties and she lunged out to grab them as they tumbled over the brick courtyard toward the bushes. But the toe of her pump snagged on the edge of a brick and she fell forward, her knee skidding over the rough surface.

Plunking down in a puddle, she examined the bloody

scrape through her torn panty hose. "Ow, ow, ow!" She fanned at her knee with her hand.

"Are you all right? Can I help you?"

A pair of scuffed cowboy boots had appeared in front of her, and her gaze slowly rose, up long legs clad in faded denim. But the owner of those legs was standing so close to her that when she reached his crotch, she was forced to stop or be caught staring. A strong, masculine hand appeared in front of her face and she silently accepted the offer of help.

Struggling to her feet, she controlled her fury at the cab driver, who'd taken her the long way home, at Louie, who had the audacity to be out of his apartment when she needed him, and at the Weather Channel, which never seemed to be able to predict the fickle weather in Seattle. "Thank you," she murmured, brushing her damp skirt and smoothing her hair back from her face. But her fingers froze in tangled strands the instant her gaze met his. Every ounce of breath left her lungs as she stared at the most startlingly handsome face she'd ever seen.

He possessed a near perfect profile, classic, the kind of face usually carved into Greek statues…a strong jaw…a straight nose. His hair, wet from the sudden rain, curled around his beard-roughened face, adding to his rugged good looks.

Dani blinked, raindrops clinging to her lashes and blurring her vision. She half expected him to disappear as quickly as he'd appeared, like some rainy day mirage. But he was still there, the crooked smile growing wider.

"That looks like a pretty nasty scrape," he said, squatting down to examine her knee. He pulled a bandana out of his pocket and dabbed at a trickle of blood. "Does it hurt?"

She swallowed hard. "Yes." She paused. "I mean, no. It's fine."

He blew on it, his breath cooling the sting and sending an unbidden shiver coursing through her body. "There. Is that better?"

He had absolutely no right to be so sexy—or to take such liberties with her knee, Dani mused. She was about to thank him and make her escape, when he rose to his feet. This time, when he held out his hand, a pair of her silk panties dangled from his index finger.

"I believe these are yours?"

She met his gaze again and saw amusement glittering in his green eyes as they dropped to her breasts. It was only then that she realized the rain had made her silk blouse nearly transparent. She plucked at the fabric, pulling it away from her skin. Then she reached out and snatched the panties from him, stuffing them in her bag. She was glad someone found her situation amusing!

"Can I give you a hand here?" he asked.

"No. Thank you. I can take care of this myself."

"You're standing in the pouring rain with underwear at your feet. Either you're some kind of street vendor or you need help."

She quickly bent down to retrieve a stray lace bra and two more pairs of panties. His insinuation that she couldn't solve a simple problem like rain-soaked underwear and a scraped knee stung more than her injury. She'd been taking care of herself since she was six years old and didn't need some urban cowboy riding to her rescue. "I've misplaced my keys," Dani explained. "And the lobby door is always locked and—"

"You live here?" he asked, handing her a bottle of shampoo.

Dani opened her mouth, ready to tell him that where she lived was none of his business. But she resisted the urge, knowing that her temper had been shortened by exhaustion.

Yes, he was incredibly attractive, and yes, he had beautiful green eyes. But it didn't take more than a few seconds to realize the guy wasn't her type.

Windswept hair and sun-burnished skin and faded denim didn't usually cause such a reaction. She was drawn to the more sophisticated end of the male spectrum—designer suits, silk ties, a man dripping with success. "I'm exhausted," she muttered to herself.

"Pardon me?"

"Nothing." In one last vain attempt, Dani searched the bottom of her overnight bag and thankfully found her keys. If she didn't get out of the rain and into the safety of her building, she might just sit down in the street and never get up. She held the keys up and jangled them. "You can be on your way now. I'll be fine."

"Let me help you," he insisted. He hoisted his backpack over his shoulder, then grabbed her garment bag and tote, his hand brushing against hers. The contact sent a tiny current shooting through her. Stunned by her reaction, she drew her hand away and pulled the door open. He gallantly grabbed the handle, holding it for her, then trailed her into the lobby.

"Thank you," Dani said. "I can get them from here."

He nodded, smiling down at her. "Well, it was nice to meet you." He chuckled softly. "Although we haven't been introduced, have we. I'm Brad Cullen."

She stared at his outstretched hand, knowing that if she touched him again she might spontaneously ignite in front of his eyes. Instead, she decided that a quick retreat was in order. "Thank you again." She waited for him to say his goodbyes and leave, but he continued to stand in front of her. "You can go now. I can carry my bags to my apartment."

"Actually, this is where I'm supposed to be," he said,

glancing around the well-appointed lobby. "A friend of mine lives in this building."

"Which apartment?" she asked as she pushed the button for the elevator.

"I don't know. Is there a directory?"

"Try the buzzers outside," she suggested as she pushed her luggage into the elevator. "Everyone has their name listed there." She turned to face him as the doors slowly closed, and for a heartbeat, she had the urge to step back out and continue her conversation with the handsome Mr. Cullen. But Dani knew better than to act on her urges. Her entire childhood had been riddled with ill-considered actions and undeniable regret. She'd put that kind of behavior behind her.

"Thanks again," she called.

With a soft sigh, she leaned back against the elevator wall and closed her eyes. She had more important things on her mind right now than a casual flirtation with a completely unsuitable cowboy wannabe. After all, her "six-million-dollar man" was waiting.

BRAD CULLEN stood in the hallway just off the elegant lobby, watching as the building manager—Louie, according to the patch on his workshirt—punched a number into his phone. He regarded Brad with a suspicious gaze. Hell, he couldn't blame the guy. After all, Brad didn't look much like a man who would have a friend in such a swanky place.

He wouldn't have expected anything less from his old college roommate, Tom Hopson. The building looked like it had been built in the early 1900s in the Beaux Arts—or maybe it was Neoclassical—style. Brad smiled to himself. He could never remember the differencc. Whatever it was, it still maintained an air of exclusivity. The lobby was ornately decorated with marble columns and elegant upholstered furniture and pretty silk flower arrangements.

He'd hoped to catch Tom in and maybe bunk on his sofa for a few days while he figured out his next move. But Louie the manager had coldly informed him that Mr. Hopson was visiting his mother in New York City.

Brad had considered walking out and finding a cheap motel room somewhere, but at the last moment, he asked Louie to call Tom. His rather spartan budget didn't include deluxe accommodations. After three months in the mountains, he was ready for civilization—good food, a soft bed, a little night life. And maybe a few attractive women to charm, above and beyond the woman he'd failed to impress on the sidewalk.

The thought of beautiful women brought him up short. The impulse was unfamiliar and unbidden. He hadn't thought of *any* woman but Josephine Millen in nearly six years. And since the first weekend in June, he'd been doing everything in his power to forget her. Brad drew a deep breath. But all that was over now. Maybe it was time to get back in the saddle.

"Mr. Hopson, this is Louie. No, no, your apartment hasn't burned down. No, there hasn't been an earthquake. I have a Mr. Brad Cullen here. He says he knows you."

It was pretty obvious what Louie thought, but Brad didn't care. Yes, Tom Hopson was gay. And Brad was as straight as an arrow. But they'd become friends when they'd been paired as roommates in their freshman dorm, a friendship cemented by their mutual love of rock-climbing. Their respective sex lives never seemed to interfere with their pursuit of difficult climbs. No doubt Louie assumed that Brad was one of Tom's "boyfriends," but he was too exhausted to try to disabuse him of the notion.

"Yes, Mr. Hopson." The manager paused, then reluctantly handed his phone to Brad. "He wants to talk to you."

Brad chuckled as he stepped into the manager's apartment. "Hey, buddy. I have to tell you, I'm insulted. The last time we spoke you said *mi casa es su casa.* And then I come all the way from Montana for a visit and you hightail it to Manhattan the moment you hear I'm in town."

"You said you'd be coming two weeks ago," Tom protested. "What was I supposed to do, hang next to the phone and wait for you to call? You're cute, cowboy, but not that cute."

"I know, I know. I'm not your type."

Tom's tone turned serious. "How are you doing?"

"Not bad. I've been doing some climbing. I did Rainier again. That's what hung me up. The weather was bad so I had to wait. I did it solo this time. It gave me a lot of time to think, and I'm thinking that getting jilted was probably the best thing that could have happened to me. Jo did me a favor. I wasn't ready to settle down."

"I thought you and Josephine were meant for each other. Your parents have been neighbors for years."

"I thought so, too. But I guess everyone was wrong." Brad sighed. Though he tried to sound flippant, the entire episode still stung. He'd thought he and Jo were meant to spend their lives together. He'd thought he had found true love. But he'd been fooled just like everyone else. "Hey, I was hoping you could put me up for a while. I'm not ready to head back to Split Rock quite yet. And I don't think my folks will track me down at your place. Besides, I want to touch base with my cousin, Alexandra Webber. She runs a daycare not too far from here. Can I bunk on your sofa?"

"No one sleeps on my sofa. It's upholstered in silk. You can sleep in the guest room. All I ask is that you water my plants and play with Mr. Whiskers."

"Mr. Whiskers?"

"My new cat. Right now he's being looked after by Louie, a cat sitter, and my neighbor across the hall, but I'm afraid of what I'll find when I get home. Mr. Whiskers gets bored easily and if he's left alone for too long, he tends to become a bit destructive. Just don't look him right in the eyes and you'll be fine."

"Thanks, buddy. I owe you one."

"Stick around for a while. Maybe we can do some climbing when I get back. Now, put Louie on the phone and let me square this with him."

Brad handed the phone to the building manger and waited while Tom talked to him. After Louie hung up the phone, he reached inside a drawer and pulled out a set of keys, then handed them to Brad. "Three-C," he said.

"My pickup is parked on the street," Brad told him.

"You can use Mr. Hopson's spot behind the building. He took his car to the airport. It's three spaces to the right of the back door."

Brad nodded, picked up his pack and started down the hall.

"And watch out for that cat," Louie called. "He's dangerous. I think he's part mountain lion. Mr. Hopson picked him up on one of his climbing trips."

"Thanks," Brad said. He strode to the elevator and pushed the button, then stepped inside.

He sure hoped the rest of Seattle's population was friendlier than the two people he'd met so far. Though he could understand Louie's suspicion, he couldn't figure why the woman he'd met outside had been so hostile. Maybe it was a city thing. Or maybe he'd lost his ability to charm the opposite sex. He smiled at the thought of her, all wet and ragged, standing in the courtyard with her underwear clutched in her hand.

Maybe he'd been out in the wild for too long, but she was just about the prettiest thing he'd ever seen. She was tall and willowy, with sun-kissed hair and legs that seemed to go on forever. And unlike Jo, who dressed in practical work shirts and jeans, this woman wore clothing to show off her figure, a skirt that molded perfectly to her backside and a silk blouse that clung to her like a second skin. An image flashed in his mind—wet silk made transparent by the rain...perfect breasts hidden by scraps of lace.

Brad groaned softly. Yes, he'd been in the wild far too long. He'd been living in a tent, catching a shower whenever he could, and doing his laundry in gas station washrooms and obliging rivers. It would be nice to spend a few nights in a real bed. He rubbed his beard, now far past a stubble. A shave would be good, too. And a long hot shower.

He found Tom's front door, then pushed the key into the lock, pausing for a moment to consider his motives. Had he decided to come to Seattle to spend some time in the city, or was this just a good place to hide out for a while? He'd put his aborted wedding to Jo in the past, but maybe he wasn't completely recovered from the shock. After all, a guy didn't get jilted like that every day—embarrassed in front of friends and family, subjected to all sorts of speculation—without getting a little bit singed.

As the eldest child of Walt and Mary Rose Cullen, Brad had had his whole life planned out for him from the time of his birth. Expectations were high. He was the one who would carry on at Split Rock, running the huge Cullen family horse-breeding operation. He was the one who'd marry Jo Millen and combine her family's land with his. He was the steady, dependable one, the one everyone in his family was counting on to do his duty.

It wasn't that he didn't love the ranch. Breeding and

training horses was a passion. But more and more of late, his father had been pushing him into the management tasks required of a ranch owner, and Brad didn't have the patience for the financial end of the business. That's why marrying Jo seemed like destiny. She'd been running the finances for her father's ranch for over five years—and she was damn good at it.

It had been a match made in heaven…and a breakup that had put him through hell. Both his parents and hers had urged him to swallow his pride and try to convince her that she'd made a mistake, that he was willing to do anything to make it work. But Brad had been burned once. He wasn't about to leap into the fire again. Fed up by a month of their constant meddling, he'd packed his stuff and made his escape, determined to make some serious decisions about the direction of his life.

He slowly lowered his pack to the floor, then glanced around the luxurious apartment. An architect by trade, Tom had a real flair for design, as well as an unfulfilled dream to have his place featured in *Architectural Digest*. The colors were muted, calming, the fabrics rich and comfortable. "I could get used to this," Brad said aloud, recalling the spartan surroundings of his room at the ranch.

Seattle wouldn't be such a bad place to hang out for a while. He'd heard the coffee here was the best in the world. There were plenty of great restaurants to try and tourist sights to see. And he'd already met a pretty girl. His mind flashed again to the woman he'd talked to out front, then lingered over the image as it drifted through his mind.

For the first time in six years, he allowed himself to consider a woman other than Jo. Hell, in those six years, he'd never once cheated on her. His social life before Jo had been active by any bachelor's standard, but once he'd committed to her, he'd been a model of fidelity. Unfortunately, she hadn't shared that particular trait.

And now there was no need to feel guilty. He'd spent the entire summer mourning what might have been. It was time to get on with his life. He was a perfectly healthy thirty-three year old man and he was completely free to start looking again—and he liked what he'd seen in the lobby. Even with her tawny hair dripping rain and her silk blouse clinging to her skin, she was beautiful—the kind of beautiful that made most other women pale in comparison. Maybe he'd ask Louie where she lived and stop by and say "hi."

But for now, he needed a shower, a shave and a good hot meal. Then he'd figure out where to go from there.

DANI KICKED her shoes off the second she closed the apartment door behind her. A soft moan slipped from her lips at the same time her bags dropped beside her. For a moment she couldn't move. She closed her eyes and leaned back against the door, certain she could fall asleep standing up if she gave herself the chance.

She glanced over at the phone sitting on an end table next to the sofa. The message light blinked incessantly and she wondered if Evie had called. A tiny sliver of guilt shot through her. She hadn't checked her messages in nearly a week; instead she'd been completely focused on work.

A knock sounded on the door, and with a groan, Dani turned around to open it. Louie stood on the other side wearing a welcoming grin, a stack of envelopes tucked under one arm and her dry cleaning hanging from the other hand. "Good to have you home, Miss O'Malley."

Dani reached out and took the cleaning from Louie, her earlier frustration with him fading. "Thanks. It's good to be home." She tossed the cleaning over the back of the sofa, then rummaged through the hangers, looking for the black cocktail dress she planned to wear to dinner that night.

"You've got lots of deliveries here," Louie said. "There have been messengers all week. They were supposed to deliver these personally, but I signed for them."

"I'll look at them later," Dani said distractedly.

"And you've had a visitor." He pulled a piece of paper from his pocket. "A Mrs. Lucille Wilson. I told her you were due back earlier today and she left this number. She's staying at a hotel south of town. She insisted that you call as soon as you arrive."

Dani took the paper from Louie's fingers and frowned. "I don't know anyone named Wilson. Are you sure she wants me?"

"The lady sure seemed anxious to talk to you. I told her you'd call her, but she wasn't happy about waiting. She stopped by twice this afternoon."

"Well, she'll have to wait a little longer. I have a dinner date and I'm due at the restaurant in a half hour." She grabbed the black dress and headed toward her bedroom. "Just drop the packages on the table by the door," she called.

The intercom buzzer sounded, causing Dani to stop short. Louie pressed the button. "Miss O'Malley's apartment."

"Is Danielle O'Malley home? This is Lucille Wilson."

"It's her," Louie whispered, pointing at the intercom. "She sure is persistent."

Dani groaned. "Tell her to come back another time. Tell her I'm not home. I have to get ready!"

"I'm sorry," Louie said into the intercom. "Miss O'Malley won't be—"

"I must see her," the woman shouted. "Now! I've tried calling her, I've sent messengers and I've waited for three days in a hotel room. I'm not leaving until I see her."

Louie glanced over at Dani. "All right," she said. "Let her in. I'll talk to her after I get dressed. She's probably one of those researchers from the university. I agreed to participate in a study years ago and now they won't leave me alone. Every year, right about this time, they show up with their questionnaires and their apologetic smiles." Another repercussion of the foster care system, Dani mused. She could never really leave it behind.

She hurried into the bedroom, tugging at her clothes as she walked. Quickly she stripped out of her damp skirt and blouse and stepped into the cocktail dress. A glance in the mirror told her she should dry her hair and redo her makeup, but she barely had time to reapply lipstick.

Grabbing the damp strands, she twisted them up into a casual knot, then secured them with bobby pins. The style revealed the creamy length of her neck and the wide expanse of her shoulders. Too sexy for a normal business meeting but exactly what she needed to tempt Jason Wentland. She removed the tiny gold hoops and replaced them with the diamond studs she'd given herself for her last birthday.

After a hurried search through a dresser drawer for the proper purse, she headed for the bathroom. She had just finished applying her lipstick when she heard Louie calling from the hallway. "Miss O'Malley?"

"I'll be out in a few minutes," she shouted.

"I—I think you'd better come out here now."

Dani cursed softly, then yanked the bathroom door open. Louie stood outside, an apologetic smile pasted on his face. "Can't she wait?" Dani asked.

"She says that she's here about Evie Gregory. And she has to see you immediately." He cleared his throat, then lowered his voice. "She has three children with her, and the little one has very sticky hands."

At the mention of Evie's name, Dani's breath caught in her throat. Her heart ground to a stop, and for a moment, she couldn't think. Slowly she walked down the hall, telling herself that everything was all right. But in her heart, she knew that something had happened to Evie. She'd had an odd feeling all week long, but had written it off to exhaustion. When she reached the living room, she took in the scene in front of her.

An elderly woman sat on the sofa, her plump figure straining her rumpled clothes. Evie's three children sat quietly beside her, their expressions dull and emotionless. With an effort Lucille Wilson stood, clutching her handbag in front of her. "Are you Danielle O'Malley?"

"What's happened to Evie?" Dani demanded, her voice trembling. "Why are her children here? Is she all right?"

"Evie died last week," Lucille Wilson said, as if she were commenting on the weather or the price of chicken at the supermarket.

A tiny cry slipped from Dani's throat and she clutched the back of a chair to keep her knees from buckling. "No," she murmured. "I just saw her last month. She said she was getting better."

"The doctors gave her three months," the woman said. "And that was six months ago."

Dani glanced at the children. Jack, Evie's twelve-year-old son, stared at his shoes. Rebecca, who was just five, wept softly, her face streaked with tears. And the baby, two-year-old Noah, didn't seem to understand what had happened. He clutched a ragged teddy bear and crawled back and forth between his siblings, whining for attention.

Hesitating slightly, Dani approached Jack, then bent down and placed her hand over his. "I'm so sorry," she said, tears filling her eyes. "Your mother and I were best friends. She was the only friend I ever had."

She fought the urge to retreat to her bedroom, to crawl into bed and let the grief overwhelm her. Instead, old instincts returned and she hardened her heart. Their friendship was never meant to last. Dani had been surprised they'd managed to keep it going this long. But the rationalization didn't help. Evie was gone, and Dani had no one left in the world who meant anything to her.

"Well, I suppose that's it then," Lucille Wilson muttered. "I've packed all their things. The bags are down in the lobby along with the baby's car seat and a portable crib. I'll ship everything else next week." She waved an envelope in the air, then dropped it on the coffee table. "This is a copy of Evie's will and a letter from her. My husband, Fred, and I were supposed to take the children. We've had them since she went into the hospital. We were all ready to take them. Had our house all fixed up for the kids. But I guess Evie thought you'd be a better mother to these three than a blood relative and she changed her will. I don't think she was in her right mind. My husband and I plan to contest your guardianship. You'll be hearing from our lawyer."

With that, the older woman turned and walked to the door. Louie gallantly pulled it open for her, then, shooting Dani an encouraging look, he followed her out. The door softly closed, leaving Dani alone with the children.

Stunned, she sank down on a chair opposite the sofa. This couldn't be right! Evie couldn't possibly have meant for her to take the children. She was a single woman with a hectic career. How was she supposed to take care of three children? "I'm sure this is all a misunderstanding," she said. "I'm sure you want to live with Mr. and Mrs. Wilson, don't you?"

"We don't know her any better than we know you," Jack muttered, his voice flat, his gaze downcast.

This was crazy! She didn't have room in her life for a

regular boyfriend. How could she make room for three children? She reached over and picked up the envelope that Lucille Wilson had tossed on the coffee table. "Just sit here for a while," she said to the children. "I'll be right back."

When she reached the safety of her bedroom, she closed the door and sat down on the bed. Tearing the envelope open, she knew she had to read what Evie had written. But she also knew it would break her heart.

Dear Dani,

I can just imagine what you're thinking right now— how there must be some mistake, how I wasn't in my right mind, how you aren't prepared to raise three children who don't belong to you. And if you really think that I've asked too much, then I leave it up to you to decide what's best for Jack, Becca and Noah. I've named you guardian, so their futures are in your hands. You're the only one I can trust with such a precious task. We promised to be best friends forever on the playground that day so long ago, and now I need my best friend to do this thing for me. If you choose to find another home for them, then I will understand. I trust that you will do what's best. But if you choose to raise my children, then I will save a special place for you in heaven. Raise them well and don't let them forget me.

Your best friend—forever and ever,

Evie

A tear fell from Dani's cheek onto the letter, smearing Evie's familiar scrawl. Dani held back a ragged sob, instead drawing a deep breath. In all the years of her friendship, Evie had never asked anything of her beyond honesty and loyalty. But could she really do this? Could she take three emotionally traumatized children and turn them into well-adjusted adults? She certainly had no examples to follow in her own unconventional life.

She did know one thing—she knew how Evie's children were feeling at this moment. Confused, abandoned and so scared they were afraid to move for fear that the world would come crashing down on top of them. To all these feelings, Dani could relate.

After refolding the letter, she stuck it back in the envelope, then reached over and tucked it beneath her pillow. She'd read the terms of Evie's will later. For now, she had to find a way to salvage what she could from a canceled dinner with her six-million-dollar man. Suddenly, her financial stability had taken on a whole new meaning. She had thought she'd finally have enough money but that was when it was just her. It would take a lot, both emotionally and financially, to keep Evie's children.

"What am I going to do?" Dani murmured, the tears tumbling down her cheeks. She drew a ragged breath. There was only one person she could turn to in a moment of crisis. Her neighbor Tom Hopson was always there for her in an emergency. And if this wasn't an emergency, she wasn't sure what was.

CHAPTER TWO

As BRAD SEARCHED for the bathroom, he slowly stripped off his clothes, dropping them along the way. He caught sight of Mr. Whiskers, who watched him with glittering eyes from behind a potted plant, but followed Tom's advice and didn't return the stare. He'd make friends later.

Like the rest of the apartment, the bathroom was right out of a decorating magazine. He was tempted by the whirlpool tub, the perfect antidote for muscles sore from sleeping on the hard ground. But the glass block shower had a strip of shower heads that looked like fun. He flipped the water on and quickly shed the rest of his clothes.

The shower was steaming when he stepped inside. Brad stood beneath the water and let it sluice over his naked body, washing away weeks of sweat and grime and campfire smoke. He furrowed his fingers through his hair, wondering if he might find someone to cut it while he was in Seattle.

He stayed in the shower until he'd worked the kinks out of nearly every sore muscle. Then, wrapping a towel around his waist, he stepped to the marble sink, wiped the steam from the mirror and searched for a can of shaving cream. But he was interrupted by a frantic knocking at the door.

With a frown, he wrapped the towel more tightly around his waist and padded through the living room. He expected to find Louie the manager on the other side with some crucial bit of information about Mr. Whiskers or specific instructions on watering the philodendron next to the phone.

But instead, he found the stunningly beautiful woman he'd met outside the building, now wearing a low-cut black dress that revealed even more of her long legs and a good measure of her cleavage.

He took in the perfect features of her face, her hazel eyes, her lush mouth, and tawny blond hair. Their gazes met, and for an instant, he felt a current pass between them, the same powerful attraction that had taken his breath away not more than an hour before. Suddenly, he worried about the effect she had on him. After all, there was only a damp towel standing between him and a potentially embarrassing reaction.

They stared at each other for a long moment, until a scream pierced the silence. It was only then that he acknowledged she held a wailing toddler. On either side of her stood a gangly but sullen boy and a little girl with a bright smile pasted on her face. The attraction he'd felt for this woman fizzled the moment he realized she was married.

At first, she seemed surprised to see him. But then she composed herself. "Where is Tom?" she shouted above the crying, pushing up on her toes to look over Brad's shoulder.

"He's not here," Brad replied. "He's visiting his mother in New York."

She groaned, her gaze slowly drifting along his naked chest to his belly, then back up again. The toddler's cries increased in volume and she made a feeble attempt to soothe him. "Right. He told me that. I was supposed to help look after his cat."

"I'm taking care of the cat," Brad said. "And the plants."

"It—it's just that he's the one who's so good with kids," she explained, a hint of hysteria creeping into her voice. Tears swam in her eyes and Brad could tell that she was teetering on the edge of control. "And I—I just needed someone to watch these three for an hour at most. I have an important business meeting and I can't get in touch with my client to cancel. I've tried to call the restaurant, but I keep getting a busy signal. And if I just leave him waiting…well, I might as well just toss six million dollars out with the morning trash. I have responsibilities and I—''

"What about your husband?" Brad interrupted.

"I'm not married," she said sharply. "Do you think if I was married I'd be standing out here asking for help?"

For some strange reason, he felt pleased rather than chastised. Maybe he'd been in the great outdoors for a little too long. Any woman, even a single mom with three kids, looked attractive to him.

"Who are you?" she asked.

"Brad Cullen. We met out on the street."

"I know. But who *are* you? Why are you here?"

"I'm an old friend of Tom's. And who are you?"

"Dani," she said distractedly, grabbing the hem of the toddler's T-shirt and gingerly wiping his nose with it. "Danielle O'Malley. I live across the hall. Tom is a friend of mine." She winced, then wiped her hand on her skirt.

Though her hair was twisted back in a knot, strands fell in loose tendrils around her cheeks and eyes, as if she'd just crawled out of bed. He fought an urge to reach out and tuck a curl behind her ear. "It's nice to meet you, Dani," he said.

"How are you with kids?" she asked, pushing aside the pleasantries.

"I'm great with kids," Brad replied, reaching out to take the toddler from her arms. Like magic, the little boy immediately stopped crying and stared up into Brad's face with wide, watery eyes. "I have five nieces and nephews. I can watch these three if you'd like. Tom can attest to my trustworthy nature."

"You can't leave us with a stranger," the older boy whispered. "You don't even know this guy."

Dani glanced at the boy and a faint blush stained her cheeks, as if she were embarrassed by her lack of judgment. "Of course I wouldn't leave you with a stranger," she murmured. "You and Becca and Noah will just have to come with me. Come on, let's go." She grabbed Noah from Brad and the little boy immediately started crying again. "We have to go. It was nice meeting you, Brad."

With that, she herded the children across the hall and they disappeared into the apartment. Brad stood in the doorway, his hand braced on his hip. She wasn't married. But she did have three children. He'd never been attracted to a woman with kids before. Brad cursed softly. "Get a grip. You've been out in the wild way too long. You don't need to be lusting after anyone right now."

Still, it wasn't hard to imagine sitting across from Danielle O'Malley in an expensive restaurant...sharing a nice bottle of wine...indulging in a sinful dessert...and then seeing just where it all led. Maybe to the plush bed in the guest room or the glass block shower or even that huge whirlpool tub.

He chuckled to himself as he stepped back inside the apartment. But as the door clicked shut behind him, he came to a sudden realization. A half-naked man in Tom Hopson's apartment. A soft groan slipped from his throat and he closed his eyes. "Geez, I hope to hell she doesn't think I'm gay."

SHE FELT AS IF she were existing in a haze. Nothing seemed real, and the more she tried to tell herself that Evie was gone, the more numb she became. Dani didn't remember helping the kids into her car or driving to the restaurant or even walking up to the front door. But now that she was here, she had to shake off her grief and tend to business. She'd just need a few minutes with Jason Wentland to make her excuses and reschedule. Then she could turn her full attention to the children.

"What are we doing here?" Jack asked, staring up at the facade of Soundings, one of Seattle's trendiest restaurants, which overlooked Puget Sound and Elliott Bay.

"I just have a quick errand to run," Dani replied as she pulled open the front door. When she scanned the bar and didn't find Jason there, she asked the maitre d' if he'd arrived.

"Mr. Wentland requested one of our best tables," the man said, looking down his nose at the children. "A table for two. He's already been seated."

"Thank you," Dani said. She directed the children to a quiet corner of the bar and sat them in a neat circle around a small cocktail table. Then she grabbed a waitress as she walked by. "I'd like to order three root beers."

"We don't have root beer," the waitress said, sending the kids a critical look. "This is Soundings."

Dani didn't need another reminder that the restaurant wasn't meant for children. She remembered all the times she'd tried to dine in restaurants with howling babies and bratty children just a few tables away. She was mortified that she might now be the cause of another diner's irritation. "All right, then how about three 7UPs with lots of cherries in them." She reached into her purse and handed the waitress a fifty. "I'm just going to be a few moments. Jack, I need you to watch your sister and brother and make sure they behave. I'll be right back and then we can go home. Can you do that for me?"

Jack nodded as Noah began to whine.

"You are going to come back, aren't you?" Becca asked, a worried frown replacing her forced smile.

Dani's heart twisted. She hesitantly reached out and rubbed her palm over the little girl's head. "Of course I am. I promise. I'll only be gone a few minutes, five at the most. I'll just be in the next room." She felt guilty leaving them there in the bar, but she had no choice. She wasn't about to drag them into the dining room. Once she finished her business, she'd be on her way.

Dani hurried back through the foyer, then paused a moment to gather her thoughts before entering the elegant dining room. Across the crowd, she caught sight of Jason Wentland and stared at him for a long moment. There had been a time when she considered him just about the sexiest man she'd ever seen. Over the past six months they'd met a number of times, and the sexual attraction between them had been electric. She'd enjoyed the tempting little games they'd played, the suggestive nature of their conversations, the little dance they'd enjoyed.

But all that seemed so unimportant now. She just wanted to do a bit of damage control before making a graceful exit. She'd think about his six million dollars and his sexy smile some other time.

Her mind flashed an image of another sexy smile. This one belonged to a half-naked man with a towel draped around his waist and his hair dripping wet. A shiver raced down her spine as she recalled the instant attraction she'd felt for Brad Cullen. He was a whole lot prettier than Jason Wentland. And he was good with children. She shook her head and scolded herself silently.

Brad Cullen was also gay. It didn't take a rocket scientist to figure out what was going on with him and Tom. And he was exactly the type of guy her neighbor was always lusting after. Oddly, she hadn't suspected when she met Brad on the street. She prided herself on her finely honed "gay-dar." Tom teased her that she was better at discerning sexual preferences than he was. All the turmoil of the day must have thrown it off.

She frowned. Cullen had mentioned that he was gay, hadn't he? She'd been so fascinated by his effect on Noah—and her reaction to his half-naked body—that she hadn't really listened to what he was saying. Of course he was gay. He was an old friend of Tom's and he was good-looking. All of Tom's good-looking friends were gay. In truth, every really great looking guy she'd met in Seattle had been gay.

Dani glanced across the restaurant at Jason Wentland, wondering if she'd somehow misjudged him. "I'm losing my mind," she muttered to herself. Taking a deep breath, she started across the room.

"Danielle," Jason said the moment he saw her. He leaned over and kissed her cheek. "I was beginning to wonder if I'd been stood up."

Smiling apologetically, Dani sat down in the chair that he pulled out. "I'm so sorry. I tried to get you on your cell phone and at your office, but I didn't have any luck. And the phone here has been busy. I had a family emergency—actually, I *have* an emergency. An emergency that's going on as we speak. So we're going to have to reschedule."

"What could be more important than our dinner?" Jason teased, sending her his most charming smile. Either he was an avowed heterosexual or he'd learned to play the game as well as she had. Dani had never been above using her sex appeal to charm a client. He poured her a glass of wine. "You can at least stay for a drink. I have some strategies I'd like to discuss with you."

Dani glanced over her shoulder. Maybe a few minutes wouldn't hurt. Jack seemed to have everything under control with his siblings. Noah wasn't screaming. She reached for her wineglass. "All right. Just a quick drink. But then

I really have to go. So, have you made any decisions about your current agency?''

''I have decided it's time for a change,'' he said, his gaze meeting hers.

Dani's hopes rose. Maybe she could salvage something from this evening. ''As I mentioned the last time we talked, I'm certain we can help increase your market share and I—''

''Excuse me.''

The cocktail waitress was standing next to the table, an uneasy smile of her face.

''We're fine,'' Jason said. ''But we would like to see menus when you have a chance.''

''Could I see you for a moment?'' the waitress asked Dani.

Dani quickly excused herself and followed the waitress back into the bar. She found Noah with his hand in a glass of soda, Jack trying to keep his brother from spilling and Becca with a unusual expression on her face. ''What's wrong?''

''She says she feels sick,'' the waitress said. ''And your little boy has already spilled one soda. You'll have to watch your kids.''

''They're not my kids,'' Dani protested. ''Not technically.''

''Well, whoever these kids belong to, you brought them here and you better take care of them or I'm going to call the manager.''

Dani bent down and looked into Becca's face. ''You don't feel well?''

Becca shook her head. ''My tummy hurts.''

''Well, you haven't had any supper yet. You're probably just hungry. Give me a few more minutes and then we'll go find something to eat.''

After ordering another round of sodas, Dani hurried back into the dining room. This time, she didn't bother to sit down. She didn't really care how this looked to Jason Wentland. She had three children to take care of. Business would have to wait until business hours. "Jason, I really have to go. I'll call you in a few days and we can discuss your ideas. Thank you for the wine and for your understanding."

Jason frowned as he stood. "I really did want to discuss this with you, Dani. Now, not later. I need to make a decision soon. Surely you can at least sit down for a few drinks." He slipped his arm around her waist and gently drew her back to the table. Suddenly, Dani felt a hand on her backside, tugging at her skirt. She pulled away, surprised at Jason's forward behavior. But Jason's hand wasn't the one she found when she turned around.

Becca stood behind her, a worried expression on her face. "I don't feel so good."

Jack joined his sister, Noah wriggling in his arms. "We have to leave. Noah is hungry and Becca has an upset tummy. And that waitress keeps staring at us."

"All right," Dani said. She glanced back at Jason to find an incredulous look on his face.

"Are these *your* children?" he asked, his words more an accusation than an inquiry.

Dani bristled at his tone. "Maybe they are," she said, tipping her chin up defensively.

"Maybe?" he asked.

"No, they are my children."

"She's our new mom," Becca said.

"I didn't realize you had children," Jason said, his tone saying much more than his words did.

"Having children in no way interferes with my ability to do my job," Dani insisted. "Our agency is very anxious to show you what we can do for Wentland Software. We believe that, with our help, you can double your market share within a year. And I'll work 24/7 to make that happen.''

She felt another tug on her skirt. "I'm going to be sick," Becca said.

Before she could even grab Becca's hand, the little girl did exactly what she promised. She bent over and threw up on Dani's designer pumps, which caused a surge of nausea to rush through Dani. "Oh, no," she said, pressing her fingers to her mouth.

Becca immediately began to cry, which set Noah off. The toddler's shrieks echoed through the entire dining room. Dani grabbed a linen napkin from the table and wiped at the front of Becca's dress, murmuring soothing words to her, the smell making her head swim. As she rose, she noticed the manager approaching and every diner in the place watching her in horror.

Quickly she gathered the children and pushed them toward the door. "I'll call you on Monday," she shouted to Jason, "and we can set up another meeting."

"I'll call you," Jason said, giving her a weak wave.

When they reached her car, Dani quickly fastened the screaming Noah into his car seat. Then she pressed her palm to Becca's forehead. She wasn't even sure what she was feeling for, but mothers always seemed to do that to a sick child. "How are you feeling? Are you going to throw up in the car?"

Becca smiled brightly. "I feel good now. My mom gives me a Popsicle after I throw up. Do you have Popsicles at your house?" She crawled in the backseat of the car and searched the floor for Noah's "blankie." He immediately grabbed it from her, stuck his thumb in his mouth and smiled.

"I hate that restaurant," Jack grumbled as she slipped into the front seat. "That waitress was really mean to us.

And that man you were talking to in the dining room was a jerk.''

"Well, I don't think we'll be going back there anytime soon," Dani said as she pushed his door closed. She just hoped that the maitre d's around town didn't have a professional hotline or she might lose her prime tables in all of Seattle's best restaurants. That could seriously hinder her ability to wine and dine potential clients.

"Who am I kidding?'' she muttered. Until she straightened out her personal life, she shouldn't even think about wining and dining clients. Dani suspected that her life was about to become very complicated, and clients were the least of her worries.

BRAD GRABBED the pillowcase and filled it full of his dirty clothes, wrinkling his nose at the odor. Tom had a designer washer/dryer in his unit, but it had too many knobs and buttons on it. Louie had informed Brad that there were coin laundry facilities in the basement. He figured the basement laundry was better than taking the risk of flooding Tom's Tuscan tile floor. Besides, what else was there to do on a Sunday morning than read the latest *Sports Illustrated* and watch his wash tumble dry?

He grabbed his last clean flannel shirt and pulled it on, not bothering with the buttons. He'd borrowed a pair of Tom's jeans and had to forgo his boxers for lack of clean underwear. Heaving the pillowcase over his shoulder, Brad stepped out into the hallway. But he stopped short as he closed the door behind him. Danielle O'Malley sat on the floor outside her apartment door, surrounded by bags of groceries and packages of disposable diapers. She'd opened a jar of peanut butter and was dipping into it with her finger as she stared vacantly at her shoes.

"Dani?" She looked up at him and he could see she'd been crying. "Are you all right?"

"No," she murmured. "But I will be. I just need a few more minutes." She rummaged through the bag next to her. "I know I bought some candy bars."

"Where are the kids?"

"They're inside watching cartoons in my bedroom…eating crackers and drinking chocolate milk…on my silk duvet cover. I'm fine with that, don't get me wrong. I'm trying to be…flexible. You should have seen how flexible I was at the grocery store, shopping with them. They couldn't decide on cereal so I bought seven boxes. And five different flavors of Popsicles. Then Becca had to have something called Fruit Roll-Ups, which I'd never heard of before. We spent a half hour racing around the store looking for those. And I won't even tell you about the mess in the snack aisle. I spent over three hundred dollars on food."

Brad set the laundry down and found a spot next to her on the floor. "And why are you out here?"

"It's quiet," Dani said. "No one's crying or throwing up or telling me what a horrible mother I'll make. I never wanted to be a mother. I have a career. I've worked hard to get where I am. Do you know I was named advertising executive of the year by the Sea-Tac Association of Marketing Professionals?"

"If you didn't want to be a mother, why did you have three kids?" Brad asked.

She glanced over at him, a look of surprise on her pretty features. "Oh, I didn't. They're not mine. I mean, I didn't give birth to them. I guess you could say I inherited them…from my best friend. She died last week and named me guardian. I don't know what she was thinking. I have absolutely no maternal instincts."

Brad frowned. So Danielle O'Malley wasn't a single

mom. She was a single woman with kids, though he wasn't sure there was much difference. "I'm sorry," he said.

"About Evie or about my lack of maternal instincts?" Dani asked.

"Both. It must be hard for you and for them. Is there anything I can do to help?"

She smiled and shook her head. "No, this is my problem. I'm going to have to deal with it myself."

"At least let me help you carry your groceries in."

She sighed softly, then leaned her head against his shoulder. "No. I think I'll just stay out here all day."

Brad turned his head slightly and drew a deep breath, inhaling the sweet scent of her hair. At the same time, she turned and caught him. She drew away and gave him a sheepish smile. "I'm sorry. I didn't mean to…I usually vent to Tom. I guess I forgot you weren't him. Even though you're…well, you're a lot like him."

Brad levered himself to his feet and then offered her a hand. "Come on. Let's unpack your groceries before the Popsicles melt."

Taking his hand, she stood up. He held on to her fingers for just a moment longer than was appropriate, long enough for her to have to pull her hand from his. She sent him a befuddled look before grabbing the grocery bag. "So, how long have you and Tom been together?"

Well, that answered a big question, Brad thought, groaning inwardly. She was under the misapprehension that he was gay. "Tom and I aren't together," he said as they stepped into her apartment.

"You're not?" she asked, glancing over her shoulder.

He shook his head. "We're just friends." He thought he saw a tiny smile curve the corners of her mouth, but he wasn't sure. In truth, it was hard to read Dani O'Malley. Though she seemed to wear her emotions on her sleeve, he sensed there was much more to her than what he saw on the surface. And he realized that he was looking forward to getting to know her a little better.

"Have the kids had lunch?" Brad asked.

"We stopped for a fast-food breakfast before shopping," Dani said as she set the grocery bags on the kitchen counter. She pulled out a package of Jell-O cups. "Look at this. You can buy Jell-O in these little containers. And macaroni and cheese and spaghetti. And they have TV dinners for kids now." She held out a frozen dinner. "Corn dogs and purple applesauce. I'd never need to cook at all. I just need to know how to read directions and turn on the microwave."

"Yeah, but this stuff isn't good for every meal." Brad flipped the box over and pointed to the nutrition label. "Look at all the sodium. That can't be good. And some of this stuff has so much sugar in it, you'll be peeling the kids off the ceiling by the end of the day. They need to have good food. Homemade dinners with meat and potatoes and—"

Brad stopped short the moment he saw her face. She looked as if she was about to start crying again. "What's wrong?"

"I don't know what I'm doing." She snatched the frozen dinner from his hands. "How am I supposed to know how much sodium a child can have? I mean, this is made for kids. Don't they know?"

"I guess not. I just know that my two nieces and three nephews aren't allowed to eat a lot of processed and packaged food."

"Everything I bought is in a package! The apples and the hamburgers and the broccoli."

"I think it's more about the additives," Brad explained, hoping to calm the edge of hysteria in her voice. "The plainer the food, the better."

"But they don't like plain food. They like junk food."

Brad grinned. "Welcome to motherhood, Danielle O'Malley. You've just joined an elite club of parents who haven't been able to figure out why stuff that's so bad for their children tastes so good."

His gentle teasing brought a smile to her face, and for that he was grateful. He liked Dani's smile. She didn't smile much, but when she did, he had to admit she was the most beautiful woman he'd ever met. He reached out and brushed a strand of hair from her eyes, not realizing what he'd done until after he'd tucked the hair behind her ear.

"I must look like a mess. I swear, I've cried more in the past two days than I have in my entire life. At a time like this, Tom would probably suggest that we go get facials."

Though Brad would have jumped at the chance to spend some time with Dani, he wasn't really a "facial" kind of guy. "Your best friend died," he said. "I think that deserves a few good cries."

She nodded. "But I have to get it together. I've got these kids and I've got to figure out what I'm going to do. I'm just not sure I can keep them. I mean, there has to be a couple out there somewhere who'd be good parents for them. At least better than me."

Brad frowned. "I just assumed you'd keep the kids."

"I don't know. I read Evie's will last night and she made me their guardian. According to the will, I'm supposed to decide what's best for them. And I can tell you that having me for a mother would not be the best thing. So I guess I'm going to have to find suitable parents."

"Do they have other relatives?"

"The grandparents are dead. The kids have an aunt and uncle who seem to want them, but I'm not sure the kids would care to live with them. They're threatening a custody suit, and I guess I have to decide whether to fight them."

"I suppose something like that could get expensive."

"I've made some good investments. And there's a small trust fund that Evie left. But it's going to take a lot more than that to put three kids through college." She drew a ragged breath. "So, I guess I have a lot to figure out." She sat down on a stool and rubbed her forehead with her fingertips. "Right now, I'm so exhausted I can't think. How do mothers make it through the day? I took them grocery shopping and I feel like I could sleep for a week." She winced as she ran her fingers through her hair. "Jelly. Noah stuck his face in my hair and his mouth was full of jelly."

"Why don't I make the kids lunch while you relax? You can take a little nap or a nice long bath."

She sent him a grateful smile. "A bath would be wonderful. But I should help you here."

Brad grabbed her shoulders and pushed her out of the kitchen. "Go. I'll finish up here and then get lunch started. Then maybe we can take the kids somewhere. Does Seattle have a zoo? Or maybe we could go up to the top of that Space Needle."

"I've never been to the Space Needle," Dani said.

"Then that's what we'll do."

He followed her down the hall to her bedroom. The kids were sprawled on her bed, watching television. "What's he doing here?" Jack asked.

"Mr. Cullen has offered to take us out this afternoon," Dani said. "He's going to make lunch for you while I take a bath."

"Come on, kids," Brad said. "I need your help in the kitchen. We're going to make lunch and then we're going to go have some fun."

Jack reluctantly crawled off the bed, then picked up Noah from the floor. Becca jumped up and joined them. "Fun?" she asked. "What kind of fun?"

"So much fun that you won't know what to do with yourself," Brad teased. He pinched the end of her nose and Becca giggled. Of the three kids, she seemed to be the one with the sunniest disposition. But he suspected that she was forcing her bright mood, hoping to make the best out of a bad situation. Jack, on the other hand, was just plain angry. Brad could see it in the set of his shoulders and the defiant tilt of his chin. As for Noah, Brad wasn't sure how much the little boy understood. He seemed to cling to anyone who'd hold him, yet didn't find any comfort in the contact.

Dani was right. If she was going to be mother to these three children, she'd need more than just ordinary parenting skills. They'd been through so much already in their young lives, and their troubles were bound to leave their mark. Brad glanced back at the kids as they followed him to the kitchen. Why was he so concerned? Hell, in a few weeks he'd move on, leaving Dani to her life. He enjoyed helping her out, but was he using her need as an excuse to avoid his own problems?

"So what do you guys want for lunch?"

"Hot dogs," Becca cried.

"Grilled cheese," Jack countered.

"Peeda," Noah shouted.

Brad frowned. "Pizza?"

"Peeda."

They decided on grilled cheese and tomato soup and a salad. Jack took care of cutting vegetables for the salad. Brad sent Becca to collect laundry and pick up Noah's toys, while he made lunch, and he occupied Noah with a collection of Dani's designer kitchen utensils, which probably hadn't been off the rack since they were purchased. By the time he'd set the table in the breakfast nook, he realized that nearly a half hour had passed and Dani hadn't emerged from her bedroom.

Brad asked Jack to set the table, then walked to the bedroom. The door was open and the room was empty. He knocked at the bathroom door but there was no answer. "Dani? Lunch is ready."

Frowning, he carefully opened the door just wide enough to talk through the crack. "Dani?" When she didn't answer, Brad began to worry so he swung the door open. She still lay in the tub, her hair wrapped in a towel, her arms draped along the sides. Her eyes were closed and her breathing was soft and even. She'd fallen asleep.

Brad wasn't sure what to do. Though the bubbles in the tub covered most of her body, there were several strategic spots where they'd dissolved, leaving a tempting view of soft flesh. "God, you're beautiful," he murmured, releasing a tightly held breath.

Guilty for staring, he dragged his gaze away from her body and focused on the ceiling. He couldn't wake her up without her knowing he'd gotten an eyeful. But then, he couldn't exactly leave her in the tub to shrivel up like a prune either.

In the end, Brad returned to the kitchen and picked Noah up off the floor, setting him on his feet. "Go find Dani," he said, handing him the lids to two saucepans. "Go find Dani."

As Noah ran through the apartment, he slammed the lids together like a pair of cymbals, creating a racket so loud that Becca had to cover her ears. Five minutes later, Dani appeared at the kitchen door, dressed in tailored trousers and a pretty sweater, her hair still wrapped in the towel. She yawned, then stretched her arms above her head. Her sweater crept up, and this time, Brad got caught staring.

"You're just in time for lunch," he said, giving the soup one last stir. "Did you have a nice bath?"

"Yes," she told him, gazing at the lunch laid out on the table. "This is wonderful. You made a salad."

"Jack made the salad," Brad said.

She turned to Jack. "Thank you. I love salad. It's my favorite thing for lunch."

Dani wandered over to the refrigerator and pulled out a bottle of water, then leaned back against the edge of the counter next to Brad, watching him flip a grilled cheese sandwich. "Tom was a fool to let you go," she said, patting him on the shoulder. "He's a bigger disaster in the kitchen than I am. He really needs a man who can cook."

Brad groaned inwardly as he watched her walk back to the table. Maybe it was for the best that she thought he was gay. He wasn't in any position to get involved with Dani O'Malley. And she certainly wasn't looking for a romance right now, not with everything she had to deal with in her life. If she thought he was gay, there wouldn't be any of the usual sexual tension and they could just be friends.

He scooped up the three grilled cheese sandwiches and set them on a plate, then carried them over to the table. Becca and Jack each reached for one, and Dani took the last, cutting it up in small pieces for Noah. As Brad watched her try to tempt the little boy, he wondered why he found her so attractive.

It wasn't just the hair or the figure or the beautiful face. There was something more elusive. Though she tried to maintain a tough facade, underneath she was uncertain and vulnerable, escaping to the hallway to hide her tears. When he was around her, he felt the undeniable urge to protect her.

Dani O'Malley was probably the most intriguing woman he'd ever met. And though they'd be nothing more than friends, he looked forward to getting to know her.

"So," Brad said, reaching for the salad. "I'm thinking we should see a little bit of Seattle this afternoon. And we should start with the Space Needle."

CHAPTER THREE

"YOU HAVE TO GET UP. Wake up, wake up."

Slowly Dani opened her eyes, squinting against the light from her bedside lamp. She glanced over at the television to see that the station had reverted to infomercials. It must be late. Pushing up on her elbow, she brushed the hair out of her eyes and came face-to-face with Jack's worried expression.

"What's wrong?"

"Noah. He's barking."

"Barking?"

"Yeah. He does that when he gets a bad cough. You have to get him the pink medicine. My mom always gives him the pink medicine."

Dani shoved the covers back and grabbed her robe. "He was fine when I put him to bed. Maybe he's just hungry. Or maybe he needs a clean diaper."

Jack grabbed her hand and pulled her toward her office-turned-guest room. "No, I checked."

By the time Dani reached the living room, she could hear Noah's cough. Jack had been right. It sounded like the little boy was barking. She stumbled through the room toward the crib, stubbing her toe on the studio couch where Jack and Becca slept. The moment she picked Noah up, he sensed her panic and began to wail. His sobs only made his coughing worse, and nothing she did could soothe him.

Jack reached up and pressed his palm to his brother's forehead. "I think he has a fever."

"Is Noah sick?"

Dani glanced down to see Becca peering up at her. "No, he's fine." She turned to Jack. "How do you know he has a fever?" Dani asked, mimicking his action. The little boy felt warm, but how warm was too warm?

"Give him the pink stuff," Jack insisted.

"I don't have the pink stuff," Dani said. "I don't even know what the pink stuff is!" Tears of frustration pushed at the corners of her eyes as Noah's cries grew louder and his coughing more uncontrolled. Why couldn't she quiet him? Did he sense her fear and her lack of confidence?

Jack rolled his eyes. "You can't just—"

"Stop!" Dani cried, holding out her hand to silence him. "Just give me a second to think." She'd call an ambulance. The paramedics would know what to do. Or better yet, she'd get dressed and take Noah to the emergency room. The hospital was just a few miles away and the doctors there were experts. Drawing a deep breath, she tried to calm her nerves. There was one other person who'd know what to do. "Go across the hall and get Brad," she ordered.

"We don't need him," Jack insisted. "I know what to do."

"Please," Dani pleaded over Noah's sobs. "Just get him."

Jack stalked out of the room, muttering beneath his breath, no doubt disparaging her abilities as a mother. But Dani wasn't about to trust a twelve-year-old with the health of his little brother. She sat down on the edge of the bed and smoothed the damp hair out of Noah's eyes.

They never should have taken the kids out yesterday afternoon. The Space Needle had been packed with tourists, all of them breathing germs on Noah. It was no wonder he'd caught a cold. "It's all right," she said. "We'll be fine." Becca sat down beside her and tried to distract her brother. When that didn't work, she slipped her hand around Dani's arm and leaned against her.

A minute later, Jack appeared at the bedroom door, quickly followed by Brad. Brad hadn't bothered with a robe and was wearing only a pair of plaid boxer shorts. Dani swallowed hard as her gaze flitted over his half-naked body.

He wasn't just gorgeous, he was perfect. Wide shoulders tapered to a narrow waist and hips. He didn't have health club abs, each muscle perfectly cut. He was lean and hard, his body obviously honed by hard work. She barely noticed Noah's crying as her gaze drifted down, past his long legs to his bare feet. Gee, he even had beautiful feet.

Dani felt a blush warm her cheeks and she turned her attention back to Noah, surprised by her unbidden reaction to Brad's body. She was tired, she was scared and she wasn't thinking straight.

"What's wrong?" Brad asked.

"I told you," Jack insisted. "He has a fever and a cough and he needs the pink medicine."

"Jack, take Becca to the kitchen," Brad ordered, "and get her a glass of milk and some crackers. You don't need to worry. Noah will be fine."

Reluctantly, Jack grabbed his sister's hand and led her out of the room. Brad closed the door behind the pair, and the moment it clicked shut, Dani felt the tears dribbling out of the corners of her eyes. Why was this happening to her? She'd never allowed herself the indulgence of tears and now she couldn't seem to stop. Was this the result of holding her emotions in check for so many years? Would she now spend the rest of her life crying at the drop of a hat?

"Oh, hell," she muttered, brushing the tears away angrily.

"Hey, it's all right." He quickly crossed the room and sat down beside her.

"I don't know what I'm doing. I feel like such a failure. Noah is sick—he could be dying—and I don't know how to help him. We should have never taken him out. We forgot his hat and it was so damp. It's my fault."

Brad smiled sympathetically, then pulled her and Noah into his embrace. "Nothing is your fault. And how can you be expected to know everything about children?" he asked, softly stroking her hair. "You've had these kids for two days."

Dani felt the warmth of his comforting arms and she snuggled closer. He smelled good, like soap, and the dusting of hair on his chest tickled her cheek. Noah's cries had subsided the moment Brad was near, and he stuck his little face in between them and sighed softly. She wasn't sure how long they all sat there on the bed, locked in a communal hug. But then Noah coughed again and Dani's worries returned.

She drew back. "I think he has a fever. Doesn't he seem a little flushed to you?"

Brad pressed his palm to Noah's forehead. "I don't know. Maybe. What should we do?"

"I thought you'd know. You're the one who's so good with kids. Do you think I should take him to the emergency room?"

Gently Brad took Noah and held him out in front of him, studying the little boy's face. Noah had stopped crying completely and now watched Brad with wide eyes. "He doesn't look that sick. He's probably hot from crying so hard."

"How can you tell?"

"Maybe we need to take his temperature. If he's really sick, he'll have a fever."

"I don't have a thermometer," Dani said. "But there's

an all-night pharmacy a few blocks from here. Maybe you could go get one?''

Brad nodded. ''All right. I'll get a thermometer and we'll take his temperature, and if it's above, say, one hundred, we'll take him to the emergency room.'' He bent close and gave her a quick kiss on the cheek, so quick that for a moment, Dani didn't even realize he'd kissed her. ''I'll be right back.''

With that he hurried out of the room. Dani watched him leave, her gaze caught by the small of his back. He wasn't just gorgeous. He was so sweet and thoughtful and dependable. ''Why are all the great guys either married or gay?'' she asked herself.

Her mind flashed an image of Jason Wentland. Just a few days ago, she thought Jason was the perfect man for her. But so much had changed in such a short time. With a new perspective, she could see Jason for the man he truly was— self-absorbed, impatient, condescending. Jason wasn't the kind of guy who'd run out in the middle of the night and get a thermometer. But Brad…he was different. ''Tom must have been crazy to let a guy like him get away.''

''Joo.''

Dani turned to Noah. His tears had stopped, and to her surprise, the little boy smiled at her. ''Are you done crying now?'' she asked.

Noah nodded his head. ''Joo.''

''Let's go get you some joo,'' Dani said, pleased that she understood his request. She didn't understand much of what Noah said, but she'd heard ''joo'' enough times to know it meant ''juice.''

Dani and the children were all sitting in the breakfast nook when Brad got back from the drugstore. Huge bags dangled from his arms and he carefully set them on the counter.

"Did you get the pink stuff?" Jack asked.

"I can only get the pink stuff with a prescription. But I got red stuff and purple stuff and yellow stuff."

Jack set his glass down and wiped his hands on his pajama bottoms. He looked over the bottles that Brad had bought, then pointed to the middle one and nodded. "That works good. I'm going to bed."

"Me, too," Becca said.

They started out of the kitchen. "Jack?" Dani called.

The boy turned. "Yeah?"

"Thanks for helping with Noah."

"Sure." With that he walked back to their room, leaving Dani and Brad alone with the toddler.

"He thinks I'm incompetent," Dani said. "He knows I don't know anything about children."

"You're their guardian, not their mother," Brad said as he began to unpack the bags. "He's going to have to cut you a little slack. Two days isn't long enough to learn how to be a parent."

"But how am I going to learn? The U of W doesn't offer graduate courses in parenthood."

Brad withdrew a thick paperback from one of the bags. "Everything you wanted to know about parenting," he said with a grin. He flipped through the book. "In 983 pages. I also got thermometers," he added, placing them on the table. "Three different kinds—one for the forehead, one for the ear and one for the...well, we'll use that one if the other two don't work. I also got a vaporizer, a cool air humidifier, alcohol wipes, Baby Tylenol, and Pedialyte. And the pharmacist says that we don't have to take him to the emergency room unless his temperature is 104. And I got this," he said, drawing a bag of Peanut M&M's out of the last bag.

"You think we should give M&M's to Noah?"

"I got the chocolate for you. You've had a rough day and I thought you could probably use something soothing."

"What? They didn't have a big bag of Valium?"

"See, things aren't so bad." He picked up one of the thermometers, opened the box and studied the directions. "You've still got your sense of humor."

Dani watched him surreptitiously. She knew better than to allow herself any romantic feelings for Brad Cullen. But it was just so hard to remember he was gay. He'd come to her rescue again and again, like some white knight. Only Brad Cullen was a knight who would rather ride off into the sunset with the prince than the princess.

She'd always respected Tom's sexuality, but there was something about Brad, about the way he looked at her, that caused her to question Brad's choice. It was just such a waste of perfectly good testosterone.

When he'd figured out the directions for the thermometer, Brad stuck it in Noah's ear, keeping the toddler's attention diverted with a series of silly faces and sounds. After a few seconds, he looked at the display and smiled. "One hundred point nine," he said.

A flood of relief washed over Dani. "Then we don't have to take him to the hospital."

"Nope. We can just give him a teaspoon of this and put him back to bed." Brad measured out some of the medicine into a syringe and popped it into Noah's mouth. The little boy smiled and smacked his lips.

"I'm going to put him to sleep in my bed," Dani said. "I can keep an eye on him…check his fever…listen to his cough."

Brad chuckled, smoothing his hand up and down her arm. "I think he'll be fine in his crib. And you need some rest."

Dani swallowed hard, the warmth of his hand penetrating her skin and warming her blood. "Thank you so much for helping out. I don't know what I would have done without you."

"You'd have figured it out," Brad said.

"No. I just don't think I'll ever be good at this." She shook her head. "I don't understand children. I don't have a reference point. I never had brothers and sisters. I never knew my father. My mother died when I was six. And I never stayed in a home long enough to learn anything from my foster mothers, so I can't understand why Evie would trust me with her children."

She glanced at Brad and immediately realized that she'd revealed far too much. It was so easy to think of him as a close friend. And now that Evie was gone, she needed someone to understand.

"Maybe Evie realized something that you didn't," Brad suggested.

"And what's that?" Dani asked, shifting Noah in her arms.

"She knew you'd have something to offer them. You'd know what they're going through. You lost your mother when you were very young, and so have they."

Dani blinked, his words sinking in. For the first time since the children had arrived, she found some insight into Evie's decision. Emotion welled up inside of her. Could she really live up to her best friend's expectations? Could she become a mother to these children? "I'm sorry. I always seem to be offloading my worries onto you."

"I don't mind."

They stared at each other for a long moment, neither one speaking. At any other time, Dani would have expected a lazy embrace and a long, passionate kiss. She blinked, snapping herself out of the brief fantasy. "I should really put Noah to bed. I've got a big day planned tomorrow. I need to start looking for a nanny for Noah and figure out what

I'm going to do about school for Becca and Jack. I've got to deal with the bedroom situation. A studio couch in the office isn't a proper bedroom. And their things should arrive soon. I'm going to have to clean out some space for toys and clothes.''

"Why don't I put Noah to bed," Brad offered.

"Thanks," Dani said. Without thinking, she pushed up on her toes and wrapped her arm around his neck, intending to give him a platonic hug. But the moment her body brushed against his, she realized she'd made a mistake. She patted him on the back and murmured a "thank you," then started to draw away.

But when their eyes met again, there was something different in his gaze. Something that looked like desire. He wanted to kiss her. She knew it instinctively, knew that if she just leaned forward slightly, he might take the initiative. A tiny sliver of apprehension shot through her. What if she was wrong? What if all the emotional upheaval of the last few days had skewed her perceptions? She knew for a fact that Brad Cullen was gay. Why would he possibly want to kiss her?

With an embarrassed smile, he took Noah from her arms. "I'll get this little guy to bed."

When she was alone again, Dani ran her fingers through her tangled hair. If she could just get a decent night's sleep, she'd be able to think straight. "Just one night," she murmured, her eyes suddenly heavy.

"DID YOU GIVE HIM THE MEDICINE?"

Brad turned from the crib to find Jack sitting up in bed. Becca was snuggled up beside her big brother, her long dark hair curled around her face. "He's going to be fine. Thanks to you."

He didn't smile, but Brad could see that Jack appreciated the compliment. "No big deal," he muttered.

Brad crossed the room and sat down on the edge of the bed. "It was a big deal. You kept your cool and you knew what to do. You're the man of this family now, and Becca and Noah are going to depend on you to do the right thing." He met the boy's gaze. "I know it's a little scary, everyone counting on you. That's kind of the way it is with me. Everyone in my family depends on me."

"I'm not scared," he said.

"Maybe not now. But if you do get scared, you can always talk to Dani."

"She doesn't know what she's doing," Jack said in a disdainful voice.

"That's why you need to cut her a little slack. Help her out."

"Why should I?" Jack asked. "She's not my mom. She's not even related."

"Maybe not. But trying a little harder is the best thing to do for your family right now."

Jack's lower lip trembled and his eyes swam with tears. "Why did this have to happen to us? Why did our mother have to die? It was bad enough when our dad died. We're orphans, you know."

Brad reached out and gathered the boy into his arms, the same way he'd done with Dani. When he'd walked through the front door of Tom's apartment a few days ago, he'd been looking for peace and quiet, time to sort out his own problems. Instead, he now found himself hip-deep in a family crisis—and the family wasn't even his. "I don't have any answers, Jack. I wish I did. But your mother chose Dani for a reason, and someday maybe you'll both understand why."

Jack brushed the tears off his cheeks and nodded. He

flopped back onto the pillow and Brad pulled the covers up to his chin. "Just give it a little time," he said. "Things will get better." He reached over to turn off the light, then walked to the door. He took a look back at Dani's "family," Noah breathing easier in the crib, Becca sprawled next to Jack. He couldn't imagine what the children were going through. He'd had the incredible luck to grow up in a whole and healthy family. But Dani knew. She shared an intimate understanding of abandonment. Many children broke under the weight of such problems, and some chose a destructive path in life. But Dani had survived and made a success of herself.

Brad walked back into the kitchen, only to find it empty, his drugstore purchases scattered over the counters. He returned to the living room, wondering if Dani had gone to bed. But then he saw her, curled up on the sofa, sound asleep. Her robe gaped open in the front, revealing the soft swell of her breast. He caught himself staring, wondering what it would feel like to press his mouth to that very spot.

Quickly, he grabbed a chenille throw from the back of a chair and covered her up, then bent down. "Dani?"

"Mmm?" She reached out and slipped her arm around his neck, her eyes still closed.

"I'm going to go now," he whispered. "I'll see you in the morning."

"Mmm. In the morning." She sighed softly and his gaze fixed on her lips. Then, without thinking, he leaned forward and kissed her, so softly that he was left wondering whether the kiss had registered at all. When he looked down at her perfect features, he knew she was asleep, her breathing deep and even.

He released a tightly held breath and sat back on his heels. "I don't know what the hell I'm doing," he murmured.

The attraction to Dani had been there from the very start, from the moment he helped her gather up her underwear in the courtyard. At first, he'd written it off as the result of a summer spent in solitude. He hadn't seen too many gorgeous women on his solo climbs. But suddenly, he found himself smack-dab in the middle of her life, trying to hold everything together for her until she was able to get back up on her feet again.

In the process, he'd forgotten all his own problems, his canceled wedding, his responsibilities at Split Rock, his family and his friends back in Montana. He'd slipped into her life and made himself indispensable. But then, Dani didn't have any expectations, she didn't make any demands. She didn't need him to be someone he wasn't.

Still, he'd have to get back to his own life sooner or later. He'd have to make some serious decisions about his future. Brad stood and stared down at Dani for a long time, fighting the urge to kiss her again, this time until she woke up and looked into his eyes, lucid and aware.

He hadn't even seen it coming, these feelings he had for her. It wasn't just a casual attraction, something that could be eased by an evening in her bed. But sooner or later, he'd have to walk away and leave her to her life. Whether he wanted to admit it or not, he belonged in Montana. He'd have to find a way to balance his father's expectations with his love for horse ranching.

Maybe it would be best to just leave. He wasn't ready for another relationship, especially with a woman who had a ready-made family. But the thought of walking away brought a surge of guilt.

He turned from the sofa, certain that if he stayed any longer, he'd somehow convince himself that he needed to kiss Dani O'Malley, really kiss her. What he felt was nothing more than a physical desire, thwarted only by her misconception that he was gay.

As he pulled open the door and stepped into the hallway, he considered telling her the truth and seeing where that revelation led. Sooner or later, he'd feel the urge again, and then he'd be forced to explain why he'd perpetuated the illusion.

Tom's apartment was dark as he walked in. Mr. Whiskers was waiting at the door and followed him into the living room. He flopped down on the sofa and grabbed the remote, tuning into one of the sports networks. Tipping his head back, he tried to put order to his thoughts. In a few hours, the sun would be up and he'd spend another day avoiding the inevitable. How long could he run away from his problems?

But the chaos in his mind was too much and he shut his eyes, listening to the animated voices debating the prospects for the NFL season. Images of Dani danced in his head, her pretty face, her damp lips, the inviting curves of her figure, the soft touch of her hands on his body. He drifted off, allowing the fantasies to focus in his head.

When the sound of the telephone ringing brought him awake, Brad was sure he hadn't fallen asleep at all. But the morning sun was already filtering through the windows, and Mr. Whiskers sat on his chest and stared into his eyes, watching him with a suspicious glint. He held his breath, wondering if it was too late to avoid the cat's gaze. Then, the cat dug its claws into his chest, hissed threateningly and leapt to the floor.

Brad rubbed his chest as he picked up the phone. "Dani?"

"Dani?"

Brad recognized Tom's voice immediately. He lay back down on the sofa, the cordless phone pressed to his ear.

"What the hell are you doing calling me this early? It's five a.m."

"Not here," Tom said. "And just who did you expect? And don't say Dani O'Malley."

"Why not?" Brad asked.

"She's my neighbor, and if you seduced her, I'm going to—"

"Hold on! I haven't seduced your neighbor."

"Good," Tom said. "So how is Mr. Whiskers?"

"He's great. We're getting along fine," Brad lied. "We're even sleeping together."

"And my plants?"

"They haven't turned brown and crispy." He made a mental note to water the plants after he hung up.

"Good. Now, would you like to tell me why you thought I was Dani?"

Brad groaned. "It's a very long story. I've just been helping her out with a few things."

"And you haven't tried to…"

"No, she thinks you and I are an item."

The laugh that came over the phone line was so loud that Brad had to take the phone away from his ear. "What's wrong?" Brad demanded. "Are you saying if I were gay, you wouldn't date me?"

"Absolutely not. First of all, you're entirely too pretty. I don't date men who look better than me. And though you have that whole Marlboro Man thing going for you, I like my men a little bit more…polished. And you live in Montana. For a gay man, that might as well be Siberia."

"I should be hurt," Brad said, his voice edged with sarcasm, "but I think I'll survive. Is there another reason you called? Or would you like to continue with the insults."

"Mother wants me to stay another week, so I just wanted to let you know that the apartment is yours until I get back.

That is, as long as you keep your boots off the sofa, wipe down the marble after you shower and stay away from Dani. She's a good friend and she'll eat you alive if you get too close.''

"Dani O'Malley?''

"She's a real tough cookie," Tom said. "A barracuda in a designer business suit.''

"Are we talking about the same Dani O'Malley?''

"Why?''

"No reason," Brad said, his curiosity suddenly piqued. "Don't worry, I have absolutely no interest in your neighbor." The last was another lie, but not a big one. After all, he wanted it to be true. He didn't want to care about anyone known as a "barracuda." But he'd never seen that side of Dani. In fact, she'd been exactly the opposite from the moment he met her—a complete mess.

"Good," Tom said. "I'll see you when I get back.''

Brad hung up the phone and let his hand rest on the receiver for a long moment. Tom was a pretty fair judge of character. Either he was off the mark completely, or Brad had been fooled by teary eyes and a pretty face.

Hell, what did he really know about Dani O'Malley anyway? Nothing beyond what he'd seen in the confines of her apartment and during a trip to the Space Needle. He never would have guessed that she'd been in foster care, that she'd been effectively orphaned at a young age. She hid that part of her past very well behind a sophisticated facade. So what else might she be hiding?

Slowly he walked to the bedroom, unbuttoning his shirt along the way. He hadn't had a lot of experience with sophisticated women. Most of the women he'd known had been pretty simple and straightforward. They were looking for a husband and family. Somehow, he suspected Dani wanted more from life than domestic bliss.

He flopped down on the bed and stared at the ceiling, knowing that the memory of his lips on hers would keep him from catching that extra hour or two of sleep. He was in over his head and it was time to admit that. He'd maintain a distance from Dani and her kids, and when it was time for him to leave, it would be simple to say goodbye.

For now, it would be best to remain the nice gay guy across the hall.

DANI ROLLED OVER on the sofa and slowly opened her eyes. She cried out softly when she came face-to-face with Noah's jam-stained smile. "Up now," he said. "Up."

She moaned softly and glanced around the room. How had he managed to get out of his crib? And how had she managed to fall asleep on the sofa? The events of the previous night slowly came back and she realized that she hadn't had more than four or five hours' sleep. But another memory drifted through her mind, the memory of a dream she'd had…a delicious dream.

Dani closed her eyes and tried to remember the details. She'd been kissing someone, but who was—oh, God. Brad. She'd been kissing Brad Cullen. And it had been a real kiss, deep and hot and wet. She touched her fingers to her lips, amazed at how real the dream had been.

"I'm having sexual fantasies about a gay man," she muttered. "Time to get a grip."

With a groan, she covered her eyes. She'd grown entirely too dependent upon him over the past couple days and he seemed to enjoy involving himself in their lives. Though the fantasies were fun, the only way to put an end to them was to put some distance between her and Brad. It was time to stand on her own two feet, to deal with her new family herself.

Pushing up from the sofa, she watched as most of Noah's

toys tumbled to the floor. He must have thrown them on top of her while she slept. A rubber duck squawked as she stepped on it, and a ragged teddy bear gave her a one-eyed stare.

"Up," Noah said.

"Up," Dani repeated. "I'm up now."

Satisfied, Noah ran back to his room. Dani glanced at the clock on the mantel. She was usually in the office by now, one of the first to get in and the last to leave. But she couldn't think about work today. She stumbled down the hall and made sure Noah was back in his crib, then crawled into her own bed, pulling the covers over her head.

Another image from her dream flashed in her mind and she realized that the dream had gone further than just a kiss. There had been a bed involved. Not her bed, but a big soft bed with down pillows and silky linens. She pinched her eyes closed and tried to remember exactly what had happened in that bed. Twisted sheets, soft moans, tangled limbs. Dani grabbed a pillow and pulled it over her face.

But she was so exhausted that she was afraid she'd fall back asleep. Reaching out, she grabbed the phone beside the bed and punched in Sam Bennett's direct line. Then she coughed softly, testing the voice she'd use.

"Hi, Sam. It's Dani."

"Dani. Where the hell are you? We've got a Mo' Joe presentation in this afternoon and you and I have to go over the agenda. Did you oversleep?"

"I'm sick," Dani said. "You're going to have to do the presentation yourself or reschedule. I'm just too ill to come in." She coughed a few times for effect, but Sam didn't seem to be buying the story.

"I can't do this myself," Sam said, shouting into his end of the phone. "You're the one they like. You can talk them into anything, and you know this concept is a little off the wall. They'll never buy it from me.''

Mo' Joe had been Dani's first account at Bennett Marks Advertising. Eight years ago, it had been a chain of three shops in the greater Seattle area, just the client for a junior account executive. Now, Mo' Joe Coffee was a nationwide phenomenon, opening a new store nearly every week and challenging Starbucks for a major share of the franchise market. And she was a senior account manager at Bennett Marks.

Dani liked to think that the success of Mo' Joe was due in large part to her guidance and finely honed marketing strategies—and the eighty-hour workweeks she put in on their behalf. Sam Bennett, her boss, believed the same thing and had relinquished more and more of the executive decisions on the account to her. Dani was sure he was grooming her for a vice presidency, a position that came with the salary and power that she coveted.

But if he found out that she now had three kids to care for, he'd look at her in a whole new light. Whether he admitted it or not, there were two tracks at Bennett Marks— the fast track, which ran straight to the top, and the ''mommy'' track, which meandered around in middle management. The mommies were allowed more freedom to come and go when needed, to tend to the demands of their families, to take six months off to have another baby. But they'd made a choice, and with that choice they understood that the travel and the late hours required to make vice president would be impossible with a family.

Dani had always considered the ''mommies'' undependable, unfocused, unable to prioritize. But it had taken her two days to understand exactly where they were coming from. How the hell could any mother put in eighty-hour workweeks when raising children sucked every ounce of energy from the body? Even if she wasn't technically a mommy, she still shouldn't have to make up lies to get a day off.

"Reschedule," she said, interrupting his pleas. "They'll understand. People get sick."

"But *you* don't get sick. I can't recall you ever missing a day of work."

"Well, now I am. I'll call in later for my messages. Goodbye, Sam." Dani quickly hung the phone up, knowing he'd keep talking until he convinced her to come in. She deserved a day off every now and then, sick or not.

"Why did you tell him you were sick?" Jack asked.

Dani spun around to find the boy watching her from the bedroom door, a sullen expression on his face. She wondered if he'd ever smile again. "It's not polite to eavesdrop," she said in a light tone. But he'd caught her in a lie and it was a horrible example to set. This was one of those times when she'd have to be a good parent. "Come here and sit down," she said, patting the bed.

Jack did as he was told, looking up at her impatiently.

"I have a lot of things to do and I didn't want to go into work today. And telling my boss I was sick was the only excuse he'd listen to. Not that it's all right to lie, but sometimes it's just…" She wanted to say "easier," but that wasn't right. "You'll understand when you're grown up and have a job."

"I understand now," Jack said. "I lie all the time when I don't feel like going to school. Sometimes you just gotta take a day off without everyone getting down on you."

Dani stared at him, surprised at Jack's insight. "That's right. I'm glad we have that straight. Now, why don't you go get your sister and brother and we'll have some breakfast and then we need to think about school."

"I don't want to go to school," Jack said.

"You don't have to go today," she said gently. "We just have to register. And maybe we'll look around a little."

He shrugged, then got up off the bed and walked out. Dani sat down and stared after him. This would be her first full day of parenthood without the help of Brad Cullen. If she couldn't cut it, then she'd have to make some difficult decisions.

Noah came toddling into the room again, this time with a training cup clutched in his chubby fingers. "Up," he cried.

"Up," Dani repeated.

She walked to the kitchen, Noah running ahead of her. As she passed the refrigerator, she grabbed a box of cereal from the counter and set it on the table. It was already nine and she hadn't even fed the kids breakfast yet. Though she'd taken the day off work, Dani was beginning to wonder whether she'd be able to get out the door by nine even if she hired a nanny. No matter how early she woke up, she'd still be rushed.

She yawned, covering her mouth with her hand. A short night's sleep on the sofa hadn't been enough, especially sleep plagued with dreams of Brad Cullen.

"Breakfast!" she called. "Jack, Becca."

A few moments later, the trio was gathered around the table in the breakfast nook. Noah easily crawled up onto the stack of phone books that doubled as a baby chair. "He climbed out of his crib this morning," Dani said.

Jack nodded. "He does that all the time. My mom used to say he was part monkey." He grabbed the cereal and dumped a handful on the counter in front of the toddler. Then he filled Becca's bowl.

"Thank you," Dani said.

He looked up at her, his expression indifferent. Dani sighed inwardly. Though they'd been together for almost three days, Dani still hadn't taken the time to sit down and talk to the children. She felt as if she were barely keeping her head above water as it was, between the meals and the laundry and the disposable diapers. Besides, the chaos was keeping her mind off Evie, off the grief that she knew was waiting right beneath the surface.

She slid in next to Becca and folded her hands. "After we enroll you in school, I think maybe we should go shopping for some new school clothes."

"I have clothes," Jack told her.

"Can I have a new dress?" Becca asked.

"Your aunt is sending your things, Jack, but I don't think they'll be here by tomorrow morning."

"I like the clothes I have," he insisted.

"I'd like a new dress," Becca said.

Dani nodded at Becca, but sensed that it wouldn't do to push Jack. At least, not on the subject of clothes. "Jack, I know that the past week has been tough on you. And I want to help you make sense of it all."

"It will never make sense," he said, anger filling his voice.

"Maybe not. But I think it might help if you had someone to talk to—if we all had someone to talk to. I'm going to make an appointment with a family counselor."

"I don't need to talk to anyone," he shouted, shoving his bowl of cereal away. "My dad's dead. My mom's dead. We're orphans." He stalked out of the room, leaving Becca with wide eyes and Noah ready to cry.

"Oh, no," Dani pleaded. She dumped more cereal in front of the toddler. "Don't cry, don't cry. Everything's fine. Jack is fine." But her words were in vain. The little boy screwed up his face and let out a howl.

"He wants blankie," Becca said.

"Run and get it for me, will you?" Dani asked. She

hurried around the table and picked Noah up from the phone books, hugging him tight and whispering soothing words. Becca returned a few moments later and handed her brother his blanket. Then she sat down beside Dani.

"Is it true?" she asked, gazing up at Dani with wide eyes.

"Is what true, sweetie?"

"Are we orphans?"

Dani smiled and nodded. "Yes, you and Jack and Noah are orphans."

The little girl drew a ragged breath. "So, what's orphans?"

This would be just the first of many questions that Dani would have to answer. None of them promised to be easy, but at least she had some experience with this one. "An orphan is a child whose parents have died. You know, I was an orphan when I was little."

They sat in the breakfast nook for a long time, talking about what it meant to be an orphan. And in the end, Dani felt as if she'd truly helped Becca understand. If she was just honest with the children and listened when they spoke, maybe things wouldn't be so bad.

CHAPTER FOUR

"THERE'S A MAN downstairs who'd like to see you."

Alexandra Webber glanced up from the baby she was feeding and smiled at Amy Tidwell. The teenager fiddled with the end of her long braid, twisting her little finger through the plait distractedly. Amy had been such a dependable employee, a real asset to Forrester Square Day Care, but lately she seemed distracted and preoccupied. Her ever-present headphones were always on her head, and she often had to be told something twice before she really heard. And though Amy usually preferred casually funky clothes, lately she'd gone overboard with the baggy look.

"Did you ask his name?" Alexandra inquired.

"He says he's an old friend," she explained. "He said he wanted to surprise you." She lowered her voice, as if the babies in the nursery were listening. "He's really cute. Real...rugged. And tall. He reminds me of a cowboy."

Alexandra only knew one person who fit that description. "Brad," she murmured. Amy's brow quirked up and Alexandra could tell she was speculating as to the extent of her boss's "friendship" with the stranger. "He's my cousin," Alexandra explained. "Our mothers were sisters and I grew up with him in Montana."

"You grew up in Montana?" Amy asked. "I thought you grew up in Kansas City."

"No, I lived there before I moved to Seattle. I grew up on a horse ranch," Alexandra said. She wondered how much Amy—or any of the employees at the day care—knew about her past. How much had Hannah and Katherine, her childhood friends and now business partners, told them? Did the staff know about the terrible fire that had killed her parents that night so many years ago?

Even now, the memories were too hard to bear. She still dreamed about that night, about the argument, the crackling flames, the grandfather clock striking four, the terror she felt. And then the sorrow when she found out that both her mother and father had perished in the fire.

A shiver skittered down her spine and she forced the memory aside as she had so many times before. To this day, she'd never read an account of the fire, never asked any questions or demanded explanations. The fire was part of her past. Someday, she'd let the memories out in the open and face what had happened. But she wasn't ready, not yet.

Alexandra stood up and carried one-year-old Mary Ellen Marino to the soft rug in the center of the room. Julia, an aide in the nursery room, sat in the middle of the rug, feeding her son, Jeremy. Alexandra settled Mary Ellen on a blanket beside Julia and handed her the half-empty jar of strained plums. "I'll be back in a bit," she said.

Hurrying down the stairs, Alexandra finger-combed her tousled red hair, then tried to brush a spot of spit up off the shoulder of her dress. She found the visitor sitting on a small plastic chair in the events room, his knees nearly touching his chin. "Brad?"

He slowly struggled to his feet, his grin wide and welcoming. "I never remember our childhood being quite this colorful. Were we ever this small?"

A flush of happiness warmed her cheeks, and with a giggle, Alexandra crossed the room and threw herself into his arms. "You're the last person I expected to see today. What are you doing here?"

"I've been doing some climbing in the Cascades," Brad said, stepping back. "And I couldn't visit Seattle without checking in. Look at you. You just get prettier every time I see you, Alvin."

Her heart warmed at his use of one of the many names he and his siblings had given her as a child. Alvin, Alfred, everything but Alexandra, as she was known to the rest of the world. She'd grown up one of the guys—Alex. "You are such a flirt," she teased, giving him a playful slap. "How long has it been? How are Uncle Walt and Aunt Mary Rose? More importantly, how are you?" She paused. "Your mother called me about the wedding. I was all packed and ready to get on the plane, but then…"

Brad smiled sheepishly. "Well, at least you didn't waste any frequent flyer miles. I suppose Jo could have called it off at the altar and really humiliated me. At least she had the good grace to do it before the rehearsal dinner. But enough about me. How about you? You've finally put down some roots, I see. Mom says you're a partner in this establishment."

Alexandra grinned. "I think maybe I've found my place here. I feel…at home. Hannah and Katherine have been great, teaching me the ropes. And I've even been looking for an apartment of my own. I think it's time for me to settle down—at least for a while."

"You? The girl who never wanted to stay in one place too long? How many different places have you lived in since you left college? Let me see, there was Chicago, and then Kansas City, and then Pittsburgh."

"Pittsburgh before Kansas City," Alexandra said. "And what are you, my cousin or my therapist?"

Brad paused, searching her face. The fire had left deep scars, emotional scars she'd kept hidden from everyone—except Brad. The nightmares that had plagued her in childhood had continued into adulthood, and it was Brad who'd suggested she seek a therapist to help her sort out the memories. "You're seeing someone?"

"A shrink?" Alexandra scoffed. "No. I don't need a shrink. I'm fine."

"Alex, you can't continue to ignore—"

"I'm fine. I've been sleeping much better lately," she lied, "and the day care has given me something to focus on. When I dream, I dream about disposable diapers and juice boxes. I'm not nearly as stressed as I used to be. Can't you tell?" She reached up and placed her palm on his check. "Stop worrying. Come on, I'll buy you a cup of coffee. There's a place just next door."

Alexandra grabbed his hand and led him back toward the front door. They passed Amy on the way and she informed the teenager that she would be back in an hour or two. After walking a few short yards to Caffeine Hy's, they both ordered a latte. When they found an empty table at the busy shop, Alexandra took a spot across from Brad, folded her hands in front of her and studied him shrewdly.

"When are you going back to Montana?" she asked.

"Is that a casual question or have you talked to my mother lately?"

"She's worried about you. How long has it been since you called home?"

Brad shrugged. "I call every few weeks. But I don't tell them where I am and I'd appreciate it if you wouldn't, oi ther. I need some time to sort this out myself—without their meddling."

"She thinks you're running away from your problems, mooning over your lost love and avoiding your responsibilities at the ranch."

"Maybe I am." Brad took a deep breath. "The way I figure, it's about time I decided what I want to do with my life. *Me,* not my parents. Hell, I've been trying to please my father since the day I was born. I'm starting to believe that's why I was so determined to marry Jo. I need a break from all that pressure.''

''You're going to climb rocks for the rest of your life?''

''Maybe.'' Brad took a sip of his coffee. ''I know a few guys who've set up a guide service on Rainier. They'd give me a job in a heartbeat.''

''But you love horse ranching. How could you give that up?''

''I love the horses,'' Brad said. ''And I love the wide open spaces in Montana. But I hate the business end of it, the bookwork, dealing with the bank, taking care of the taxes. That kind of stuff consumes all my time and I barely get a chance to get out of the office. That's not horse ranching, that's bean counting.''

''Have you talked to Jo since…the breakup?''

Brad shook his head. ''Hell, no. And I don't want to. I don't need a reminder of what a sap I was. I was in love with her and she was messing around with some rodeo cowboy. I heard she ran off to Vegas with him.''

''Is that why you decided to take off?''

''A guy can only be humiliated so many times before he has to take a stand,'' Brad joked.

Alexandra reached out and took his hands. ''I'm not sure I should tell you this.''

He frowned. ''I'm not sure I want to hear this. What is it?''

''Your mom told me that Jo is back home. I guess the thing with the bull rider is over. Your mom seems to think there's a chance you'll work things out if you'd only go home.''

''I don't think that's going to happen. I've moved on.''

''You've found someone else?'' Alexandra asked. He

paused, as if trying to decide what to tell her. "I won't tell anyone." She held out the little finger of her right hand. "Pinky swear."

Brad hooked his finger over hers and chuckled. "Well, there's this woman. I've been staying at Tom Hopson's apartment while he's out of town. He was my college roommate, remember?"

Alexandra nodded.

"She lives across the hall and we meet the first day I was in Seattle. I chased down a pair of her panties."

Alexandra gasped. "You what?"

"She's beautiful and smart. And she thinks I'm gay." He held up his hand. "Don't ask."

"Are you planning to let her in on the truth?"

"It's kind of nice not to have that whole sex thing hanging over us. Besides, she's got enough to think about right now. She just became guardian to three kids and she could use a friend a whole lot more than a lover. So that's what I've been doing. Helping her out with the kids."

"She's got kids." Alexandra slowly nodded. "Ah, I see where this is leading. She's got kids and I've got a day-care center. I feel like there's a favor in here somewhere."

"There is," Brad said. "She needs child care for two of the kids. Becca is five and Noah is two. Becca would be just half days since she'll be in kindergarten. I'm hoping you can help her out. Just until she gets on her feet."

"You really care about this woman."

"No," Brad said. "I'm just doing a favor for a friend."

"Well, we have plenty of openings. And we have a kindergarten here. But if…"

"Dani," Brad said.

"If Dani would like Becca in public school kindergarten, we can arrange for the school bus to pick her up and drop her off here. I can give you a fee schedule and a copy of our brochure. We'd be happy to have Becca and Noah.''

''Great. Dani's going to be so relieved. This whole thing has been hard on her. Losing her best friend, inheriting a family, trying to learn how to be a parent.''

''Are you sure you're not falling for her?''

''As long as I'm gay, we're just friends.''

Alexandra smiled and nodded. ''It's so great to have you here. And as long as you're gay, maybe you and I can go shopping this afternoon. I need a new outfit and I'd love to get your input. What do you think? Would I look good in orange?''

Brad growled playfully, then reached across the table and ruffled her hair, the way he'd done when they were kids. ''Only if you'll help me shop for something decent to wear. All I have along are jeans and T-shirts. I need something a little nicer if I'm going to be staying in Seattle for a while.''

Alexandra observed him shrewdly. From the time they were kids, she'd been able to read Brad. And if she knew one thing for certain, her cousin was in serious denial. Heck, he lived in jeans. He'd tried to convince Jo to wear denim for their wedding, and now he was interested in dressing up?

Brad had feelings for this Dani O'Malley, whether he was ready to admit it or not. She smiled to herself. Well, if she had two of Dani's children at the day care, that would give her plenty of time to check the woman out. Jo Millen wasn't the one for Brad, but perhaps Dani O'Malley was.

''ALL RIGHT, let's see how you all look. It's your first day of school so you have to look just right.''

Dani stood back and evaluated Jack, Becca and Noah. After she'd registered Jack and Becca for school yesterday, she'd come home to find Brad waiting with brochures for a local day care center. They'd all toured Forrester Square Day Care the next day and followed that with a trip to the mall for new clothes. Jack wore a baggy shirt that Dani knew was popular with the skateboard crowd, and cargo pants with a multitude of pockets. His old backpack was slung across one shoulder, filled with everything a seventh grader needed at Thomas Edison Middle School. But from his gloomy attitude, it was clear he wasn't excited about his first day at a new school.

Becca could hardly contain her elation. She'd had her first taste of kindergarten in the weeks before her mother had died and missed it desperately. She'd barely slept the night before and couldn't stop talking about how much fun she was going to have and how many new friends she'd find. She'd chosen a Barbie backpack, a pretty flowered dress and shiny red shoes for her first day.

As for Noah, he wore the cutest little corduroy pants and airplane T-shirt, already stained with grape juice, and seemed to be completely oblivious to the importance of the day.

"I'm going to drop Jack off at school," Dani said, "and Becca, you and Noah are going to the day care with Brad. Remember, Becca, when you visited the day care yesterday and you met your teacher, Mrs. Perez? Well, she's going to introduce you to a whole bunch of new friends."

"What about real school?" Becca cried.

"A bus will pick you up at day care and you'll go to school after lunch. Your teacher there is Miss Wisnicki. And after school, you'll go back to the day-care center. Then, after I pick Jack up from school, I'll come to the day care and pick you two up. And then we'll go home." Dani took a deep breath. "I know it sounds complicated, but we'll get used to it." Sooner or later, she'd have to find a way to make this work on her own. But for now, she'd gratefully accepted Brad's help.

He'd already done so much for the children, finding a terrific day care for Noah and Becca, taking Jack shopping for school supplies, and helping Becca decide which socks to wear with her new dress. She'd come to depend on him over the past few days, and he'd been so generous with his time, making her life much more manageable. But Dani couldn't depend on Brad forever. She couldn't depend on anyone but herself. Like the others, he'd walk away and she'd have to stand on her own two feet. The sooner she did that, the better it would be for all of them.

"The three of you look wonderful," Dani said with a smile. "You're going to make all sorts of friends."

A knock sounded on the door of her apartment, and a moment later, Brad stepped inside. "Hey, is everyone ready to go?" he shouted.

The children hurried out of the bedroom and greeted Brad. Dani stopped short when she saw him. He wasn't dressed in his usual jeans and flannel shirt. Today, he wore a pair of pressed khakis and a crisp Oxford cloth shirt, unbuttoned at the neck. If she didn't already know he was a cowboy, she might never have guessed. She wondered at the change, wondered if he'd met someone—some man—here in Seattle whom he wanted to impress.

An unbidden surge of jealousy shot through her and she pushed it aside. He wasn't her cowboy. She had no right to such feelings. Still, her dependency on him had given her claim to his time, time he'd so generously provided. If he found someone else to occupy his time, then he'd have less for them. Dani cursed silently. It was time to let go.

"You look nice," she said, keeping her tone light. "Do you have something planned for today?"

He shrugged. "I've got a lunch date," he said. "But I can pick up the kids from school if you'd like."

Dani shook her head. "I already told the children that I'd be picking them up."

"It's no trouble," Brad said.

"No," she replied, a bit more firmly than she wanted to. "I have to do this. It's my responsibility. It's best that we get into some kind of schedule and the sooner the better."

"Then why don't I make dinner for us tonight? You'll all be tired and hungry after a long day. And I've got time to make my world-famous bunkhouse chili."

Dani sighed. Brad had become attached to the children. Perhaps it would be best to make the break slowly. Besides, she didn't want to seem ungrateful. "All right," she said. "We should be home before five."

He sent her a smile and Dani held her breath, unable to stop the flood of warmth that raced through her. This crazy attraction to him would have to stop. There was no future in it. Yes, Brad Cullen was incredibly attractive and kind and understanding and sexy. But he wasn't about to come over to the dark side simply because she had strange, erotic dreams about him.

"Come on, Jack," she said. "We better leave or you'll be late."

Jack muttered something, then bid goodbye to his siblings. Dani knelt down beside Becca and kissed her on the cheek. "You're going to have a wonderful time," she told the girl. "And you're going to make lots of new friends." Then she gave Noah a hug. "Be a good boy today."

She expected him to start crying as he usually did when she was near. But to Dani's relief, Noah was beginning to trust her. Little by little, the boy had became more comfortable, and now he sent her a sweet smile. A smile that warmed her heart. "You won't have any trouble," she said. "You'll charm all the ladies at the day care."

"They'll be fine," Brad said, helping her to her feet. He rubbed her arm, leaving a warm brand on her skin. "Alex will make sure they settle in."

Dani fought the urge to step into his arms and lose herself in his strong embrace. She needed a little reassurance right now, the kind of reassurance that only he seemed able to provide. Today would be another difficult day. Her worries about the children would hang over her until she picked them up that afternoon. And after two days of feigned illness, she'd have to figure out how to tell Sam Bennett that she suddenly had other obligations beyond her sixteen-hour workdays.

With a forced a smile, she met Brad's gaze for a long moment. "Let's go."

She hurried to the elevator, Jack silently striding along behind her. Dani wanted to encourage him as she had Becca and Noah, but she knew exactly what he was going through—the sick knot in his stomach, the dry mouth, the face that would ache by the end of the day from trying to smile.

When they got in the car, Jack immediately turned on the radio, choosing a local hip-hop station. Dani focused on traffic, but her mind filled with memories of her own childhood. Of the long string of schools, a new school with every new set of foster parents. Until she met Evie, she hadn't really cared where she landed. But once she had a real friend and began to excel in her studies, the social workers had decided it was best to leave her in the same school.

That had been when her life had changed and she'd taken control of her future. She'd been just about Jack's age. Dani often wondered at the powers of fate. What if she hadn't been forced to stand at that fence on that particular day? What would life have held for her?

She pulled up to the curb in front of the school, then turned to Jack. "Are you going to be all right?"

He nodded, his expression distracted, indifferent.

"I know how difficult this is, Jack. I went to a lot of new schools when I was a kid."

"You did?"

"I remember this one day in particular. I was at another new school and there was a group of girls who were picking on me because I was the new kid. I was sure I'd never make any friends. I hadn't in the past. But then I met this really nice girl on the playground and she turned out to be my very best friend."

He smiled wanly. "Was that my mom?"

"Yeah. Maybe you'll be lucky and find a good friend on your first day. But I know if it doesn't happen today, it will happen very soon. Because you're a really good kid and someone will figure that out."

Jack opened the car door and stepped out. For an instant, Dani considered calling him back. Maybe it was too soon. It hadn't even been two weeks since his mother died. And she knew how tough the day would be. But then Jack turned, straightened his spine, and walked up the sidewalk to the front door of the school. She watched him until he was swallowed up by the crowd. Then she said a silent little prayer that at least one person would talk to him during the day.

As she put the car into gear and drove away, Dani thought of all the comforting things she could have said. This parent stuff was confusing and nerve-racking. She'd thought her own childhood was painful enough, but watching another child go through it all over again was just as bad.

By the time she reached the office, she'd turned her

thoughts to the next problem on the list. She'd considered keeping the kids a secret from Sam, but though the idea was good in theory, it would be nearly impossible to execute. Like the working mothers at the agency, she needed a little flexibility in her schedule and understanding from her boss.

Dani glanced at her watch, pleased that she'd managed to get to work before nine. Tomorrow, if they all got ready just fifteen minutes earlier, she'd be able to drop Noah and Becca off at the day care and then swing by Jack's school on the way to work. "Organization," she stated as she pulled into the parking lot. "That's what it's going to take. That and a very loud alarm clock."

As Dani strode through the lobby, she felt like a stranger walking into unfamiliar territory. At first, she thought the odd feeling came from two weeks in L.A. But it was something more. She wasn't the same person who'd walked out of the office two weeks ago. Since last Friday, her life had been turned upside down, her priorities called into question. She owed it to Evie to put her children first, to make a good home for them while they were still grieving. Yet she'd spent years building a career that had been the most important thing in her life. Still, if anyone could do it all, she could.

"Good morning, Laurie," Dani said, snatching up her messages from her assistant as she passed.

"Sam is waiting in your office," Laurie said.

"I figured he would be," Dani called over her shoulder as she pushed open the door. "Morning, Sam."

Her boss glanced down at his watch. "It's almost nine. Where the hell have you been?"

"Good morning to you, too," she said, tossing her coat over one of her guest chairs. "How did the meeting go Monday?"

"Terrible. They balked on the concept and they seem to

be confused about the media buys we proposed. You've got a lot of damage control to do here, Dani.''

Dani sat down in her chair and looked through the story boards for the new Mo' Joe campaign. ''Don't worry. I'll talk to Rick and get this all straightened out. The campaign looks great.''

Sam tossed the Tuesday business section of the *Seattle Times* on her desk. ''Yesterday's paper. Page three, second column.''

''What is it?''

''Jason Wentland announced on Monday morning that he was taking his advertising to Davich Walters. I thought you told me he was a sure thing. Six million dollars and those idiots at Davich Walters got his account. Their guys still think puns are the height of creativity.''

Dani sighed. ''I'm sorry.''

''Didn't you have a dinner meeting with him on Friday?''

''Well, I was supposed to, but I had to reschedule. I guess he wasn't interested in what we had to offer.''

Sam cursed softly. ''Dani, what the hell is going on with you? That meeting was important. You had a chance to reel that guy in. You usually don't mess up like this.''

''I've had a lot on my mind,'' she replied, looking for an opening, a way to break her big news.

''What could possibly have been more important than work.''

There it was, Dani thought. She drew a deep breath. ''My best friend died and left me her three children.'' She probably should have softened the revelation a bit more, but she was known for her direct approach when it came to business. ''They were at my apartment when I got back Friday night and I've been trying to get them settled ever since.''

''Three children?'' He stared at her as if she'd sprouted horns and a tail. ''You have three children now?''

"Yes. I'm their guardian and it's up to me to decide where they should live."

"Then this is just a temporary thing," Sam said.

"I don't know," Dani murmured. "Maybe not. They might be staying with me permanently. I'll have to see how things go."

"You can't be serious. You don't have the time for one child, much less three. You have a career here, and I don't have to tell you that we have plans for you at Bennett Marks."

"And those plans don't have to change," Dani said. "Once I work all the kinks out, I can devote my full attention to work. I think, given the chance, I can balance my job with caring for the children. I just have to get everything organized." Dani knew she was stretching the truth a bit. With three children, her life would never be completely organized. But she had to at least give it a try.

"You can't divide your energies and expect to be as effective as you were," Sam said.

"And why is that, Sam? Will being around children suddenly suck all the intelligence out of my head?"

"Don't be ridiculous. This has nothing to do with intelligence. It has to do with priorities. Plenty of working mothers have tried to juggle both. Believe me. You'll have to make choices, Dani, and when you have children, work can't come first. There are only so many sick days I'll tolerate."

"I can do it all," Dani said. "And I'll prove it to you."

"I wish I could believe that," Sam said. He slowly stood, finished with his attempt to convince her of what she already knew was true. "I told the guys at Mo' Joe that you'd call them as soon as you got in.

As her boss stalked out of the office, Dani sank back into her chair. Everything she'd worked for, all the long hours and endless travel, didn't mean anything to Sam Bennett. She was the one who'd built Mo' Joe into a multimillion dollar account. She was the one who'd put the creative team together and developed the marketing strategies. And the reward was supposed to be a vice presidency.

But now, in the blink of an eye, she was suddenly a different person, a less competent person, simply because she had children to care for. But how could she care for these children if she didn't have job security? Where would they all be if Sam Bennett decided that another account manager could better handle the Mo' Joe business?

Dani rubbed her temples, trying to ease the stress and clear her head. She'd make this work. Heck, if she could put herself through college and build a successful career, she could certainly figure out a way to get that vice presidency!

"I'm going to do it, no matter what Sam Bennett says." She sighed softly. "I have to."

BRAD HEARD the front door of Dani's apartment open. The sound of running footsteps filled the air, and a few seconds later, Jack, Becca and Noah appeared in the kitchen.

"I'm starving," Becca cried.

"Do we have any chips?" Jack asked.

"Joo," Noah demanded.

Brad picked up an apple and tossed it to Jack. "Eat that," he said. He grabbed another from the bowl and presented it to Becca. "Where's Dani?"

"She's gone to lie down," Jack replied.

Brad wiped his hands on a dish towel and grabbed a bottle of wine he'd opened. Then he picked up a pair of glasses and headed into the living room. He found her stretched out on the sofa, her shoes still on, her arm thrown over her eyes.

"Supper is almost ready," he said.

She didn't uncover her eyes. "I'm really not very hungry."

Brad picked her feet up from the end of the sofa and sat down. Then he pulled off her shoes and gently massaged her feet. "Bad day at work?"

"Horrible. The worst. Oh, that feels good."

The simple act of touching her, even her feet, brought an unbidden surge of desire. But now that he'd started, he couldn't just stop. Instead, he grit his teeth and slipped his hands up to her ankles. "Would you like to tell me about it?"

"No," she said.

"Come on," Brad encouraged her. "You'll feel better after you eat. One taste of my chili and you'll feel much better."

"I said, I'm not hungry," Dani repeated. She pulled her feet away and sat up, raking her hand through her hair. "I don't need you to make dinner or clean the apartment or solve all my problems. I don't need you to worry about the children or try to coax me out of a bad mood. I—I don't need you."

The vehemence of her words stunned him. "Dani, what's this all about? If you had a bad day, don't take it out on me."

"This is exactly what I don't need right now," she said.

"Right," Brad said. "You don't need anybody or anything. Never mind that I care about you and the kids, that I want to help."

"Why?" she demanded. "What's in it for you?"

"There's nothing in it for me. Does there have to be?"

"Do you have some crazy idea that we're going to be a family?" she asked, lowering her voice so the children couldn't hear. "That I'm going to go out and work and you're going to stay home and cook and we'll live happily ever after.'' She stood up. ''Someday you're going to make some man a great wife, is that what you want to hear?''

Her comment stung, and Brad didn't try to quell the surge of anger. He followed her to her bedroom, where she angrily pulled off her jacket and hung it in the closet. ''I know you had a tough childhood and I know that you're not used to asking for help.''

''You don't know anything about me,'' Dani muttered.

He saw the hard, angry expression on her face and realized that maybe she was right. Maybe he didn't know Dani O'Malley at all. Tom's characterization of her filtered through his mind. ''I guess no one will ever get to know you then. Not if you keep pushing them away. Is that what you're going to do with the kids?''

''What I choose to do with those children is none of your business. They're my responsibility, not yours.'' She pushed past him and stalked to the kitchen. But Brad wasn't ready to let the issue go. He caught up with her just as she was opening the refrigerator door. Grabbing her arm, he spun her around to face him. She tipped her chin up, sending him a withering look. ''What?'' she demanded.

''Aw, hell,'' he muttered.

One moment he had decided the best course of action was to just walk away from the fight. And the next, his mouth was on hers. A tiny gasp slipped from her lips and he felt her try to pull away. But Brad wasn't about to let her go until she was quite clear about his feelings. Forget acquaintances and friendships and all the other polite little words for their relationship. From now on, she'd know exactly where he was coming from.

As he deepened the kiss, Dani went soft in his arms and he knew she wanted this as much as he did. His tongue teased at her mouth, and she hesitantly opened beneath the gentle assault. This was not a thank-you kiss, not a platonic kiss or a kiss stolen while she slept. No, there wasn't any way she could mistake this kiss for anything less than an expression of pure need.

He needed to taste her, to feel her body pressed against his, to set her pulse racing and her mind spinning. When he finally drew away, Brad was pleased. He'd done all right. He suspected that Dani had just been kissed more completely than she'd ever been kissed in her life.

She opened her mouth to speak, then snapped it shut again.

"There," he said. "I'm glad we cleared that up. And now I'd better be going. The chili is done. There's cornbread in the oven and shredded cheese in the fridge."

He walked back through the kitchen, only to find three faces staring at him from the table.

"You kissed her," Becca whispered.

Brad smiled at her wide-eyed expression, raising his eyebrows. "I guess I did."

"Does that mean you're going to marry her?"

"Don't be dumb," Jack whispered. "People who kiss don't always get married."

"Lizzie Martin kissed you last summer and she said you were going to marry her."

Squatting down in front of Becca, Brad took her hands in his. "I just needed to let Dani know something and the only way to do it was to kiss her."

The little girl sighed. "It was just like *Lady and the Tramp,* only without the noodles."

"Next time, I'll remember the noodles," Brad teased. He tweaked her nose then straightened. "Enjoy your dinner. You can tell me about school another time."

He glanced back over his shoulder at Dani. She was leaning against the counter, her hands braced behind her as if she were about to crumple in a heap on the tile floor. Then he walked to the door, certain that in time, she'd have something to say to him about their kiss. After all, on a scale of one to ten, he had to admit it ranked right up there with his best work.

It wasn't hard to kiss Dani. Her lips, her eyes, everything about her tempted him at every turn. If the kids hadn't been watching, he might have continued to kiss her for the rest of the night. Hell, he might have scooped her up into his arms and carried her to the bedroom.

He closed the apartment door behind him, then leaned back against it, wondering if he ought to go back inside and explain himself. Brad shook his head. If that kiss hadn't said everything he wanted to say, then to hell with it. She wasn't a naive woman. The ball was now in her court. She'd have to make the next move.

Pushing off the door, he crossed the hall and stepped inside Tom's apartment. But in the silent interior, memories of the kiss lingered, swirling in his head until he felt drunk with the thought of it. It had been a long time since he'd felt such instant desire, such overwhelming passion.

He couldn't recall it ever being that way with Jo—except maybe those first few months. Their relationship had been more comfortable and easy than intense. They rarely argued. There had even been times when Brad wondered how deep Jo's feelings really ran, since she never seemed to be bothered by anything in their relationship. Maybe he should have trusted his doubts. There had been something missing, and now he knew exactly what it was—fire.

Love ought to be a little dangerous, Brad mused. It ought to be risky and scary and overwhelming. If not, how could a person know the depth of their feelings. He sat down on the sofa and kicked his feet up, not bothering to remove his boots or heed Tom's warning about the silk-covered cushions.

But Brad couldn't stay still. He felt caged, frustrated and confused. Every instinct told him to run, to get as far away from Dani O'Malley as he could. Not five months ago, his life had been turned upside down by a woman he thought he knew better than anyone. Why would he suddenly trust his heart to a woman he knew nothing about?

With a soft curse, Brad grabbed his jacket and headed toward the elevator. Had he been back at Split Rock, he would have taken Riot, his horse, out for a long, hard ride. But there weren't any horses worth riding in the city of Seattle, so a brisk walk would have to do.

When the elevator opened at the lobby, he stepped out. Louie, the building manager, stood at the door, polishing the glass until it gleamed. "Working late?" Brad called.

Louie stopped polishing and rubbed a kink out of his back. "This seems to be the only time I can clean this door without people traipsing through and messing it all up again." He picked up a rag and spray bottle. "Look at that," he said, pointing to a spot further down. "Jelly. Since those kids moved in here, I've had to polish this door twice a day."

"They do have a way of making life a little more exciting, don't they," Brad said.

"Exciting?" Louie scoffed. "Those little ankle-biters are too much damn work."

"You ever been married, Louie?"

The man shook his head and smiled. "Nope. My lady is this building. From the minute I walked into her, I knew we'd be together forever. Did you know they hired a guy from France to carve the crown molding in this lobby? And these floors. Well, they don't make floors like that anymore.

And that mahogany paneling in the elevator was imported. It used to be in some palace in Europe.''

"It must be nice to love your work," Brad said.

Louie nodded. "What do you do?''

"My family owns a ranch in Montana. We breed horses.''

"Humph," Louie replied.

"You don't like horses?''

"Nah. I just figured a guy like you would be involved in a different line of work. You know, hair dressing or fashion design or one of them artsy jobs like Mr. Hopson has.''

Brad wondered if he ought to illuminate Louie now that he'd made his preferences clear to Dani. "Nope. Just horses.''

Louie nodded. "If you're a horse guy, what are you doing in Seattle? We don't have a whole lotta horses around here.''

"I'm just taking a break," Brad said. "Trying to figure out what I want to do with my life.''

"If you don't like ranching, maybe you ought to give architecture a try. Seems to be working out for Mr. Hopson.''

Brad shook his head. "I'm no good at the math.''

"Yeah, me neither," Louie said. "I guess guys like us are just meant to work with our hands instead of our heads.''

"Maybe so." Brad smiled, then started toward the front door. If only it were that simple. Maybe it was for Louie, but Brad had choices to make. The ranch was his to run, but he wasn't interested in the business of running it. He liked the work, the barns and the pastures, riding the fence-lines and breaking the stock. Dusty work, his dad called it. His three younger brothers and only sister were satisfied to make the ranch an occasional occupation. But by virtue of the order of his birth, he was expected to give up work he loved for days spent sitting at a desk and poring over bank statements and trucking invoices and vet bills.

As he strolled down the sidewalk, Brad thought about what he'd say to his father. Hell, maybe he just shouldn't go back. He'd saved some money and invested wisely. He had enough for a down payment on a place of his own. He'd have to start small, but the notion appealed to him. After all, it was the easiest solution. His father would have to understand a man's need to make something for himself.

He turned the idea over and over in his head, trying to picture the kind of place he'd like. But the landscape didn't look like the rugged vistas of Montana. Instead he saw lush green hills and thick forests and the heavy mists that rolled off the Pacific.

"Washington," he murmured. "I wonder if they raise many horses in this state."

Brad sighed softly. Was he really interested in Washington for its horse-raising potential? Or was he contemplating a place where he could be closer to Dani O'Malley and her kids. He cursed softly. "Don't go jumping the gun, there, cowboy."

Like Jack said, just because he kissed Dani didn't mean he was going to marry her.

CHAPTER FIVE

DANI ADJUSTED the wicker laundry basket under her arm, then stepped into the elevator, pushing the button to the basement of her apartment building. For children who didn't have a huge wardrobe, she sure spent a lot of time doing laundry. At first, she had thought about sending everything out to her dry cleaners, but at the rate Noah went through shirts and Becca went through socks, she'd be flat broke before Christmas. She had learned one thing about toddlers in the past week—they didn't care if they wore a juice-stained shirt. So she'd started leaving Noah in his dirty shirt until bedtime.

In truth, that wasn't all she'd learned. Since her argument with Brad last night, she'd been forced to deal with all things family on her own. And though it had only been a day, she felt pretty proud of her efforts. She'd made it to work on time, that morning and the kids had made it to school dressed in clean clothes, and no one had gone hungry.

She didn't need Brad Cullen. At least not as a baby-sitter or stand-in husband. But that didn't mean she'd forgotten the kiss they'd shared in her kitchen. The wonderful, mind-numbing, toe-curling kiss that had taken her breath away and made her knees turn to pudding.

Though the kids and work occupied her thoughts for most of the day, every free moment had been filled with memories of his lips on hers, of his tongue invading her mouth and taking possession of her senses. For a gay guy, he sure knew how to kiss women.

Dani leaned back against the mahogany paneling and sighed. But that wasn't the only thing that occupied her brain. If Brad was gay, why would he even kiss her at all? She drew in a sharp breath. Unless he'd realized that she harbored a secret crush on him. Dani groaned. Maybe it had been a pity kiss, or maybe he'd meant to taunt her with her silly attraction.

The elevator doors opened and she stepped out. As she walked down the hall, the telltale sound of the washers working echoed against the concrete walls. If there weren't two or three free, she'd be doing her laundry all evening. But as she entered the room, Dani found only one person doing laundry on a Thursday night—Brad Cullen.

He stood in front of one of the washers, his back to her. He was dressed in just his jeans, his back and arms bare. She stood behind him, watching the play of muscle across his shoulders as he flipped the pages of a newspaper. He didn't notice her entrance. She quickly turned, hoping to make an escape before he looked up, but then he put the newspaper down and glanced over his shoulder and she was caught in midflight.

Dani cursed beneath her breath. This was her apartment building and her laundry room! She had every right to do her laundry whenever she wanted. And he had no right to walk around half-naked. Gathering her resolve, she strolled inside and slid her basket onto the floor in front of an empty washer.

He watched her every move, silent and indifferent, as if he was waiting for her to start the conversation. Somehow she sensed that he was thinking about exactly the same thing she was—the kiss they'd shared. A tiny shiver skittered down her spine. How could she have possibly thought he was gay? She'd replayed their conversations over and over again, trying to pinpoint the exact moment when she'd made that assumption, and could only conclude she'd missed something big.

She had managed to avoid him for almost forty-eight hours, which was pretty good, considering he lived across the hall. But that didn't mean she hadn't been tempted to cross that boundary and demand an explanation—or borrow a cup of sugar. If he was gay, then maybe the kiss had been a lapse in judgment. And if he wasn't gay, then he'd been carrying out a rather elaborate charade, for what reason, she didn't know.

There was one other explanation, she mused. Dani cleared her throat and pointed at the washer he was standing in front of. "Are you using that one?"

"No," Brad said.

He moved aside, forcing Dani to brush up against him as she opened the lid. Her elbow skimmed his rib cage and the contact of skin against skin sent her heart racing. She risked a glance up at him and found his gaze intently fixed on hers.

"Can I give you a hand?" he offered.

"No, I'm fine."

She reached past him again, but as she did, she dropped one of Becca's dresses onto the floor. They both bent down at the same time, and when they stood, Dani found herself just inches from his body. Her gaze dropped to the smooth expanse of his chest and she clutched the dress, fighting an impulse to reach out and run her palm over his skin, then gauge his reaction.

"How are the kids?" Brad asked, his lips so close to her temple that she could feel the warmth of his breath.

"They're fine."

"And how are you? I haven't seen you around."

"I'm fine, too."

He nodded, then reached over her shoulder and grabbed a handful of laundry from her basket. For a heartbeat, his chest pressed against her breasts. Dani should have stepped back, but the contact made her lose every bit of her resolve.

When he finished loading her laundry, he held out his hand. "Do you have quarters?"

She reached into her pocket and handed him four. He put them into the machine and waited. "Soap?"

Dani blinked, catching herself in an idle contemplation of his left bicep. With a silent curse, she reached into the laundry basket and grabbed the detergent, pouring a measure into the machine. He sent her a devilish grin, then shoved the quarters in, dropped the top and pushed the button. "I guess that's a first step," he said.

"A first step?"

"You're allowing me to help you with the laundry."

"You're not helping," she said. "You're..." She drew a deep breath. "In the way."

"So, are we going to talk about it?" Brad asked.

"About what?"

"You've forgotten already? I thought I did a little better than that."

Dani bristled at his teasing tone. "I don't know what's going on with you, but I do know what's going on with me. I have three children to take care of and a career to deal with, and I don't have any time for your silly games."

"Games?"

"The kiss. Do I have to say it? You kissed me...in my kitchen. Yes, I remember."

His smile grew wider. "Ah, the kiss. I'm glad you brought that up."

Dani gasped. "I didn't bring it up! But now that it is brought up, it can't happen again. It won't."

"Why not?"

"I'm not going to be caught in the middle of your sexual identity crisis. I know there are some men who…go both ways. Dipping your toe in the hetero pool may be exciting for you, but I don't want to be a part of it. I have enough problems of my own without adding yours to the mix."

"I didn't kiss you to cause problems," Brad said. "I actually thought it might solve a few."

She drew a deep breath and met his eyes. "Why did you kiss me?"

He stepped closer, his gaze dropping to her mouth. "Because I'd been thinking about it since we first met." He reached out and dragged his thumb across her lower lip. "Are you telling me you never thought about it?"

"You're gay," she said. "Thinking about kissing you would have been a waste of perfectly good brain cells." She drew away from him and grabbed her laundry basket. "I have to go. Jack is watching Becca and Noah."

"I'm not gay!" he called after her.

Dani rushed out of the laundry room, her heart pounding. There, he'd said it. He wasn't gay. But the admission didn't seem to make her feel any better. In truth, it made her feel even more confused. Because if Brad Cullen wasn't gay, then there was nothing keeping him from kissing her again…and again and again.

She didn't bother to wait for the elevator, afraid that he might follow her. Instead she ran up the stairs to the lobby. Her heart slammed in her chest but it wasn't from the climb. She closed her eyes and pulled open the door to the lobby.

Louie was polishing the glass front doors as she came out. He waved at her. "Hey there, Miss O'Malley.

"Hi, Louie." She walked to the elevator, then remembered another thing on her to-do list—besides figuring out if Brad Cullen was gay or straight. "Louie, I'm going to do some redecorating in my apartment. Maybe some painting and wallpaper. I want to turn my office into a bedroom for the kids. And I've got to move some of my furniture down into storage.''

''So the kids are going to stay?'' he asked.

Dani nodded. ''For a while at least. Until I decide what to do. I'm not going to make any rash decisions. They've been through enough already.''

''Well, Mrs. Marston wants me to paint her kitchen, and then I've got the Wellmans' floors to refinish. I wouldn't be able to get to it for a few weeks.''

''Can we at least move some of the stuff out of my office? The kids have to crawl over boxes just to get to the bed.''

''Yeah. Hey, maybe I can get Brad Cullen to give me a hand.''

''No,'' Dani said. ''I don't want you to ask him to help. I've already imposed on him enough.''

''I thought you two were friends.''

''I think he might want to be a little more than friends,'' she muttered.

Louie frowned. ''You do know he's gay, don't you, Miss O'Malley?''

''That's what I thought. But he isn't.''

''Yes, he is,'' Louie insisted.

Dani slowly shook her head. ''No, Louie, I'm pretty sure he's not.''

''But he told me he was. And I heard him talking on the phone about his boyfriend, Joe. He was telling Mr. Hopson how they'd just broken up. We were talking yesterday. He's thinking of leaving his horse ranch to become a hairdresser.''

An image of Brad Cullen working in a beauty salon flashed in her mind and she couldn't help but giggle.

"That's ridiculous." Either he was gay or he wasn't—or he was both. And it was about time she knew for sure. She dropped the laundry basket on the floor, then hurried to the stairs. She found him where she'd left him, leaning against the washing machine.

With a soft curse, she strode up to him, slipped her arms around his neck and kissed him. She kissed him like she'd never kissed a man before, focusing every ounce of her effort into eliciting a response. At first, he registered surprise, but it didn't take more than a moment for Brad to match her, opening his mouth and meeting her tongue. With a low groan, he grabbed her waist and pulled her against him.

His hands slid up to her face and he furrowed his hands through her hair, molding her mouth to his, his kiss turning intense. Slowly, Dani realized that she'd lost all control of the situation. The kiss was supposed to be a challenge, a way to settle things once and for all. But the moment their lips met, she'd lost herself in a wave of sensation, desire nearly drowning her.

With every ounce of resolve she still possessed, Dani drew back. "You're not gay!" she accused.

He grinned. "No, I'm not gay."

"Not at all?"

"Not a bit," he said.

She tried to keep her voice calm, but this was serious business. He'd been playing some bizarre little sex game with her, acting like her friend and confidant and all the time lusting after her. Making her want him, yet letting her believe she couldn't have him. Without thinking, she raised her hand, ready to slap the smirk off his face.

But Brad was too quick and grabbed her wrist. He drew her hand to his lips and kissed the center of her palm, drawing his tongue along to the tip of her index finger. Dani groaned inwardly and tried to keep her mind on the matter at hand. Men had kissed her before, but not one of them had caused quite the reaction that Brad had.

"If—if you're not gay, then who is Joe?"

He seemed surprised by the mention of the man's name. "Joe? How do you know about Joe?"

"Louie told me you were talking about your ex-boyfriend on the phone. He said that you'd just broken up. Did you break up because you didn't want to be gay anymore?"

"I'm not gay," he repeated. "Jo is my fiancée. *Was* my fiancée. Josephine Millen. She dumped me the night before our wedding."

"And that's why you became gay?"

"Dani, listen to me." To emphasize his point, he took her face between his hands and forced her gaze to meet his. "I'm not gay. I've never been gay. Never even considered being gay."

"But you and Tom are—"

"College roommates."

"Oh," she said. This changed everything. Sure, she'd had some pretty interesting fantasies about Brad Cullen, but he'd been gay then. Now that he wasn't, those fantasies seemed a little closer to reality. Silently Dani cursed. This was crazy! "Why couldn't you have just stayed gay?"

Brad laughed. "Why would I do that?"

"Because it made things a lot easier. You were my friend and now you're...you're...I don't know what you are."

"I'm a man," he said, brushing another kiss across her lips.

"And I suppose I'm a woman?" she asked.

"Wow. What a lucky break," he teased.

"You knew what I thought, yet you continued this little charade of yours. I suppose you found the whole thing very amusing."

"No, that's not the word I'd use to describe it. Distracting might be a bit closer to the truth. And on occasion, a little painful. But I thought it made things easier."

"Kissing me was painful?" Dani asked.

"No. Trying to keep from kissing you was painful."

Dani swallowed hard, her gaze locked with his. He was about to kiss her again, she could feel it in every nerve of her body. And if he did, she'd find some way to forgive him for his deception or to rationalize his reasons, which she still didn't understand. "I—I have to go. The kids are alone upstairs and I—I have to go."

She ran out of the room and took the stairs two at a time. But as she climbed up to the third floor, Dani knew that as long as Brad Cullen was living across the hall, she'd never be far enough away from him to feel completely at ease.

"THIS IS A PICTURE of your mom and me," Dani said, pulling a photo booth strip out of an old shoe box. "We were on a field trip, I can't remember where. I think we were about thirteen." She turned to Jack. "About your age."

"What about my age?" Becca asked, leaning over the box.

"I don't have any photos from when I was five," Dani said. "My mom didn't have a camera." Actually, there had been a camera in the house and her mother had taken pictures. But she'd destroyed them all in one of her depressive episodes, wiping away Dani's entire childhood in a bonfire in their backyard.

"Our mom was pretty," Becca said.

"She was," Dani agreed. "And she used to wear the prettiest dresses. She had one dress that looked like a rainbow. I'll always remember it."

"I'm scared I'll forget her," Becca said. "Do you think she forgot us?"

Dani slipped her arm around Becca's shoulders. "Oh, honey, never. Your mother will always be with you. All you have to do is look in the mirror and you'll see her eyes and her smile. And if that doesn't work, we'll just look at the pictures."

Becca nodded. "And Mommy said that I can see her in my dreams."

"Well, then, we'll just have to find a photo to put next to your bed. There must be some albums in the boxes that your aunt sent. Tomorrow, we'll unpack everything and we'll find them."

"I don't remember my daddy. I was three when he died."

"I remember him," Jack said. "We used to play football in the backyard and he took me fishing. He was really tall."

Dani looked at Noah, who was curled up next to Becca on the sofa, his thumb in his mouth. He'd never known his father and would only have vague memories of his mother at best. Suddenly, the impact of their situation hit her full force. She felt a surge of emotion but fought back her tears. She'd cried enough and her tears were only confusing the children.

"I think it's time for bed," she announced. "Jack, why don't you help Noah get into his pajamas. Then you can watch some television in my room until it's your bedtime." She kissed Becca on the cheek and smiled at Noah. "I'll be in to read your story in a little while."

She watched as they all crawled off the sofa and headed to their room. The tears that threatened a few moments ago now pooled at the corners of her eyes, and with a soft sob, Dani ran to the front door and escaped to the safety of the hallway. With her back against the wall, she slowly slid down until her knees were under her chin.

Exhaustion overwhelmed her, and suddenly she wasn't sure she could go on. She was just barely keeping things together at work, and the housework never seemed to end. She only slept a few hours each night, her mind was plagued with worries about the children. She'd taken to examining every move she made with them, every word she spoke, assessing both action and reaction, wondering if she was somehow creating lifelong scars from which they could never recover. Parenting must come more naturally to biological parents. But she felt as if she were lost in an unfamiliar world without a map.

Every day that passed, she was faced with the realization that no matter how hard she tried, she might not make a good mother to Evie's children. She pressed her forehead to her knees and let the tears come. Admitting failure wasn't part of her nature. But right now, it was the only thing she could do.

The door across the hall opened. Dani gazed up at Brad and quickly brushed the tears off her cheeks. He looked so handsome, dressed in jeans, a crisp shirt, and a sports jacket, ready for a Friday night out.

"Hey, what's wrong?" he asked, squatting down in front of her.

"Nothing," she said, her voice still shaky. "Don't mind me. I just needed to be alone for a few minutes." She stared at the front of his shirt. "Are you going out?"

"I'm meeting my cousin Alex for a drink. But I've got some time."

"Go," Dani said. "I'll be fine."

He shook his head. "I'm not going to leave you out here in the hall. Tell me what's wrong."

"It's nothing. It's…it's…everything."

"Tell me," he urged, sitting down beside her. "Tell me."

She drew a ragged breath and wiped her runny nose with her fingers. "I—I listen to what these children are going through. They're confused and they feel abandoned, and I'm just putting a Band-Aid on the problem. I don't know if I can help them, Brad. I'm afraid that by the time I realize I can't, it's going to be too late. They'll be so messed up, nothing will save them.'' She paused to brush away another tear. ''Maybe they need to have parents who will help them cope. A father and mother who know how to deal with these problems.''

''You want to put them in foster care?''

''I know there are lots of great foster parents out there,'' Dani said. ''And I'm sure some of my foster parents were wonderful people. I was the problem, not them. I couldn't trust anybody. I wouldn't allow myself to love anyone or depend on anyone. And I was so angry. I don't want that to happen to Evie's children and I think it might.''

He slipped his arm around her shoulders. ''You do the best you can, Dani. And you love them. Parenting is a risk even in the most perfect situation.''

''There are a lot of childless couples who are looking to adopt. They could stay together and they'd be in a happy home.''

''Maybe you just need some more time to adjust,'' Brad said, reaching up to brush her hair from her face. ''It's only been a week. You can't turn into Supermom that quickly. Sometimes the cape and blue tights need some adjustments.'' He smoothed his hand over her cheek, then bent closer and gave her a soft kiss. ''You'll be all right. I promise.''

''I hate to cry. I never cry.''

''Sometimes it's a good thing.''

''I just feel so…so much,'' she said, pressing her hand to her heart. ''I always used to have everything under control, no surprises, no emotional upheaval. I thought I had a great life, and I used to pity all those people who had so much drama in theirs. And now I'm one of them."

"And that's not a bad thing," he said.

Dani nodded, her gaze fixed on his mouth. She leaned forward again, needing just a bit more reassurance. Brad took his cue and kissed her again and Dani felt her bleak mood dissolve in the face of desire. With a soft sigh, she opened beneath him, losing herself in the taste and warmth of his mouth. How had she become addicted to this so quickly? One day he was gay, and the next she was necking with him on the hallway floor. In the past she'd had such control with the men in her life, but Brad was different.

The day she'd met him had been a day of profound changes in her life—Evie's death, the children's arrival. The woman she had been was gradually being replaced with someone different—someone softer, someone needier. Though every instinct told her to bury that woman deep inside of her, she couldn't.

He drew back and pressed his forehead against hers. "We have to stop meeting like this."

"That's probably a good idea. After all, you'll be leaving soon."

"Right. Tom's coming back in another week."

"A week," she said. The past week had felt like a life-time, but the next would probably fly by faster than she wanted. Especially if all she could think about was kissing Brad Cullen again. "We'll miss you."

"I'm not leaving yet," Brad said. "Until I do, let me help you with the kids. You're upset because you're tired and overwhelmed. Let me make it a little easier for you while I can."

Dani knew she should refuse. Another week with Brad in their lives would make it all the harder to watch him leave. But his solid presence gave her the confidence she needed to master this new life of hers. When she degenerated into an emotional mess, he always knew what to say to make her feel better. In just a short week, she'd come to need him more than she'd ever needed another human being in her life.

"Why do you want to do this?"

"Because, unless you haven't noticed, I like you. And I like the kids."

She reached up and brushed the last traces of tears from her cheek. "I like you, too," she admitted. "But I'm afraid the kids might become attached to you."

He stared into her eyes for a long moment, then nodded. "I understand. You're probably right."

"Or maybe I'm wrong," she said with a rueful smile.

"Why don't we just play it by ear?"

"If we kept things platonic, maybe it would be all right," Dani rationalized. "And I am a better parent when you're around. I guess that's good for the children."

"So platonic means no more…"

Dani nodded. "I think that would be for the best. I don't want to confuse them. You're my friend and a neighbor, and when you leave, we'll say goodbye and go on with our lives."

That would be a lot easier said than done, Dani mused. After Brad went back to Montana, it would be a long time before she'd be able to go to sleep without dreaming about him.

"Wow," Alex said. "These are some pretty ritzy digs for a cowboy like you." She strolled through Tom Hopson's apartment, examining the decor with a shrewd eye, picking up a small statue of a cat that looked a bit Egyptian to Brad.

He laughed, then pointed to the sofa. "Silk. I wouldn't

know the difference between that and a sow's ear, but I do know not to put my feet on it.''

"See?" Alex teased. "You're getting the hang of this city life. You're even starting to dress like a city slicker. Have you given up your blue jeans and boots? Or are you just trying to impress Dani O'Malley?"

Alex always did have the ability to cut right to the truth of the matter. And the truth was that since he'd seen Dani in the hallway a few hours earlier, he hadn't been able to get her off his mind. She liked him—maybe more than she wanted to. After all, why make a pact to keep things platonic if there wasn't something more to her feelings? That thought alone had teased at his mind all evening. "What if I was trying to impress her?" Brad asked. "There's nothing wrong with that."

"No, I suppose not. But this really isn't you, is it?" She reached out and rubbed his new black sweater between her thumb and forefinger. "Nice. Is it cashmere?"

"No," Brad said, slapping at her hand playfully. "I think it's cotton."

"And very fashionable." She paused, a serious look coming over her face. "So what is going on with you? I see Dani at the day care, but beyond saying 'hello' and 'goodbye,' she doesn't offer any details on your love life."

"We don't have a love life," Brad said. "We're friends and that's all."

"Are you still gay or have you come out of the closet?" Alex giggled. "Wait, I already know the answer to that. You've bought so many new clothes you were forced out of the closet. Or maybe the new wardrobe is to maintain the illusion that you're gay?"

"Ha, ha," Brad said. "She knows I'm straight, and since she found out, it's been pretty good between us." He got up from the sofa. "Do you want a glass of wine? Tom has a whole refrigerator full of the stuff."

Alex followed him into the kitchen, then grabbed the bottle he'd taken from the small refrigerator near the sink. "This looks like pretty pricey wine. Are you sure we should drink it?"

"I'm going to have a beer," Brad said.

Alex jumped up on the granite counter. "I'll have a beer, too. Do you have anything to eat?"

"I thought you said you weren't hungry. We could have gone out to dinner."

"I wasn't, but now I am," Alex said.

"I have some leftover chili that I made for Dani and the kids earlier this week. The kids weren't too crazy about it, so she gave some of it back to me. It should still be good. Want some?"

"Still trying to feed me meat?"

"You grew up in cattle country," Brad teased. "You're a disgrace to the Cullen family with your crazy eating habits. I thought maybe you'd changed your ways."

"Nope."

"Then, I've got some cheese and crackers."

Brad handed her a beer, but she waved her hand at the glass, preferring instead to drink right from the bottle. She watched him as he grabbed a box of crackers and dumped them on a plate. "How have you been doing?" he asked as he sliced the cheese.

"Fine."

"That's the same answer you gave me the last time I asked. If you're not going to talk to a shrink, then you could at least talk to me."

"All right. It's nice to be working with Hannah and Katherine. Even though I was only six when I moved away, we've stayed such good friends. Living with Katherine has been nice, too, although I'm going to start looking for a place of my own. And the kids at the day care, they're…''

''Nice? So everything is nice. Have you had any nightmares lately?''

''Nothing new. Just the same old thing.''

''The fire?''

Alex nodded. ''It's so frustrating because I have the same nightmare over and over again. And I keep thinking that I'll figure out what it means or maybe why I'm having it. Or something different will happen and it will all make sense.''

''Tell me about it. Tell me the dream.''

''It's night and it's really dark in the house. Sometimes I hear the fire first, sometimes I feel the heat or smell the smoke. But after a moment, it's all there and it's hard to breathe. There are people there, too. Sometimes it's like there's a party going on. I hear them talking, or maybe they're part of another dream. I don't recognize the voices and what they say doesn't make any sense.'' She paused. ''You know, I bought this book on conscious dreaming once, hoping that I could put myself in the middle of the dream and ask all the questions, but it didn't work.''

''What happens next?'' Brad asked.

''The flames…they're everywhere. I can't see. I have to get out…my hands are gripping the railing on the upper landing…but I can't move. I know if I don't try soon it will be too late. I'm looking into the fire below and I see people, but they're blurry, or maybe it's just the flames. And then the clock strikes…four times, slowly, and that's it.''

''That's all?''

''Then my real memories begin. I remember standing outside and watching the fire.''

''So what did the police say happened? Did the fire department do an investigation? There must have been stories published in the papers."

"I don't know," Alex said. "I've never tried to find out."

"Maybe you should," Brad suggested. "Knowing the details might help you make sense of your dream."

"I just want to forget it all," Alex said. "My parents died in that fire. I don't need to know anything else."

Brad reached out and took her hand, then gave it a squeeze. "Maybe not," he said.

Alex drew a deep breath and pasted a bright smile on her face. "Well, now that we have that out of the way, let's talk about something much more interesting. Like you and Dani O'Malley."

"You two have a lot in common," Brad said.

"I don't think so. She's tall and sophisticated and blond. I'm short and boring and I have red hair."

"She lost her parents when she was six. Or at least her mother. She never knew her father. She grew up in the foster care system. Maybe you're not so different."

"And maybe that's why you're so attracted to her."

"How so?" Brad asked.

"It was the same thing with me when I came to live at the ranch. You wanted to fix me, to make everything all better. Face it, Brad, you're not happy unless you're taking care of everyone. Maybe that's what you want to do for her."

"That's not true. In fact, that's exactly why I left Split Rock. I got tired of taking care of everyone." He was silent a moment, then sighed. "You're right. But that's going to stop. It's just that I feel compelled to help Dani because, unlike my family, she really needs my help. She's all alone in the world and she has these children who are as scarred as she is. They deserve to have someone looking out for them.''

"You're talking about this like it's something that might last," Alex said.

"Is that stupid? I know it is. A few months ago, I was on my way to the altar. I'm not ready to jump back into a relationship again. But I can't seem to help myself."

"You're a good guy, Brad. There aren't many left like you."

He took another sip of his beer, then leaned back on the kitchen island. "I went out today and looked at a ranch about fifty miles west of here."

"A ranch? You already have a ranch. Split Rock."

Brad shook his head. "I don't know if I'm going back. I've been thinking I might like to start my own operation. Something small."

"And something close to Seattle?" Alex sighed. "I'd assume that wouldn't be because you want to be closer to me."

"Washington isn't Montana. Land prices here are ridiculously high and I wouldn't have a large place."

"Don't you think you're moving awfully fast here?"

"I wasn't in love with Jo," Brad said. "I thought I was, but I wasn't. I know that now."

"And you are in love with Dani?"

"No. I mean, I'm not sure. But I could be. I'm just exploring my options here. I haven't made any decisions."

"Don't you think it's time you talked to your parents. How long has it been since you called home?"

"Not since I got to Seattle. You haven't told them I'm here, have you?"

"I may have mentioned it." Alex shrugged. "All right, I told Mary Rose that I'd seen you and that you're alive and doing just fine. She's your mother and she was worried.

But I think she figures since you came to see me, you're about ready to come home. If that's not true, you'd better let her know.''

"I will. I promise. Just as soon as I have it all figured out myself.''

A knock sounded at the front door and Brad straightened, setting his beer on the counter.

"Are you expecting company?'' Alex asked.

"No. It's probably Dani. I'll be right back.'' Brad strode through the hallway to the foyer, then opened the door. As he'd expected, Dani was there. Her hair was pulled up on top of her head in a casual ponytail and she wore faded jeans and a T-shirt. He fought an impulse to pull her into his arms and steal a quick kiss.

"Hi,'' she said, smiling.

"Hi. Is everything all right?''

"Yeah. I just needed to borrow a screwdriver. I'm putting together a new dresser for the kids. I don't know what made me think I could do it myself. I'm not very handy.''

"I can help you,'' Brad said.

"Hi, Dani.''

Brad turned to find Alex standing behind him.

"Oh, hi,'' Dani said, her gaze dropping down to the beer Alex was holding. "I'm sorry. I didn't mean to interrupt.''

"You didn't,'' Alex said, setting the beer on a marble-topped table. "I was just going. I've got to stop at the day care and pick up some work, and Katherine will probably be ready to get some dinner. Say 'hi' to Becca and Noah for me, all right?'' Alex rose up on tiptoe and gave Brad a quick kiss on the cheek. "Call me,'' she said, sending him a sly smile.

"Not if you call me first,'' Brad said.

He waited until Alex stepped inside the elevator before he grabbed Dani around the waist and pulled her against him. Without giving her a chance to protest, he kissed her. A tiny sigh slipped from her and she wrapped her arms around his neck and kissed him back.

When he drew away, she smiled, then slowly opened her eyes. "Is this what I'm going to have to do every time I want to borrow something?" she asked.

"Maybe."

"I'll have to make sure I run out of sugar soon. And I'm out of eggs. Do you have a flashlight I could borrow?"

Brad growled then kissed her again, pulling her tight against his body. His hands smoothed along her spine to her hips. Gently he pressed her back against the doorjamb, then nuzzled her neck. "Have you had dinner yet?"

Dani shook her head. "Just snacks. But I have a frozen pizza."

He moved on to her shoulder, pulling aside her T-shirt until he found warm skin. "I'm not in the mood for pizza. Why don't we take the kids out?"

"They ate a few hours ago. We could send out for Chinese and you could help me put that damn dresser together?"

He stepped back and gazed down into her eyes. "That might cost you."

"What happened to our platonic plan?" Dani asked.

"We'll start that tomorrow."

CHAPTER SIX

"I WANNA PUSH THE BUTTON!" Becca cried.

"Jack, let your sister push the button," Dani said, shuffling the children into the elevator. She reached out to grab the groceries they'd picked up that morning and kicked the package of disposable diapers through the elevator door. "All right, Becca. Push 'three.'"

Becca sent her older brother a smug smile then punched the proper button with her finger. The elevator doors closed and they rode up, Noah wriggling in Dani's arms and Jack sulking in the corner, hiding behind the grocery bag he held. She'd had a long morning of errands and the Saturday morning traffic had been a tangle. But she'd gotten them up and dressed and, to Dani's surprise, the routine was getting a bit easier.

"As soon as you get your coat off, I want you to start your math homework," Dani said to Jack. "You're not going to leave it until the last minute again."

"I have the whole weekend," Jack complained. "Why do I have to do it on Saturday morning?"

"Because we're all getting organized, and that includes you," Dani replied. The elevator doors opened and Becca and Noah ran out. Dani followed and Jack lagged behind, doing his best imitation of a surly teenager. But as they turned the corner in the hall, they all stopped. The hall was cluttered with camping equipment, and it was gathered in front of Dani's apartment.

"Brad!" Becca cried as she ran inside the open apartment door.

Dani stumbled over a line of sleeping bags, then stubbed her toe on a campstove, before she was able to follow her inside. "What is this?" she said, staring at a huge tent that he'd set up in the living room.

"The Cascade Family Model 417," Brad said, glancing up from the doorway to the tent. "Rip-stop nylon, reinforced floor, self-standing tent that sleeps six comfortably."

"I can see it's a tent," Dani said. "What's it doing in my living room?"

"Wow," Jack said, slowly circling the dark green monstrosity. "This is cool."

"I thought we could take the kids camping. I've got the perfect spot in the Cascades, just an hour or so away. We can do some hiking and maybe some fishing and come back tomorrow evening."

Dani swallowed hard. "Camping? I don't camp." Besides, after the kiss they'd shared last night in Tom's apartment, Dani wasn't sure she should be spending any time at all with Brad, especially in the confines of the Cascade Family Model 417. A tiny shiver raced down her spine at the thought of his mouth touching hers. So much for trying to keep things platonic. "I really…well, I've never camped before."

"That's the great thing about camping," Brad said. "You don't need any special skills. You just need to dress warmly and have an adventurous spirit."

"But I have work to do. I have to write a marketing report this weekend."

"Come on," Brad teased. "You don't really have to work, do you?"

"Yeah," Jack said. "I want to go camping."

"Me, too, me, too," Becca cried. "I want to go. It'll be fun."

"We can't take Noah—he's too young," Dani said. The hard ground, the cold nights, the close quarters. Somehow it didn't sound like fun. It sounded like sheer torture.

"This is the perfect time for Noah to go," Brad told her. "It will start him appreciating nature early in his life. And don't worry. I'll take care of everything. You and the children just have to have fun, that's all."

Becca skipped over to Dani's side and grabbed her hand. "Please? I've never been camping."

"How about you, Jack?" Dani asked.

"Yeah, I'd like to go," he said, managing a hopeful smile.

This was the first thing Jack had been enthusiastic about since he'd come to live with her. Maybe it was a chance to experience something fun with the children, a chance to create new memories. Surely she could put aside her reservations and try to have a good time. "All right."

Brad grinned, then winked at her. "You'll have a great time, I promise. Now get your things together. You'll need warm clothes, hats and jackets, and sturdy shoes. Bring extra pairs of socks." He reached behind the tent and handed Jack a backpack on an aluminum frame. "This is for you," he said. "You need to carry your stuff and Becca's." He handed another to Dani. "You'll carry your things and Noah's. We're leaving in an hour."

As they got ready for their trip, Dani had to admit that the adventure would be good for the children. Anything to get them out of their normal routine. The weather had been pleasant enough for October, and Brad had promised they weren't going too far away. If it rained, they'd come home.

When her own pack was stuffed, she helped Jack rearrange his, then made the children dress in warmer clothes.

They were nearly ready to leave when the phone rang. Dani's first impulse was to let the machine pick it up. But old habits died hard, and she grabbed up the cordless and punched the button.

"Dani? It's Sam."

Why on earth had she answered? "Sam, it's Saturday morning. What problem could have possibly come up that couldn't wait until Monday morning?"

"Well, there's the problem that you usually come into work on Saturdays," Sam said. "And you usually stay late on Fridays. I needed to talk to you before you left."

Dani walked into her bedroom and closed the door behind her. "I had to pick the kids up from school. I have to leave early every day."

"And you come in late every day," Sam said. "When am I supposed to meet with you?"

"Between the hours of nine and four," Dani said. There was a long pause on the other end of the line and Dani knew what was coming next. Sam Bennett had never been a patient man.

"I need you to come back in. We have to go over the data for the marketing report before our meeting Monday morning. I have creative I need to discuss with you, and I want you to be in on the pitch for the Milano Prego restaurant chain."

"I can't come back in," Dani said. "I'm about to leave on a little trip with the children."

Sam cleared his throat. "You don't understand. I'm not asking you. I'm telling you. It's about time you got your priorities straight, Dani. If you expect to be handed a vice presidency, this is not the way to go about it."

Dani felt her temper rise at his demand. Handed a vice presidency? No one needed to *hand* it to her, she'd earned it. She slowly ran her fingers through her hair. "I'm not coming in. I'll get the report done and we'll present it on Monday. I've got all the data I need.''

"That's not good enough," Sam said.

"Well, if it's not good enough, then I don't know what to say. Do you want me to quit?'' The line was silent and Dani felt her heart stop. She hadn't meant to make the threat, but now that it was out, she couldn't take it back.

"Maybe that would be best," Sam said.

"Maybe it would," Dani replied stubbornly. "So that's it then. I quit. I'll come in on Monday and pick up my things.''

"I'll have them packed for you.''

The line went dead, and in that instant, the impact of her decision hit her full force. Slowly she lowered herself to the edge of the bed, her senses numb, her mind spinning. She felt dizzy and nauseous, as if she'd just stepped off a carnival ride that had been spinning for the last eight years. "Oh, God," she moaned, bending over her knees.

A soft knock sounded at the door. "Are you all right?" Brad asked.

Dani glanced up from a careful study of her pedicure—a pedicure she hadn't had time for in two weeks and now couldn't afford. "No, I'm not.''

"Who was that on the phone?''

"My boss. He wanted me to come in to work.''

"When?''

"Now. Today.''

Brad nodded. "Are you going to go? Hey, if you have to work, I could take the kids by myself.''

Dani raised her shoulders and then let them drop. "I don't have to work. I just quit." She covered her face with her hands. "Oh, God, I can't believe it. I've been working there since I got out of college. My whole life has been about Bennett Marks and now I've thrown it all away. He just backed me against a wall and I said what he wanted to hear. I have three children to care for and I don't have a job." Dani started to laugh, the sound bordering on hysterical. "What was I thinking?"

Brad sat down next to her and draped his arm around her shoulders, pulling her close. He kissed the top of her head. "You were thinking of the children."

"No, I wasn't. If I was thinking of them, I wouldn't have quit."

"So what are you going to do?" Brad asked.

She drew a deep breath and let it out slowly, trying to get used to the fact that she was suddenly unemployed. "I have some savings. And Evie left that trust fund for the kids, so that will help pay for groceries in an emergency, although I wanted to save that for their college fund. And I have a retirement plan I could cash in. We're not going to be out on the street tomorrow, but I'm going to have to find a cheaper place to live."

"Tell you what," Brad said. "Why don't we forget about all this for the weekend. Let's go camping and you can think about it when you get back." He reached under her chin and tipped her face up. He stared into her eyes for a long moment. "Everything will be all right," he told her. "I promise." And when he finally kissed her, his lips were warm and soothing.

It was exactly what she needed to banish all the worries from her head. With a sigh, she wrapped her arms around his neck, needing just a little more encouragement. Dani knew they'd made a promise to keep their relationship platonic, but now that promise seemed silly. After all, what harm was there in an occasional kiss.

When he drew away, Brad gazed down into her eyes and brushed a strand of hair from her temple. "You'll be all right," he repeated, his attention dropping to her mouth.

"I could always go in on Monday and beg for my job back."

"That's Monday," he said, stealing another kiss. "You don't need to decide now."

"Or I could look for a new job. There are a bunch of smaller agencies that would probably kill to have me walk in the door. I'll find something more…family friendly."

"Mmm," he said, nuzzling her neck.

"Or maybe I should go right to Mo' Joe and see if they'll hire me. I know everything there is to know about the company. I could step into virtually any job there. And they have a very good attitude about families. They have their own day care at the corporate headquarters."

"You could do all of that," Brad said. "You can do anything you set your mind to."

Dani smiled, then laughed softly. At that moment, the future didn't seem so bleak. "Evie used to say that."

"I think she'd approve of what you did."

She turned the thought over in her mind. "I think so, too." She leaned into Brad and smiled. "I don't know what I'd do without you."

He grabbed her hand and pulled her up from the bed, then led her to the door. "Wait 'til I get you out in the wild. Then I'll really show you my stuff."

The prospect of camping suddenly seemed a lot more interesting, Dani mused.

THE CAMPFIRE HISSED and crackled in the silence of the night, sending sparks up into the air. Brad stared into the flames, watching them waver in the chilly air. Dani sat next to him, wrapped in a sleeping bag, her back against an old log, her head on his shoulder. The kids were already asleep in the tent, wrapped snugly in sleeping bags.

They'd spent the afternoon in the great outdoors, just as

Brad had promised. They'd hiked around a small lake, the kids racing ahead on the trail to discover something new around each bend. Later, he took Becca and Jack fishing while Noah napped in the tent. And then, he'd cooked them all a campfire dinner and roasted marshmallows. The children had been exhausted by the activity and crawled in the tent before eight, leaving Brad and Dani to share the evening alone.

"This is the perfect antidote," she murmured, staring into the flames. "It feels like I left all my troubles behind in Seattle. Maybe I should just pack the kids up and we can live out in the wild. I bet we could live pretty cheaply in a tent."

Brad stretched his legs out in front of him, resting his feet near the fire, then linked his hands behind his head. "I could live in a tent," he said. "I did live in a tent before I got to Seattle. I camped in this very spot. I thought it was just about the most perfect place I'd seen."

"It is beautiful," Dani agreed, gazing up at the sky. "I've never been an outdoorsy person. The closest I got to hiking was taking the garbage."

"You'll learn to love it," Brad said. "I wish I could show you Split Rock. There are some spots on the ranch that rival this. You should bring the kids out to Montana sometime."

A long silence grew between them, and Brad chided himself for even bringing the subject up. Neither one of them had mentioned the future. It had been assumed that he'd stay until Tom returned and then they'd part ways. But now he'd changed the plan. Hell, why not? It was a friendly invitation. There was no reason to read anything more into it than that.

"When are you going to go home?" she asked, sending him a sideways glance.

"What? Are you anxious to get rid of me?"

"Not at all. I was just wondering why—if you have a home, and family who cares about you—you're here with me?"

"I'm exactly where I want to be," Brad said.

"The truth," Dani insisted.

He shrugged. "The truth is, I'm not ready to go back. I've got a life all planned out for me there. My father wants me to manage Split Rock. My brothers and sister want me to make their lives easier. And my mother, well, she wants me to marry Jo."

"I thought she walked out on you."

"She's back. I guess that rodeo cowboy wasn't the man of her dreams. She ran off with a bull rider and I ran off to the woods."

"Do you love her?"

"No," Brad said, shaking his head. He was surprised at how easily the answer came. Jo Millen barely entered his thoughts these days. Instead, he'd been consumed with fantasies of tawny hair and hazel eyes, and legs that seemed to go on forever. "I don't know if I ever loved her. I see my life a lot more clearly when I'm away from Split Rock."

Dani nodded. "I'm starting to think that maybe it's better not to have a plan in life. I mean, look at me. I didn't plan on having three kids. I didn't plan on quitting my job. And I never planned on going camping."

"But you like it, right?"

"I like being here with you," Dani admitted. "You're very…warm."

Chuckling, Brad pulled her closer, then kissed her. Somewhere along the way, they'd dropped the platonic plan and moved on to something ressembling romance. It seemed so natural to kiss her, so effortless. He craved the taste of her mouth and the touch of her tongue, the scent of her hair and the sound of her voice. When she was near, he wanted to soak her in, like sunshine on a cloudy day.

It had taken him a year to fall in love with Jo, and only a moment to fall out of love with her. With Dani, it was the opposite. He had shared more with her in just a over a week than he could have ever imagined. But it was what they had yet to experience that occupied his thoughts now.

He slipped his hands around her waist and pulled her down on top of him, his mouth still on hers. They'd kissed before, but this time it was different. Desire crackled between them like an electric current, the sensation of her body against his setting every nerve on edge, the cold heightening his awareness.

She wriggled around until the sleeping bag enveloped them in a cocoon, leaving no need for the layers of clothes they wore. Brad pulled her jacket open, then did the same with his, anxious to share her warmth. She stared down into his eyes, her breath coming in short gasps, clouding in front of her face.

The silence of the night made it seem as if they were the only two people on earth. With nothing but the stars and the inky sky above them, the walls between them began to fall away and desire took over. With every little sigh from Dani, he ventured a bit further, searching for soft skin and warm flesh.

Urged on by his touch, Dani found warm places for her hands as well, unbuttoning his flannel shirt and smoothing her hands over his chest. His blood heated with every heartbeat and Brad felt himself grow hard with desire, her body pressing against his erection. Groaning, he pulled her beneath him, pushing aside the sleeping bag.

The cold air caused her to shiver, but didn't stop her gentle exploration of his body. She finished unbuttoning his shirt, then pushed it off his shoulders, her lips trailing after her fingers. Brad reached down and pulled her leg up along his hip, wondering where they would stop and knowing it wouldn't be easy when they did.

He'd never felt such desire for a woman, and not just the need for physical release. With Dani he felt a hunger to strip away all the barriers between them, to know her as no one else did. She had obviously had experience with men, but Brad suspected that she'd kept a certain part of herself in check.

He rolled back, settling himself beside her. Drawing a deep breath, he tried to slow his heartbeat and quell his desire. But Dani didn't want to wait. Her gaze fixed on his, she sat up and pulled her sweater over her head, then tossed it aside. She wore just a thin T-shirt beneath, her breasts outlined by the tight fabric, her nipples peaked from the cold.

The light from the campfire flickered, casting her skin in gold, creating a strange, magical atmosphere around them. He reached out and slid his hand along her ribs, then cupped her breast in his palm. Dani smiled and closed her eyes, tipping her head back.

God, she was beautiful, Brad mused. Everything about her made him need her more. Up until now he'd considered himself a normal guy, with normal desires. But Dani made him feel more, an insatiable hunger to possess her. Whether a simple kiss or an intimate caress, each seemed to spark the same reaction.

Leaning forward, he drew her to him again, kissing her deeply, his tongue invading her mouth. And when he'd left her breathless, Brad traced a path from her neck to her breast, teasing at her nipple through the thin fabric. He knew if he wanted, they could continue undressing and make love under the stars. But Brad didn't want to be just the next on Dani's list of lovers.

Though she tempted him, he didn't allow himself to step over the edge. By the time the fire had died down and dissolved to embers, they'd snuggled back beneath the sleeping bag.

"I could stay out here forever," she confided, nuzzling her cold face into the curve of his neck.

"So could I."

"We're going to have to leave sooner or later. The kids have school. But until we do, this is good."

"Then you've decided it's all right to need me?" he asked. "Even if it's just for warmth?"

"I have. You know, that goes way back. It's not just you. I've never really needed anyone before. Except for Evie." She was quiet a moment. "It's a little scary."

"Why is that?"

"I'm just used to being on my own. After my mom died, I couldn't allow myself to care about anyone. It was safer that way." She laughed softly. "After I met Evie, things changed. She believed in me, and I wanted to show her she was right. I worked my way through college and got a good job and tried to become a different person."

"And did you?"

"Maybe on the outside. The designer suits and expensive shoes, the hairstyle and the jewelry. Nobody would have suspected I was a poor foster kid from Portland."

"I'm sorry about that," Brad said. "About what you had to go through."

She rubbed her hand over his bare chest. "Don't be. It wasn't your fault. It wasn't anyone's fault." She reached out and took his hand, then wove her fingers through his. "I used to think I'd made a pretty good life for myself. But since the children came, I've realized all I really had was a good job and a nice apartment. That wasn't a life."

"And this is?" He kissed her again, lingering over her mouth for a long moment.

"It's a lot closer. I never know what's going to happen from day to day. That used to scare me, but it doesn't anymore."

Brad turned her around and nestled her backside into his lap, wrapping his arms around her body.

"And what about this?" His hands found a spot underneath her T-shirt, his palms resting on smooth, warm skin. "Does this scare you?"

"No," she murmured, taking his hand and sliding it up to her breast. "It doesn't."

Brad sighed softly. He'd spent months out here alone, trying to figure a future for himself. And now, it felt like he'd finally found a place where he belonged—in Dani O'Malley's arms.

He wasn't sure how long he would stay, but for now, that didn't matter. Dani needed him and he needed her. That was enough.

"I'VE GOT COFFEE," Hannah Richards said as she walked into the office at Forrester Square Day Care. Alexandra Webber and Katherine Kinard both looked up from their desks in the ground-floor office. The sun had just set on the cool October evening, but the three of them had scheduled a quick meeting before they left for the day.

Katherine had called the meeting and Hannah assumed it was to discuss their budget for the next year. She had all the figures ready, along with income and expense projections. But as she passed out the lattes, Hannah saw a look pass between Alexandra and Katherine. "What?" she said.

Alexandra took a quick sip of her coffee. "Sit down. We need to talk about Amy."

"Our Amy? Amy Tidwell?"

Katherine nodded and leaned back in her chair. "Alexandra mentioned to me yesterday that Amy's been a little distracted lately. I've noticed that she's been late for work on more than one occasion, and when she is here, she seems to be somewhere else."

"Well, she has been a little spacey lately," Hannah said. "But she's a teenager. Doesn't that go with the territory?"

"We think you should talk to her," Alexandra said. "Tell her that we're concerned and that she needs to try a bit harder to focus. See if you can get her to talk. Find out if there's some problem she's having."

Hannah gnawed on her lower lip as she considered the impact of her partner's request. She knew precisely what was bothering the teenager, but had been sworn to secrecy. Now she felt disloyal to her business partners. "She's always been a good worker. She's wonderful with the children, very kind and patient. And she takes her job seriously."

"I think you should point that out to her," Alexandra said. "And that's why we're concerned that she seems distracted lately. Hannah, you know her better than either of us. Maybe she'll open up to you. Maybe there are problems at home."

Hannah shrugged, knowing that the assumption was the truth. But Amy's problems at home were just a part of what the teenager faced. "Her father is a businessman, and from what Amy has told me, he's pretty focused on his work. Amy's mother died when she was little and he's raised her alone. I get the feeling that he's got pretty high expectations for her—honor roll, prestigious college, a high-income career. Amy's mentioned to me that she'd like to be a teacher. Maybe he's pressuring her to do something else with her life."

"I thought it might have something to do with boys,"

Alexandra suggested. "She's got a boyfriend. He picks her up every now and then, but she's never introduced us. He looks like a nice guy. But maybe there's some trouble there." She sighed. "This is all just speculation."

"All right," Hannah said. "I'll talk to her."

Katherine nodded. "Good. Amy's stocking art supplies and Carmen left early today, so now's the best time to speak to her. Let us know what she says."

Hannah stood and grabbed her coffee, then slowly walked out of the office. Katherine usually took the lead in personnel matters, but since Alexandra had joined them, she'd proven to be particularly competent in that area. Hannah was an equal partner in the day care, and though she preferred to handle financial matters, she had to share responsibility for anything and everything that affected the children.

She found Amy sitting on the floor in the kindergarten room, sorting construction paper by color. As usual, her headphones were on and she was bobbing along to a song that only she could hear. Hannah sat down at one of the tables and watched the teenager for a long moment. When she finished with the construction paper, Amy struggled to her feet, then pressed her hand against her belly. When she turned and saw Hannah, she quickly let her hand drop to her side.

Amy took the headphones off her ears. "Hi," she said. "Did you need something?"

"Sit down," Hannah said, her gaze flitting between Amy's face and her abdomen. She couldn't hide the pregnancy forever. Sooner or later, someone would notice. Hannah's mind wandered back to a time when that fear had gripped her own life, when she'd been pregnant and all alone with her secret.

The teenager did as she was told, tossing her long braid over her shoulder. "What's up?"

Hannah took a deep breath, wondering just how she ought to broach the subject. When she couldn't think of a smooth entry, she decided a pointed statement might have the effect she sought. "Katherine and Alexandra asked that I talk to you. They've noticed that you've been a bit…distracted lately."

"Do they know?" Amy asked, sucking in a sharp breath.

Hannah shook her head. "I haven't told anyone about your pregnancy, Amy. But you're not going to be able to hide it forever. You're five months along. The baggy clothes can't conceal it much longer."

Amy's gaze dropped to her lap and she sighed raggedly. "I thought I'd figure out what to do before anyone guessed." She glanced up. "They're going to fire me, aren't they."

"No, no, they won't." Hannah reached out and grasped Amy's hands. "I promise. But Alexandra and Katherine are going to have to know. You and Will need to decide what you're going to do."

"I saw some ads in the paper. People wanting to adopt. But Will isn't sure we should give up the baby."

"Whether you decide to keep the baby or not, you need to tell your father."

"I know. But every time I think about it, I start to cry."

"You don't know how he's going to react."

"Yes, I do. He's going to kill me. Then he'll kill Will." She twisted her fingers through the cord of her headset. "He'll probably kick me out of the house and never talk to me again."

"I felt the same way when I got pregnant." Hannah had never told a single soul about her own unplanned pregnancy, but it seemed right to reveal that secret now. Amy needed her help, and if the teenager understood that Hannah was speaking from experience, maybe she'd realize how important her decisions were. "I'll keep your secret if you'll keep mine," she said with a smile.

"You were pregnant?" Amy asked.

"I was. And unmarried. And just like you, I was scared of what my parents would say and I didn't know where to turn."

"How old were you?"

"I was a junior in college and I fell hard for this guy. He was handsome and dangerous and I was sure I was in love with him. When I found out about the baby, I tried to call him, but he never called me back. I'm not even sure he would have cared. So I gave the baby up for adoption. I never told anyone. Not even my parents."

"And they never found out?"

Hannah shook her head. "But I want to tell you, Amy, that looking back on it, I should have told them. If I had, maybe they would have helped and I would have kept the baby. And maybe I would have raised my son and been sure that he was growing up in a happy home. But I couldn't disappoint my parents. I was afraid to tell them. So I gave up an entire lifetime with my baby. I regret that now."

"Have you ever thought about finding your baby?" Amy asked.

"Every day. But I made a decision back then not to, a decision I can't change. I don't want you to be forced into doing the same."

"But if I tell my father, he might make me give up the baby."

"You're eighteen, Amy. He can't make you do anything. If you tell him and he kicks you out, then at least you know where you stand with him."

"I wish I had a mother to talk to," Amy said. "Maybe she would understand."

"You can always talk to me. And you can confide in Will, can't you?"

Her eyes filled with tears. "Every time I talk to him, we end up arguing. I know Will wants to go to college and get his degree, but he keeps telling me that the baby is his responsibility. He'd marry me if I said yes, even though he knows my dad hates him." She brushed a tear from her cheek and forced a smile. "What are you going to tell Alexandra and Katherine?"

"I'm going to tell them that you and I talked and you promised that you're going to try harder at work. And you will try harder. The rest you're going to have to tell them yourself. Your secret is safe with me."

Amy nodded. "I will tell them soon. Maybe it will give me practice for telling my dad."

Hannah rose to her feet. "If you'd like me to be there when you tell Alexandra and Katherine, I will."

"Thanks," Amy said.

"You'd better get back to work. Carmen's going to want her art projects laid out before she gets in tomorrow. What is it, jack o'-lanterns or autumn leaves?"

"Leaves," Amy told her.

Placing her hand on Amy's shoulder, Hannah gave it a squeeze, then slowly walked to the door. But Amy's voice stopped her.

"You should try to find him," she said.

Hannah turned. "What?"

"Find him. You don't have to talk to him or see him, but at least you'd know he was all right. You'd know he was happy. Maybe that would help."

Hannah nodded, then walked from the room, emotion welling up inside of her. How many times had she thought about her son over the past few months? She'd hoped that working for the day care would help soothe the aching emptiness she felt. But being around children only made the loss more acute.

She'd tried so desperately to put her past behind her, to forget about the son she'd given away and the man who had fathered him. But she'd formed a picture of the boy in her mind, a slender child with jet-black hair and pale blue eyes. Sometimes she saw him as a miniature version of his father, rather than herself. Other times, he was blond like her. But she had no way of knowing if her pictures of him were close to reality. If she walked by her son on the streets of Seattle, she wouldn't even recognize him.

"No," Hannah said a loud, as she wandered back to the office. "No, no, no." If she found her son, she'd feel compelled to see him. And if she saw him, she'd want to talk to him. There would be no going back after that.

She brushed away an errant tear. But maybe there was a way she could find out if he was safe without learning where he was. She could contact the adoption agency. Maybe they'd give her a few details, enough to ease her mind.

"No," she repeated, as if saying the word would convince her.

"No, what?"

Hannah glanced up to find Alexandra and Katherine staring at her from behind their desks. "No...problem," Hannah said. "I talked to Amy and there won't be any problems anymore."

"Did she tell you why she's so preoccupied?"

"Just the usual teenage stuff," Hannah lied. "Boyfriend, classes, grades. She promised she'd try harder."

"Good," Katherine said. "Thanks for talking to her."

Hannah sat back down at her desk and stared at the payroll she had been working on. But her mind wasn't on social security deductions and federal income tax withholding. The numbers blurred in front of her eyes and she bit back a sob. Even if she decided to find him, she might not succeed. Where would she start? The adoption agency would never give her an address. Once the adoption was final, all the files were sealed. Could she find something on the Internet?

Confronting the past might bring back more pain and anguish than she could handle. Hannah placed her palms on her desk and drew a deep breath. She'd made her decision long ago and that decision had been final. Once again, she would put her past behind her and get on with the future. And maybe someday, if her son came looking for her, her questions would all be answered.

Until then, she would just have to wait and believe that her son was happy and safe.

CHAPTER SEVEN

"SO ARE YOU GOING TO HANG around until I get back?" Tom asked.

Brad sat down on the silk-covered sofa, the phone pressed to his ear. "Tell me again why you're staying in New York."

"Business. I've got a chance to pitch a project here in Manhattan. A chance to do something with a little bit of tradition to it. You can stay at the apartment for as long as you'd like. In fact, I'd appreciate it if you'd stay. Mr. Whiskers likes having company."

"I still can't look him in the eye without him sinking his claws into my leg or arm. But he's started sleeping with me," Brad said. "Although, I don't think it's me. He's just looking for a warm body."

"Aren't we all," Tom joked. "So how are things going with Dani? Are you sleeping with her yet?"

Brad would have liked nothing more than to confide in Tom, but he held his tongue. Hell, he wasn't quite sure what was happening between them, beyond a very strong sexual attraction. He didn't need to get involved with another woman. Right now he needed to figure out his own life.

"Everything's great. We're getting to know each other. She's doing really well with the children. You'll like them. They're great kids."

"You two. I just can't figure."

"Don't go dusting off your bridesmaid's dress yet," Brad teased. "I'm telling you, we're just friends."

"I'll call you before I fly home," Tom said. "And keep your feet off the sofa."

Brad turned off the phone and set it on the coffee table, then leaned back into the soft cushions of the sofa. His time with Dani had always had a limit and he'd accepted that. Since they'd returned from camping in the Cascades, he'd been preparing himself to leave by the end of the week. He wasn't sure where he planned to go—maybe back to Split Rock, or maybe he'd find another quiet spot to hide out for a while. But now that had all changed. He had another two weeks to avoid his family. Who knew where he and Dani might be by the end of October?

Maybe it was time to admit the truth—he wasn't just attracted to Dani, he was falling in love with her. But was this all just a little vacation from real life, something interesting to occupy his time and keep him from facing his own problems? Would these feelings last in the real world?

He shook his head. Dani was smart and sophisticated, a businesswoman who seemed to thrive in the city. He preferred a life in "Big Sky" country. Most couples had a few speedbumps to overcome on the road to love, whereas he and Dani had about six hundred miles of geography between them, including two or three major mountain ranges.

Besides, what would her job prospects be on a ranch in Montana? About as good as *his* would be in the city of Seattle. Hell, he and Jo Millen had been made for each other and they couldn't make it work. What chance did he have with Dani?

Brad stood up and looked around the apartment. Maybe it would be best to just pack up and leave, before it became impossible to walk away. Dani probably had the right idea all along. If he didn't learn to depend on her, then he wouldn't be hurt when she was no longer there. But somehow Brad knew that six-hundred miles would not put an end to his feelings for her—or for Jack, Becca and Noah.

His mind wandered back to his conversation with Alex. Sometimes she knew him better than he knew himself. He did seem to take on more responsibility than he really had to, and Dani and the children were a prime example. But with Dani, he didn't feel resentful. She didn't take his help for granted.

But was what he felt for her really love or just an overwhelming sense of responsibility? He liked the fact she needed him, but he couldn't confuse that kind of need with love. He had to see this relationship for what it really was. The only problem with that was he didn't know what it was—at least not yet.

He glanced at his watch. Dani had driven the kids to school that morning, even though she wasn't on her way to work afterward. She'd already set up three interviews, one for later that afternoon, and had a list two pages long of other businesses she intended to contact. She was determined to find a job that was more flexible with the hours, yet still offered a good career track.

"Everyone needs to take a break for lunch," Brad said to himself. Maybe it was time to find out exactly where he stood with Dani O'Malley. If he was going to make decisions about the rest of his life, he needed to get the facts. And the fact was, he was falling in love with Dani. But how did she feel about him?

He buttoned his shirt, then headed across the hall. Dani answered his knock at the door, but she didn't look as if she'd been job-hunting. Her hair was tangled and tinged with white goo, the same goo that covered her T-shirt and jeans. She held a long strip of wallpaper border and Brad assumed that the goo was paste.

"What are you doing?"

"I'm wallpapering," Dani said in a bright voice. "Usually I hire Louie to do things like this. He's kind of an all-around handyman. But I thought I'd save a little money. Now that I've quit my job, I've got to watch my pennies."

"Do you know what you're doing?"

"I bought a book," she said. She held it up, but when she put it down, her fingers stuck to the pages. With a soft curse, she shook her hand until the book tumbled to the floor. "I'm making a mess of this. But it's going to look great when it's done."

"Would you like some help?"

Dani laughed, then shook her head. "I'm perfectly capable of putting up a wallpaper border on my own."

"Actually, I've helped my mother do it. And it's definitely a two-person job."

A tiny frown furrowed her brow and then she groaned and strode back toward the children's room. She crumpled the sticky paper up and tried to toss it on the floor, but like the book, it stuck to her hands. "Why am I doing this?" she said, shaking it off. "I should be out looking for a job right now. Instead, I'm putting up a wallpaper border like some deranged Martha Stewart. I'm not Martha Stewart."

"You're a mom who wants to make a nice bedroom for her children," Brad said.

She glanced over at him, the smile returning to her face. "I do," she said. "I want to make a good home for Evie's children." She slowly sat down on the sofa. "I didn't realize it until now, Because I've been so caught up in all that's been going on. But when it comes right down to it, I want the children to stay with me."

"Then you've made a decision," Brad said.

She nodded. "I guess I have. I'm going to keep the children with me. I mean, if they want to stay with me. I need to ask them. No one ever asked me what I wanted when I was a kid, so I owe them that much. I know it's going to be hard. I've got to find the right job. And we can't stay here forever. We'll need an extra bedroom, and the rent is more than I can afford right now.''

Brad squatted down and picked up the crumpled wallpaper, decorated with skateboards and socccr balls. If only his decisions about his future came as easily as Dani's did. She was going to keep the children, but did she want to keep him as well? ''How's Becca going to like this pattern?''

Dani shrugged. ''She's not. But I couldn't very well put ballerinas and bunnies up. When I find a different place, she'll have her own room and we'll decorate it any way she wants. Evie had a pretty pink canopy bed, and I always loved lying on it. Maybe I'll get a bed like that for Becca.'' She reached out and plucked at the wallpaper in his hand. ''Until then, I need them to know that this is home.''

''Then why don't you let me help you?'' Brad asked, grabbing Dani around the waist and pulling her up against him with one arm.

''I've heard that couples shouldn't work on home improvement projects together.''

''Are we a couple?'' Brad asked.

Dani shrugged. ''Until it's time for you to go home, I guess we are.''

Brad brushed a kiss across her lips. He didn't blame Dani for her pragmatic approach to relationships. She'd learned from her experiences in childhood. People came and people went, and so would he. ''Hand me that book,'' he said. ''Between the two of us, we should be able to get this job done.''

''It's a lot more difficult that it seems. I stick it up on the wall and it falls down on my head. That's why I have so much paste in my hair. I'm not even sure industrial adhesive would keep that damn border on the wall.''

A knock sounded at the front door and Dani sighed. ''That's Louie to the rescue,'' she said. ''I called him and asked if he could bring up some stronger glue.''

''You called him before me?'' Brad asked. ''Ouch. That hurts.''

''I was going to pump him for free advice and then call you in for the heavy work,'' she said as she walked into the living room. Brad followed her, enjoying the view from behind. Dani really ought to wear blue jeans more often. Those tailored trousers she usually wore did nothing to show off her figure.

She pulled open the door. A man in a suit stood in the hallway. ''Are you Danielle O'Malley?'' he asked.

''I tried to stop him,'' Louie said, peering over the man's shoulder. ''I told him we should buzz you first.''

''Consider yourself served.'' He held out an envelope and Dani took it from his fingers. ''Have a nice day.'' With that, the man turned around and strode back to the elevator.

''Are you in some kind of trouble?'' Louie asked.

''I—I don't think so,'' Dani replied. She slipped her finger beneath the flap and pulled out a sheaf of papers, holding the document by the edges with her sticky fingers. But she just stared at it for a long moment, then handed it to Brad.

''It's a summons to appear in family court in Portland,'' he said. ''Someone is contesting your guardianship of the children.''

Dani nodded. ''Fred and Lucille Wilson,'' she murmured. ''Lucille is the one who brought the kids to Seattle. She's the children's aunt, John Gregory's older sister. She threatened she was going to do this, but I didn't take her seriously. She hasn't even tried to contact the kids since she left them here. I thought she'd changed her mind.''

"What are you going to do?" Brad asked.

"You need to get a lawyer," Louie said. "Mr. Kelly in 4-E is a bigshot lawyer. He could help you out. He gets home at seven."

"Thank you, Louie," she said. Dani grabbed the door and slowly closed it, then wandered over to the sofa. She sat down, her gaze fixed straight ahead. "I should have known this was coming. Things were just going too well."

Brad sat down beside her. "Hey, don't think like that."

"It's the story of my life," Dani said. "The good things always get taken away."

"Damn it, Dani, don't do this to yourself. You're past all that. You're in charge of your own life now."

"What do you know about my life," she snapped. "You walked into it—what?—thirteen days ago? You don't know anything about me. It isn't supposed to be easy for me. Somehow, that was in the plan from the beginning."

"That sounds like self-pity to me."

"I think I'm allowed," she said. She shook her head. "I don't feel like working on the wallpaper right now. I just want to be alone." She looked at him. "I'll be all right. Just go."

Brad cursed beneath his breath. He wanted to stay with her, to say all the right things, to make her feel better. But he knew one thing about Dani. Once she pushed someone away, it was better to retreat and come back later than to fight with her.

"I'll talk to you later," he said.

"Later," she repeated, her gaze still fixed on the document.

DANI SLID THE pizza out of the oven and onto the cutting board, then carried it over to the table. She handed Jack the pizza wheel, grabbed a spoon and sat down next to Noah. She knew she'd have to talk to the children, to prepare them. They'd had a big enough shock when they turned up on her doorstep. She wasn't going to do that to them again.

"There's something I need to talk to you guys about," she said, feeding Noah another spoonful of applesauce.

"Are we going camping again?" Becca asked.

"That was cool," Jack said, smiling. "I liked that hike we took around the lake. I was telling Charlie about that today at school and he likes stuff like that. Maybe sometime Brad could take us, just the guys."

"Is Charlie a friend?" Dani asked.

"Yeah, he's in math and English with me. And we've been playing basketball at recess. And he's got the best board."

"Board?"

"Skateboard. He lives just a few blocks from school so he rides his board to school. He knows this really great shop downtown that sells lots of dope gear. Can we go down there this week?"

"Sure," Dani said. "Why don't you ask him what the place is called and the name of the street? We'll go down on Saturday."

Jack grinned. "Cool."

His attitude was slowly shifting, she mused. He was beginning to settle in and make friends and he wasn't nearly as belligerent and moody as he'd been when he'd arrived. Dani actually saw a lot of Evie in her son, his wry sense of humor, his curiosity and his smile.

"There is something else that I need to talk to you about," she said. "Yesterday, while you were at school, I got a…a letter from your Uncle Fred and Aunt Lucille. They want you to come and live with them."

A long silence descended over the table and Dani looked from Jack to Becca to Noah.

"No way," Jack finally said, his voice hard and emotionless.

Becca wrinkled her nose. "She smells funny. And she makes us eat vegetables."

"Well, that's not such a bad thing," Dani said, feeding Noah another spoonful. "We should eat more vegetables, ourselves."

"Yuck," Becca said.

Dani smiled at her. "I want to know what you want."

"What do you care?" Jack asked, pushing his pizza around his plate.

"When I was younger, I moved from home to home. And no one ever asked what I wanted, whether I wanted to stay or go. Now I need to know that from you. If you want to stay with me, then I'm going to make it happen. But if you want to live with the Wilsons, then—" She swallowed hard, trying to control her emotions. "Then that's all right, too. Or if you want to live with a whole new set of parents, then that's what will happen. But now is the time to tell me."

"I wanna stay here," Becca said. "I like it here. I like my school and my teacher and the day care. And I like you."

Dani smiled. "I like you, too." She turned to Jack. "How about you?"

"How do I know you won't change your mind later?"

"I'm not going to do that," Dani said. "If you decide you want to stay with me, then I'm going to fight as hard as I can to keep you here."

Jack stared at his plate. "Yeah. I want to stay here."

She hadn't realized how much their answer meant to her. The dread she'd been feeling all day long dissolved and Dani was strengthened by their decision. If it took every penny of her savings to win the custody suit, then that was fine. She was going to find a way to make this work.

"And I think Brad should live with us," Becca said. "I think he should be the dad and you should be the mom."

It sounded so simple when Becca said it. And in truth, it would probably be the answer to all her problems. But to make it happen, she'd have to convince a virtual stranger they were meant for each other. Dani's powers of persuasion were finely honed, but she'd never tried to talk a man into happily ever after.

She turned the notion over in her head. What would marriage to Brad be like? She'd have someone to depend upon, someone to help with the children, to take up some of the stress in her day-to-day life. But marrying him because it was convenient would backfire sooner or later.

A man and a woman were supposed to marry because they loved each other. For Dani, that was a problem. She wasn't sure what love was supposed to feel like. She couldn't remember loving her mother. And though she knew she loved Evie, that was a different kind of love. Of all the men in her life, there hadn't been one she'd even come close to loving.

So how would she know? Would there ever come a time in her life when she was sure? Somehow, she knew that Brad would be long gone before she figured it all out.

"Can he be the dad?" Becca asked.

"I don't think so," Dani told her, smiling. "Brad is our friend. He's just visiting here. He lives far away, in Montana. And he's supposed to leave in a few days. So it would be just me. And you guys."

Jack nodded. "Okay."

Dani got up from the table and walked to the kitchen to get the milk. As she reached into the refrigerator, her hand trembled and she clutched her fingers in front of her. Until that moment, she hadn't realized how much she'd come to care about Evie's children. Every time she looked at them, she saw Evie, and though it was painful at first, lately she'd found it almost comforting. But what was even more comforting was that they cared about her, maybe as much as she cared about them.

Dani grabbed the milk jug and carried it back to the table, then poured a glass for Jack and Becca. She took a slice of pizza and put it on her plate. "I'm going to give Brad a piece of pizza," she said. "I'll be back in a second."

"Can you ask him if we can go camping before he leaves?" Jack asked.

Dani walked to the front door, then stepped out into the hallway. Before she knocked, she quickly smoothed through her hair. When he answered, she held out the plate. "We were just having some dinner," she said. "I thought you might like a piece of pizza."

Brad took the plate from her hand. "Thanks."

"And I wanted to apologize. For yesterday. You were only trying to help and I shouldn't have snapped at you." She drew a deep breath. "You've done so much for us and I didn't want you to leave without knowing how much I appreciated it."

He nodded, then smiled crookedly. "Actually, I'm not going to be leaving just yet. Tom called to say he'll be staying in New York until the end of the month."

Dani tried to hide her surprise—and her delight. She'd grown used to having Brad around, and she'd grown addicted to his kisses. A couple more weeks of both wouldn't be the worst thing in the world. And maybe he'd be able to help her through the custody suit. "Good," she said. "I'm sure Tom would appreciate you taking care of Mr. Whiskers."

"So, how are the kids?"

"I haven't told them about the custody suit, but I did talk to them about where they wanted to live, and if they wanted to live with the Wilsons. I tried to make them understand that I'd listen to what they had to say and take their wishes into consideration." She forced a smile. "I wanted them to choose me."

"Did they?" Brad asked, stroking her cheek with his fingertips.

Dani nodded. "The thought of losing them just hurts. It makes me feel sick inside. At first, I thought it was just an instinct to win. I have that problem. I have to succeed at all costs. But that's not it. These children mean something to me. I've grown...attached."

"And you're surprised it happened," Brad added.

Dani nodded. "Isn't that a sad thing? I mean, I was attached to Evie, I know that. But I never told her. I was afraid if I said it out loud, she would go away." She straightened. "And then she did, before I had a chance to tell her."

"She knew," Brad said. "She left her children in your care."

"I know that now." She looked up at him. "Would you like to come over for dinner? We have pizza. And ice cream for dessert."

"That would be great. Let me go get a shirt." He disappeared into the apartment, then came back a few minutes later. "Maybe I should go out and get a video. Pizza and a video. A real family Friday night."

"It's Thursday night," Dani said. "Besides, the children watch too much television already. Tonight I'm going to introduce them to the game of Monopoly. As a former business executive, I think I'll be able to teach them a few things."

As they both walked back to Dani's kitchen, Brad

grabbed her hand and gave it a squeeze, a silent show of affection that set Dani's pulse racing. Two more weeks, she mused. A lot could happen in two weeks.

"Hey, guys," Brad said as he walked into the kitchen. "What are you up to tonight?"

"We're having pizza," Becca said with her mouth full.

"And then I hear you're going to play Monopoly." He snatched a piece of sausage from her plate and popped it in his mouth. "Monopoly is for sissies. I say we play poker."

"Yeah!" Jack said.

"I don't know how to play poker," Becca complained.

"Then I'll teach you. Back on the ranch, me and the guys play poker every Friday night. We play for money. Do you guys have money?"

Dani shot him a warning look. "I don't think gambling is the best thing to be teaching them, do you?"

"All right. We'll play for…" He glanced around the kitchen table, then walked over to a cupboard and pulled out a bag. "Mini-marshmallows. Hey, me and the guys play for marshmallows all the time."

"Let's play," Jack said.

"Do you have cards?" Brad asked.

"I think I have a deck in my bedside table," Dani said. "I play solitaire when I can't sleep."

She went to retrieve the cards, but on her way back to the kitchen, Brad met her in the living room. He pulled her into a corner, away from the eyes of the children, and gave her a quick kiss.

"What was that for?" Dani asked.

"I figured I'd want to do that at least once during our card game. I didn't want to crawl over the table to do it."

Dani gave him a playful shove. "You better not. I'm letting you teach my children how to gamble. That's where it stops." She paused. "They're getting attached to you.

We have to be careful they don't get the wrong idea. Becca mentioned that if I'm going to be their mother, then maybe you could be their father. I don't want them to think that's an option.''

"Of course not," Brad said. "I understand."

They walked back into the kitchen and sat down at the table. Jack pushed the pizza box out of the way and rearranged the glasses and silverware. "This is a very simple game," Brad said as he shuffled the cards. He dealt five hands of five cards.

"Noah can't play," Jack said.

"This is a very simple *family* game," Brad said. "We'll turn Noah's cards up so everyone can see what he has."

Dani sat back and watched as Brad patiently explained the rules of the game. Becca was too young to remember them all, but he helped her along, reminding her of the different hands. He advised her on her bets, and as they played hand after hand, he found a way to let one of them win.

He'd make a wonderful father, she thought. It was a shame he didn't have children of his own. And it was even sadder because her children needed a male influence in their lives, especially Jack. Though the twelve-year-old kept a wary distance from Dani, he seemed to thrive in Brad's company.

Dani cleared her throat as she placed her two-marshmallow bet in the center of the table. "Jack, didn't you want to ask Brad something?"

Jack scowled. "But I thought you—"

"Brad told me he's going to be staying for another two weeks. You can ask him."

The boy seemed almost nervous, wriggling around on his chair. "I wanted to know if you could take me camping again. Me and my friend Charlie from school."

A slow smile curved Brad's lips. "Sure. Maybe next weekend. We could take everyone. And I've got a two-man tent that you and your buddy could use."

"Really? We could stay in a tent by ourselves?"

"Sure. If that's all right with Dani?"

Jack turned to her. "I think that would be fine," she said. "Why don't you and Brad plan the trip and let me and Becca and Noah know where you're going to take us."

"Can we go back to the same place?" Jack asked Brad.

"It's getting colder in the Cascades," Brad said. "But I know of this really nice island off the coast. You can only get there by boat."

"We don't have a boat," Jack said.

"I know where I can get one," Brad said.

Jack grinned and turned back to his cards. "Cool."

THE LAW OFFICE was located on the eighteenth floor of a downtown Seattle high-rise. Dani and Brad rode the elevator up, Brad whistling along with the piped-in music. He'd never seen her so uneasy. She reached over and grabbed his hand, weaving her fingers through his.

"I'm nervous."

"You'll be fine. She's just going to listen to your story, that's all."

"But what if she doesn't want to take the case?"

"Then we'll find another lawyer."

They walked into the office together and approached the receptionist. "Dani O'Malley to see Elizabeth Winters."

"She's expecting you," the receptionist said, glancing at Brad. "You can go back."

"I'll just wait out here," Brad said, pointing to a comfortable chair in the corner.

"No," Dani said, clutching his arm. "I want you to come

with me. I need you in there. I'm not sure I can do this on my own."

"All right," he said.

When it came to things outside motherhood, Dani was the picture of confidence. Dressed in her designer business suit, she looked as if she'd put on her armor and was ready to go into battle. But when he looked into her eyes, he could see the vulnerability there. She was afraid of losing the children she'd come to love and she felt as defenseless as she had when she was a child.

Brad wanted to gather her into his arms and hold her until she stopped trembling. But a woman stepped out of an office halfway down the hall. "Ms. O'Malley?" She extended her hand. "Hello. I'm Elizabeth Winters."

"Hi," Dani said, shaking the lawyer's hand.

Brad did the same. "Brad Cullen. I'm a friend of Dani's."

"You look worried," Elizabeth said, pointing to the guest chairs in front of her desk. "You don't have to be. I'm on your side. Please, sit down." She took her spot behind the desk, then picked up the papers that Dani had given her.

"I've read the summons you messengered over and I think we're going to be spending some time in court. The Wilsons have grounds for challenging your guardianship. They are blood relatives, and Evie rewrote her will right before she died, when she was heavily medicated. However, they do admit that they have not been an active part of the children's lives. They claim Evie cut them off from the children after her husband died. From what I understand, there was a disagreement over John Gregory's estate."

"She never said anything to me about that." Dani forced a smile. "Evie and I didn't really stay in touch. We talked on the phone three or four times a year—usually she called on holidays. And she sent me cards and letters. I'm ashamed to say that I didn't always reciprocate.'' She paused. ''I should have.''

''Well, the Wilsons don't have any way of knowing that. But we also don't have any way of knowing how close they were to the children before John Gregory died.''

''Jack says that he doesn't know the Wilsons at all. Why would they want the children?''

''They don't have children of their own and John was Lucille Wilson's only sibling. I get the sense that the family never approved of him marrying Evie Marshall.''

''I don't think they were at her wedding. At least, I don't remember meeting them.''

''So, tell me about yourself,'' Elizabeth said, sitting back in her chair. ''I understand you're single. Are you two involved?''

''Oh, no,'' Dani told her. ''We're just friends. Brad is living across the hall from me. He's staying there while the regular tenant is visiting his mother. He's been a great help.''

''So you're not romantically involved?'' Elizabeth asked.

''Does that really make a difference?'' Brad wondered

''Are you sleeping together?''

''No!'' Dani cried.

''I had to ask. Your personal life will be scrutinized. You'll have to defend your suitability as a parent. Especially because you'll be a single parent. Now, what do you do for a living?''

''I'm between jobs right now.''

''And you don't have any regular means of financial support?''

''I have savings and a stock portfolio and a retirement account. I have some jewelry I can sell if I have to.''

''It won't look good that you're unemployed,'' she said.

"But she quit work because her job was taking her away from the children," Brad objected.

"And there's the rub. If you work, Dani, you don't have time for the children, and if you don't work, you can't provide financial security for them. And where do you live?"

"I have an apartment in Queen Anne. It's only got two bedrooms, but I'm thinking I might look for a house. Something with a yard where the children can play."

"I wouldn't jump into any real estate transactions right now," Elizabeth said.

"Are you saying we won't win?" Dani asked.

"I'm just trying to prepare you for the fight."

Elizabeth continued to grill Dani, asking her personal questions, probing to get the most detailed answers out of her. Every so often, she'd ask for Brad's opinion, telling him that an objective viewpoint would be valuable to her.

"Is there anything else you'd like to tell me?"

"I spoke to the children a few days ago and I asked where they wanted to go," Dani explained, "with the Wilsons or with me, or with different parents altogether. They want to stay with me."

"Well, if it were just Jack, that might make a difference, but Becca and Noah are too young to make any decisions for themselves. Now, I want to talk to the children and I'd like to visit your home. The preliminary hearing is the week after next, so we need to be ready to counter anything they throw at us."

"Why so soon?" Dani asked.

"In a case like this, it would cause more harm to the children if they stayed with you and then the custody was reversed. It would be more difficult to take them out of a familiar environment and move them again. They've already become attached to you."

"We're going to lose this, aren't we," Dani said.

"No," the lawyer replied. "Not if I can help it. I just need to make sure we're prepared. And it would help if you'd get a job before we go to court. A flexible job that pays well and includes benefits would be the best, as impossible as that sounds. Now, I'll schedule depositions for the end of the month. We'll need to drive down to Portland, but we'll only need a day. For now, I want you to go home and make a list of all the reasons you think you should keep the children. And then, I want you to list all the reasons why you shouldn't. Be honest. We'll talk again next week."

She stood up, calling an end to the meeting. Brad looked at his watch and realized they hadn't even spent fifteen minutes together. Dani glanced over at him uneasily. He took her hand and they walked out of the office, neither one of them speaking.

When they got to Dani's car, she gave him the keys, then slid into the passenger seat. Brad got behind the wheel, but waited. She'd closed her eyes and leaned her head back on the headrest. "It's going to be all right," he told her.

"I knew I wouldn't make a good mother. I've known it all along and she just confirmed it."

"Dani, don't get ahead of yourself here."

"This is going to cost so much."

"Don't worry about the money. I've got plenty if you need some."

"Not money. I'm willing to pay whatever it takes. It's going to cost in other ways."

He pulled her into his embrace and pressed his lips to her hair.

"Maybe I should let them go." She said. "Maybe they would be better off with the Wilsons."

"You can't think that way. Evie gave the children to you. She made that decision for a reason. And you need to remind yourself of that."

"We need to go pick up the children. Jack will be finished with school soon and I want to get the kids from the day care. Maybe I shouldn't send them there anymore. That might look bad. I mean, if I'm home, I should be taking care of them, right? I just wanted them to make friends and have other kids to play with. Was that wrong?"

He wanted to soothe her worries, but he knew there wasn't anything he could say that would make a difference. The reality was that she could very well lose in court. "Dani, you need to relax. This is going to take a long time and a lot of energy to sort out. And you've got to keep it together or the kids are going to start worrying."

"I'm going to lose them," Dani said. A tear slipped from the corner of her eye and trickled down her cheek. "I've tried to do everything right, but it's not going to make a difference."

He reached over for her, but she drew away, hugging herself as if that might create a shield around her. Brad cursed silently, angry at the circumstances that had brought her so much pain and caused her defenses to rise again. As he drove out of the parking lot, he could almost feel the wall rising between them. He'd give her time to adjust, but he'd be damned if he'd let her face this alone.

CHAPTER EIGHT

BRAD TUGGED AT THE KNOT in his silk tie, wincing as the starched collar of his dress shirt chafed at his neck. The suit was brand new, purchased that very afternoon from one of the fancy department stores that Alex had suggested. Though the sleeves were a bit long and the pants had been quickly hemmed, he thought he looked pretty damn good for a common cowboy.

He took a deep breath and rapped on Dani's door. He hadn't bothered to call ahead. The element of surprise was probably his best advantage. If Dani didn't have time to think, then she couldn't possibly refuse him.

A few seconds later, the door swung open. Jack stood on the other side, his eyes wide with surprise.

"Don't say a word," Brad warned, pointing at him with the bouquet of roses that he'd brought along.

A wry smile quirked the boy's lips. "Is it Halloween already? What are you going as—Businessman?"

"Can't a guy wear a suit if he wants?"

Jack stepped aside as Brad walked into Dani's apartment. "Why? Are you trying to impress her?"

Brad turned and sent Jack a withering glare. "No. We're just going out, and fancy restaurants don't like it if you wear jeans and cowboy boots. Besides, Dani prefers sophisticated men."

"You're going out? Dani's already in her robe and slippers. Maybe she forgot."

It was barely 6:00 p.m. She must have had a pretty bad day to be in her robe already. She'd had three interviews set up and she hadn't run across the hall to tell him she'd found a new job. Maybe this wasn't such a great idea. "She doesn't know yet. It's a surprise. My cousin Alex is going to come over and baby-sit and—"

"Brad?"

He turned around and found Dani standing in the middle of the living room, a look of pure astonishment on her face. As Jack had said, she was dressed in a pretty silk robe. Underneath, a body-skimming T-shirt and baggy silk pajama bottoms completed the look. Her hair was pulled up into a haphazard ponytail, tendrils falling around her face. "Hi," he murmured, his gaze fixing on her pretty features, scrubbed clean of the makeup she usually wore.

She slowly walked toward him, the silk clinging to her curves as she moved. "What is this? Do you have a date or something?"

"I do," Brad said. His reply caused an uneasy expression to cross her features and he thought he saw a hint of jealousy in her eyes. He held out the roses. "With you, I thought we could go out. Maybe have some dinner." He reached into his pocket and produced two tickets.

She examined them closely. "Shakespeare? I didn't know you liked Shakespeare."

"You don't know a lot of things about me," he said. "Maybe it's time you found out." Their gazes met and held for a long moment. If Jack weren't standing between them, he might have tossed the roses aside and kissed her. But he fought the impulse. "So are you going to come out with me?"

"What about the children?"

"I can baby-sit," Jack said. "I'm old enough."

"I asked Alex to watch the kids," Brad said, "to give

Jack a break. She'll be here in a few minutes. Now, go put on a pretty dress and some perfume and we'll be ready to go. I've got a reservation for six-thirty.''

Dani glanced back and forth between Jack and Brad, then grinned. ''All right. After the day I've had, I could use a night out. I never thought it would be so hard to find a job. I'm an experienced advertising executive with a great track record and I—'' She paused, as if realizing she'd been rambling, then smiled. ''I'll just be a second.'' She spun around and hurried down the hallway to her bedroom.

With a sigh of relief, Brad sat down on the sofa. He'd been right to ask her on the spur of the moment. Lately, Dani felt her life was all about schedules and interviews. Doing something spontaneous was a stroke of brilliance on his part. And so was the suit, he mused as he smoothed his hand over the tailored lapel. She had obviously been impressed.

Jack sat down next to him. ''So you really like her, huh?''

Brad sent him a sideways glance. ''Yeah, I like her.''

''Do you like her like her? Or do you *like* her like her?''

''What's the difference?'' Brad knew it was something only a preteen would know, but he was interested anyway.

''Do you wanna kiss her all the time?''

Brad frowned. All the time. But he couldn't say that out loud. ''Is that any of your business?''

''It is,'' Jack said, his expression turning serious. ''If she falls in love with you, then she won't want us. She'll want her own family and she'll send us away.''

A gasp of surprise escaped from Brad. ''Is that what you think?''

''It's true,'' Jack said, his eyes wide and honest. ''She's not really our mother. She can send us away whenever she wants. To an orphanage. Or to the Wilsons. She says she won't, but she could.''

"And it's your job to protect this family, right? You're the one who has to take the responsibility for Becca and Noah.''

"Who else will? Not her.''

"You've got to give Dani a chance. You lost your mom, she lost her best friend. She's just as scared and hurt as you are. It's going to take some time for all of you to adjust. Believe me, her feelings for you have nothing to do with whatever she feels for me.''

Brad wanted to reassure him that everything would be all right, that he and his siblings would live happily ever after with Dani...but he couldn't. He didn't know what the future held for them, especially with the custody suit looming on the horizon. He drew a deep breath. There was a way to help, a way to increase the odds that Dani would win the custody suit. Brad shook his head, knowing that the idea was ridiculous at best. Still, he couldn't seem to put the notion out of his head, not since the appointment with Dani's attorney.

"I'm not scared,'' Jack said, stiffening his spine and tipping his chin up. "Becca, she's scared. But she's always smiling like everything's going to be fine. Even when Mom died, she kept smiling. She thinks if she's a good girl, then Dani will want us.''

"People deal with death in different ways,'' Brad said. "Even Noah is struggling with this. When he got here, he cried all the time.''

"He still cries at night. I think he has bad dreams,'' Jack said. "And he's sucking his thumb again. He hasn't done that in a long time.''

Brad reached out and slipped his arm around the boy's shoulders. "I know this is hard, Jack. If you need to talk about this, you can always come to me. Anytime. I think I know a little bit of what you're going through.''

"Did your parents die?" Jack asked.

"No. I don't know about that part. But I know about feeling like you're responsible for everything and everyone. Having so many expectations resting on your shoulders that you feel like you don't have a life of your own, you don't have any choices. But you can't run away from your fears, Jack. You have to face them head-on. I've been running away for four months now, and sooner or later I'm going to have to face my problems."

"When?" he asked.

Brad shrugged. "I don't know. Soon."

"I'm ready!"

They both stood and slowly turned. Dani wore a sexy black dress that revealed both her long legs and her smooth shoulders. She did a little pirouette in front of them, then clutched her handbag to her chest. Just then a knock sounded on the door. Jack ran over and opened it, finding Alex on the other side.

Brad walked over to them. "Jack, this is my cousin Alex. Alex, this is Becca and Noah's older brother, Jack."

"Hi," Jack said, taking the hand she offered.

"Hi," Alex said. "We met already, the day Dani brought the kids to see the day care, remember?"

"Jack's a pretty good poker player," Brad commented. "And Alex likes a good game of poker. When we were young, she used to take my allowance from me every week. Don't let her talk you into a game."

"I could beat her," Jack said, gazing at Alex shrewdly.

"You think you can beat me? Get the cards and we'll see."

Jack glanced over at Brad, and Brad smiled. "Are we cool?"

The boy nodded, then ran off.

"Where are the other two?" Alex asked.

"They're watching a video in the bedroom," Dani said. "Becca is coloring and Noah's eating goldfish crackers. They'll be thrilled to see you."

"Well, I'll go check up on them. You two had better get going. And have fun."

Brad helped Dani slip into her coat, then placed his hand on the small of her back as they walked out, trying hard to remember all the manners his mother had drilled into his head when he was a kid. When they reached the elevator, he punched the button. Then he turned, forgetting etiquette completely. Grabbing her, he pulled her against him and brought his mouth down on hers. He lost himself in a long and lingering kiss, running his fingers through her silken hair and inhaling the scent of her perfume. When he finally drew away, Brad sighed, pressing his forehead to hers. "There," he murmured. "That's better."

"You look very...different," she said, running her palms over the lapels of his jacket. "Handsome, but different."

"Do you like it?"

She frowned. "I'm not sure I like you in a suit."

"This suit cost me a month's salary," Brad said. "You'd better like it."

She reached up and dragged a finger along his freshly shaved cheek. "I was getting used to the cowboy in you."

Brad chuckled, then loosened his tie and unbuttoned his collar. "Good, because this shirt and tie are killing me." He grabbed her hand. "Come on, we'll be late for our reservations."

They took Dani's car to the restaurant instead of his pickup, and as he drove through evening traffic, his mind wound back to his conversation with Jack. He should take his own advice and solve his own problems before he tried to solve Dani's. But hers were so much more immediate. The ranch could wait. It wasn't as if it was going anywhere.

"This evening is exactly what I needed," she said as he pulled into the restaurant parking lot. "I was getting too wrapped up in the custody suit. And this hunt for a job."

"How's that going?" Brad asked.

"Not great. I was so optimistic when I started. But I think I may have overestimated my value in the job market. When I explain I'm looking for a flexible schedule and no travel, they look at me like I've just asked them to give me their firstborn." She glanced over at him. "I have to find a job. And right now, it looks like I'm probably going to have to take the first thing that's offered."

"Maybe not," Brad said. "You never know what might come along."

"Like a bag filled with a million dollars? I'm not holding my breath."

He pulled up to the valet parking attendant, then hopped out of the car and tossed the guy Dani's keys. Brad jogged around to the passenger side and opened her door, offering his hand to help her out. His gaze fell to her ankles, then moved up to the curve of her thigh as she stepped out of the car.

Why the hell had he insisted on dinner out? He could have cooked for her in Tom's apartment, nixed the suit and tie and had her all to himself. Brad groaned silently as she tucked her hand in the crook of his arm. Considering his need to drag her into his arms, this promised to be a very long evening.

The maitre d' seated them immediately at a small candlelit table against the windows. "I've dined here a number of times, but I've never been given such a good table," Dani commented. "How'd you manage?"

"Charm, wit and bribery were involved," Brad said.

"You didn't have to do that."

Brad reached across the table and grabbed her hands. "Dani, there's something I wanted to talk to you about."

"This sounds serious," she said, frowning. "What is it?"

He drew a deep breath and gathered his thoughts. Ever since they'd visited the lawyer, he'd been turning the idea over in his head, working up the courage to mention it. "Remember the other day when we were in the lawyer's office. She mentioned that you'd have a better chance of keeping the children if you were married."

"She didn't say that," Dani objected.

"Well, not exactly. But she said being a single mother was a disadvantage."

"But I'm not married."

"You have to admit, marriage would give you an edge. A young married couple would probably have a better chance than a couple over the age of fifty."

She smiled. "What? Are you going to volunteer for the job?"

He hesitated, then nodded. "Yeah. I thought I might."

Dani's eyes went wide and she gasped. "You're offering to marry me?"

"Yes," he said.

"No!" she cried, jumping to her feet and laughing nervously. She realized how loudly she'd spoken and glanced around at the other patrons in the restaurant. Two spots of color blazed on her cheeks and she slowly sat back down.

"No? Is that your answer?" Brad asked.

"Yes," she whispered. "We can't get married. Marriage is a huge step. We're supposed to date and then we're supposed to live together and then we get engaged, and after a few years, we start planning the wedding." She shook her head. "That's not what I meant! Not *we*—a couple. A random couple. A couple is supposed to date and—well, not us."

"It doesn't have to work that way all the time. Haven't you ever heard of love at first sight?"

"Are you in love with me?"

Brad opened his mouth, then snapped it shut. His first instinct had been to say "yes." But he hadn't taken the time to fully consider the question, either before or after Dani had posed it, and he didn't want to lie to her. He felt as if he loved her, but then he'd thought he loved Jo Millen. All he'd really been concerned about was helping Dani. "That's not the issue here. We're talking about a way for you to get custody of the children."

She frowned. "So, it would be like a business arrangement?"

"Yeah," Brad said, relieved that the conversation had shifted from love to business. "Exactly like a business arrangement."

"All right," she said in a measured tone. "Then what are you getting out of the arrangement? I know what I'm getting, but a business arrangement usually involves the exchange of goods or services. What do you expect in return?"

"Well, I hadn't thought much about it." That wasn't true. He had thought a lot about the pleasures he and Dani might share, had they been tied to each other legally. It didn't have to be all about business. "There wouldn't have to be an equal exchange. I'd just have the satisfaction of knowing that Evie's children ended up in a good home."

"And what happens if and when I get custody of the children? Would we get a divorce?"

"I hadn't thought about that, either. We'd have to work out all the details."

Dani stared down at the table, her fingers fiddling with

her fork. At that moment, Brad would have given his best broodmare to know what was going through her head. Was she actually considering his offer? And what if she accepted? Good Lord, what had ever possessed him to make the offer anyway?

"I guess I have to at least think about it," Dani said. "I have to be practical here. I'm willing to do whatever it takes to keep Evie's children. If it takes marriage, then that's what it takes."

"Right."

Dani sent him a weak smile, then rubbed her arms. "Do you mind if we go? I'm really not very hungry right now."

"I'm not, either," Brad said, a sick feeling settling into his stomach. So much for dating. He'd been out of the loop so long, he'd forgotten the appropriate behavior for such an important social situation. After all, who the hell proposed marriage on a first date?

DANI STARED OUT THE WINDOW of the car, watching the lights of one of the many ferries that crossed the calm waters of Elliott Bay into Puget Sound. She followed the boat's path until it disappeared behind the landscape. She was almost afraid to talk, afraid that they'd be forced to discuss Brad's rather impromptu proposal.

Of all her expectations for this evening, she certainly hadn't expected a marriage proposal. Romance, conversation, a little wine, maybe. Even some uncontrolled passion before the night was over. But not a proposal. What could he have been thinking? They barely knew each other. He lived in Montana and she lived in Seattle.

"Alex said she could stay until midnight," he told her. "And the children are probably already in bed. Tom has a whole refrigerator full of wine and I've got some Chinese take-out left over. Why don't we have dinner upstairs? If you're actually considering my proposal, maybe we should...get to know each other a little better?''

"What difference does it make?" she said, trying to affect a teasing tone, but failing miserably. "Since it's just a business proposition, we should be able to cover all the contingencies in a contract."

Brad pulled the car over to the curb, screeching to a stop. "Can we just forget I ever asked you to marry me? I just wanted to help. I felt compelled to help. It's a problem I have."

Dani could see the regret in his tense expression, in the way he clutched the steering wheel with his white-knuckled hands. "No, I'm sorry, I should have been more gracious. It was a very generous offer. It just took me by surprise."

"It kind of took me by surprise, too."

"Then it's forgotten," she said. "We won't mention it again, all right?"

Brad nodded, put the car back into gear and drove the three short blocks to Dani's apartment. He pulled back into her parking spot barely a half hour after they left it. When he turned off the ignition, he shifted in his seat to face Dani.

She glanced up at him and smiled. "I suppose I ought to thank you for such a nice date." A giggle slipped from her lips. "But it was pretty awful."

Grinning, Brad reached out and smoothed his hand over her cheek. "It was pretty bad, wasn't it. It's been a long time since I've been on a date, but even I know that wasn't my best effort."

"Why don't we just rewind and go back to the beginning of the evening and start again," Dani suggested. "We should have stuck to dinner at Tom's apartment and a video."

Brad got out of the car, but this time, Dani didn't wait for him to open her door. Instead, she hopped out and grabbed his hand, then strolled with him to the back door of her building. They rode the elevator up to the third floor, but when they stepped out, she didn't head for her own apartment. She wasn't ready to go home quite yet.

As soon as Brad unlocked the door to Tom's apartment, she stepped inside. And the instant the door closed, she turned to face him, wrapping her arms around his neck. "Maybe instead of ending this date with a kiss, we could begin it with a kiss?"

With a low groan, he grabbed her around the waist and pressed her back against the wall. Then he brought his mouth down on hers, kissing her deeply and thoroughly. Dani sighed softly and buried her hands in his hair, causing him to deepen his kiss.

He'd touched her many times in the past week, but it had always been with a measure of reserve, knowing they couldn't go too far. But this was the first time they'd been completely free to see where a simple caress might lead. And Dani wasn't about to let the opportunity pass her by.

He trailed a line of kisses from her mouth to her neck, pushing her coat open and letting it fall to the floor. The moment his lips touched her shoulder, she realized that she'd chosen the right dress. It exposed the maximum amount of skin without looking too obvious.

Brad's efforts to do away with a layer of clothing didn't go unnoticed, and Dani quickly dispatched his suit jacket and silk tie in the same way. When she moved to the buttons of his shirt, she was almost desperate to put her hands on his skin and he was just as desperate to oblige. His mouth still caressing her shoulder, Brad tugged his shirt out of the waistband of his trousers and tore it off.

Once his hands were free he cupped her face and began a determined assault on her mouth. There was something about kissing Brad that she found addictive. The way he almost overpowered her, so potent and irresistible. She felt like a woman when he touched her, and though she'd kissed her share of men, not one had ever caused such an intense longing.

But Dani wasn't content to stop at kissing. Her hands smoothed over his chest, and desire flooded her body, seeping into her limbs and making her knees weak. And when her lips followed her touch, Brad tipped his head back and closed his eyes. A low groan slipped from his throat when she circled his nipple with her tongue.

"When I said we should get to know each other a little better, this wasn't exactly what I had in mind," Brad murmured.

"What did you have in mind?" she asked.

"I can't remember," he said. "But I guess this will do."

Dani grinned, then reached for his belt buckle. She quickly undid it, glancing up at him. "Maybe we should have some wine." She turned and walked toward the kitchen, taking his belt with her and letting it drag on the floor behind her in a silent invitation to follow.

She'd never been quite so bold with a man. Nor had she felt so at ease with seduction. Brad knew the real Dani O'Malley. He'd seen her at her worst and it hadn't scared him away. If there was ever a man meant to completely possess her body, he was the one. And if he tried, she didn't intend to stop him.

Brad caught up with her in the kitchen. She bent over and peered into Tom's wine cooler, giving Brad a tantalizing view of her backside. "What would you like? How about champagne?" She pulled out a bottle and handed it to him. "Open it."

"Are you sure Tom won't mind?"

She examined the bottle and then shrugged. "It's expensive, but nothing we can't replace. I'll get glasses." She walked over to a glass-paned cabinet, then stood on her tiptoes to grab two crystal champagne flutes. Her skirt rose as she reached, providing another nice view, and she heard Brad draw a deep breath. When she turned back, his attention was focused on the cork.

The children usually served as a buffer between them. Even when they were asleep in the other room, Dani knew there was always a chance they might walk in. Now, being completely alone with Brad caused an anticipation that was exciting on its own.

The cork popped and she held a glass out. When it was filled, she smiled and took a sip. "I suspect you're used to this," he said as he filled his own glass. "Expensive champagne."

"Oh, yes. It's part of the strategy of a successful advertising executive," she said. "Wine and dine the client. Smile and laugh at all the jokes, but be all about business. Look good and be smart. I was the best. I could talk just about anyone into just about anything."

"You haven't lost your touch," he said. "I'll do whatever you ask."

She smiled. "Now it all seems so…unimportant. Who cares if I get the account? Who cares if I'm vice president? All that matters is if Jack gets an A on his math quiz or Becca has the right color socks to go with her dress or Noah says a new word. I've gone completely soft."

Brad drew his thumb over her damp lower lip. "I like soft."

She smiled ruefully and ran her finger along his chest. "And I like hard."

He groaned, then kissed her neck. "You are bad," he teased her.

"I used to be bad. Now I'm the mother of three."

Brad slipped his finger under the thin strap of her dress

and pushed it off her shoulder, placing a kiss where it was. "I thought we weren't going to talk about the children." He pushed the other strap off and then stepped back. "You're beautiful," he said.

"Flattery will get you everywhere." She turned and walked over to the doorway into the kitchen, then turned the dimmer down. The halogen lights above the island faded until the kitchen was draped in shadows. As she walked back to him, Dani slipped the straps of her dress over her arms and shimmied out of it, revealing a sexy strapless bra and lace panties.

Brad gave another groan as she moved to stand in front of him. Dani picked up her champagne glass from the counter and took a sip, watching him over the rim. From the moment they'd walked into the apartment, she'd known what was going to happen. If it didn't happen tonight, then it wouldn't happen at all. Brad would be going back to Montana soon and she wanted him to remember her on those lonely nights at the ranch.

Dani boosted herself up on the counter again and grabbed the champagne bottle to refill Brad's glass. But the look in his eyes was enough to tell her he wasn't interested in champagne. He stepped between her legs and pulled them up against his hips, then slid her forward until she was teetering on the edge.

"I think I've had enough," he said.

"Champagne?"

"Mmm." He kissed the base of her neck, lingering there.

"What is it you want?" Dani asked, hoping against hope it would be what she wanted, too.

"This," he said, letting his mouth drift down to the swell above her breast. "And this." He kissed her belly.

Dani tipped her head back and closed her eyes, losing herself in the sensation of his lips on her bare skin. He kissed her hip and then the inside of her thigh. Then he removed her shoe and kissed the arch of her foot, sending a shiver racing through her body.

He slid his palm up along her leg to her rib cage and then her neck, and when he straightened, he kissed her again, his mouth hot and demanding. Though she and Brad had tested their desire for each other, until this instant, Dani hadn't realized how much he really wanted her—with an intensity that made her relinquish every inhibition she still possessed. And she wanted him.

Gently she pulled, pulling his mouth from hers. "Make love to me, cowboy," she murmured.

"Here?"

"Anywhere."

Brad didn't waste any time. He picked her up, wrapping her legs around his waist, and carried her to the living room. But he stopped at the sofa. "Hmm. Silk. Tom would probably kill me."

"The bedroom," Dani said, nuzzling her face into his neck. "That might be good."

With a grin, Brad pressed her back against the wall, kissing her long and hard. At that moment, Dani figured the hall would be as good as the bedroom, but he started walking again, kissing her as he went. When they reached the guest room, they tumbled down onto the bed in a tangle of limbs and expensive bedding.

But what started as playful suddenly turned serious. Brad stared down into her eyes, his expression clouded with desire. Dani held her breath, waiting, wanting him to take the lead. She'd never really made love. Before this it had been about sex, physical need and inevitable release. But with Brad there was something more. She wanted to know him in the most intimate way. To touch him in a way no one else had.

To that end, she reached down and worked at the waistband of his trousers. But when her hand brushed against his erection, he sucked in a sharp breath and groaned. A tiny thrill raced through her at his reaction. But he didn't allow her to go any further. He grabbed her hands, then pinned them above her head.

Stymied, Dani wriggled beneath him. "Shh," he whispered. With deliberate care, he clasped her wrists with one hand and trailed his other hand along her body. When he reached her bra, he deftly pushed aside the lace. Dani watched him, anticipating the feel of his mouth on her nipple. But when it happened, the anticipation was replaced by a wave of sensation that made her head swim.

Sighing softly, she arched back into the pillows. But while Brad's lips teased, his hand slid down further, this time pushing aside her panties. A current raced from her core to the tips of her fingers and toes, setting every nerve on fire. He drew her closer to completion, then let the need ebb, teasing and tantalizing her with every flick of his finger and his tongue.

Any attempt at self-control was now gone, and Dani found herself at his mercy. She wanted to touch him, but her inability to do so made the seduction even more exciting. On and on, he explored her body. She didn't notice when he finally rid her of her sexy underwear, only that after it was gone, she felt an even greater need to touch him. She was completely naked, lying beside him, and he still wore his trousers and shoes.

"Stop," she murmured, breathless.

Brad froze, then pushed up on his elbow. "Stop?"

Dani rolled off the bed and stood beside it. By the look on his face, he obviously thought she was having second thoughts. To soothe his fears, Dani smiled, then held her hand out. He took it and she pulled him to his feet. "I think you're a little overdressed," she said.

A slow grin curved his lips. "Sorry. I've never had very good fashion sense."

"Maybe I should help you." She bent down and untied his shoes, then pulled them off his feet. With a deliberately provocative move, she straightened against his body and handed him the shoes. "Thanks," he murmured, his gaze fixed on her body, his hands now occupied with his shoes.

"Socks," she said, bending over again. Dani knew he was growing impatient with her little game. But if he could tease her the way he'd done, then she could return the favor. When his feet were bare, she reached up and stuffed his socks into his shoes, letting her breasts skim along his chest. "There. Much better."

With a soft growl, Brad threw his shoes across the room. Then he reached for his waistband, but Dani slapped his hands away. She undid the button, then slowly lowered the zipper. Grabbing the fabric at his hips, she tugged the trousers down, his boxers coming with them. And when she'd thrown them in the direction of his shoes and socks, Dani slowly rose, allowing her body to slide along his, her breasts grazing his hard shaft, her lips skimming along his smooth chest.

"Much better," she said. "I really didn't like the suit. Now you may proceed."

Brad chuckled, then grabbed her around the waist and threw her down on the bed. He pinned her hands above her head again, but this time he stretched out on top of her, their bodies pressed together, their fingers tangled. Dani drew her legs up alongside his hips and his erection grazed the dampness between her legs.

Suddenly, she needed to feel him inside of her, that intimate connection she craved. As if he could read her mind,

Brad reached over and grabbed a condom from the drawer of the bedside table. Dani arched her brow as he handed it to her. "I was optimistic," he told her.

She tore open the package, then sheathed him. "Optimistic would have been a box of twelve."

"In the drawer," he murmured, pulling her on top of him.

Dani looked down at Brad, at the man who'd ridden to her rescue so many times since they'd met, at the smile she'd grown so accustomed to. She reached out and smoothed his hair out of his eyes, then leaned down and kissed him. This was what passion was supposed to feel like, she mused. The need racing through her took her breath away.

She wanted to tell him how she felt, she wanted to express that need in more than just a soft moan or an arch of her back. But in the end, Dani let her body speak for her. Her hands splayed over his chest, her knees pressed against his hips. As if they'd made love many times before, they found each other, Brad slipping inside of her, burying himself to the hilt.

He closed his eyes as she began to move above him, slowly at first and then with a more determined rhythm. Dani watched his face, the pleasure marking his handsome features. With every stroke, she let go of a little bit of her past, all the barriers she'd built to protect herself. She felt powerful, yet completely vulnerable. But she wasn't afraid.

Dani slid her hands up to his face and drew her thumb along his lower lip. He opened his eyes, looking at her through a haze of desire. And in that instant, she knew he was close. She wanted him then, wanted to possess his body as well as his soul. But Brad had other ideas.

He sat up, wrapping her legs around his waist again. And then he slipped his hand between them and touched her, while he was still buried deep inside. They watched each other, their movements ever so slight, but just enough to drive them forward. And when they were both ready, Dani arched against him, tumbling over the edge, her body spasming around him. He buried his face in the curve of her neck and followed her, shuddering as he reached his peak.

They held each other close until their hearts slowed and their breathing returned to normal. And then Brad drew her down onto the bed and wrapped his arms around her. Dani sighed and nestled against his warm body, closing her eyes. She felt…perfect. Content. As if she could stay in his bed forever.

As she listened to his soft breathing, felt his heart thud beneath her fingers, Dani let her mind wander. She'd never believed in romance, but now she could imagine herself falling in love with Brad Cullen. It would be so easy to just drop the last of her defenses and allow him into her heart. An image of them together, with the children, drifted through her thoughts, and this time she didn't push it aside. If she could be happy with any man, she could be happy with Brad.

He gently stroked her back, the warmth of his hand lulling her to sleep. Dani wasn't sure how long she dozed, but she was awake when one of Tom's antique clocks chimed twelve.

She drew a deep breath and pushed up, bracing herself on her outstretched arm. Brad's eyes were closed and his breathing was deep and even. At first, she thought about letting him sleep. But then she leaned over him and brushed a kiss across his mouth. When he didn't wake, she kissed him again and a moment later his hand tangled in her hair, keeping her close.

"What time is it?" he asked.

"It's late," Dani replied. "I have to go. Your cousin has to work tomorrow."

Brad groaned, then rolled over on his stomach. "I know you have to go, but I wish you could stay."

"I'll talk to you tomorrow," she said.

"I could always sneak into your apartment after Alex leaves. We could set the alarm and I could sneak out before the kids wake up."

Though the offer was tempting, Dani knew that getting Brad to leave her bed would be as hard as getting herself to leave his. "I don't think that would be a good idea." She crawled off the bed, then grabbed her underwear and tugged it on. "Where's my dress?"

"I'll get it," Brad said, sitting up.

"No. Go back to sleep. I'll see you in the morning. You're going to take the children to school, right?"

"Mmm-hmm." He yawned. "Are you sure you can't stay?"

"I'm sure," Dani said, giving him another kiss. She walked to the bedroom door, then took one last look back at the naked man lying across the bed. With every lover in her past, she'd been able to maintain control and then walk away. Passion had had its limits. But she couldn't do that with Brad. In bed and out of bed, he owned her soul.

Dani ran a hand across her tangled hair. She'd always known that Brad would leave sooner or later, and she'd been fine with that. But now, the thought of him disappearing from her life caused a dull ache to settle in around her heart. If she was falling in love with him, she'd have to put a stop to it right here and now—or risk regretting this night forever.

CHAPTER NINE

THE WATER SLUICED over her naked body and Dani tipped her face up into the shower. She'd barely slept a wink last night. Though her body had been pleasantly exhausted by the time spent in Brad's bed, her mind couldn't stop working once she got back to her own.

Making love to Brad had seemed like such a good idea at the time. She'd been curious and tantalized and captivated by the prospect of tumbling into bed with him. From the moment they'd met out on the street, the moment he'd dangled her underwear in front of her face, she'd thought he was one of the sexiest men she'd ever laid eyes on. And that opinion hadn't changed...except maybe when she'd thought he was gay.

There was something about him that she found irresistible. Maybe it was the cowboy charm, the easygoing manner and the lazy smiles. Or maybe it was more about the physical—the long, muscular legs and broad chest, the hair that seemed to be kissed by the sun and blown by the wind. Whatever it was, she'd been hooked.

All he had to do was pull her into his arms and kiss her and she lost all ability to reason. But when she really thought about it, it wasn't the sex or his incredible body, his charm or his sense of humor. Brad was just so...solid. There might have been a time when she found that type of man boring. But her tastes in men had seriously shifted over the past few weeks.

An image of Brad, lying beside her, naked and aroused, flashed in her mind, and Dani felt her knees weaken again and her heart skip a beat. She'd never thrown inhibition aside as she'd done last night, allowing her mind and body to be overwhelmed by desire. The thought of what they'd done together was a bit disconcerting considering her normally controlled behavior in the bedroom.

As Dani ran her hands over her soap-slicked body, she recalled the effect that his caress had had on her. She craved his touch, so much that she'd been willing to forget who she was, surrendering to the sensations of his hands on her skin, of his mouth on her breast, of his desire deep inside of her.

Still, Brad was just a man, and men had always occupied a singular place in her life. They were great companions and interesting dates and essential lovers, but beyond that, they were temporary pleasures at best. Not one of the men from her past had ever wanted to be more...until Brad.

Dani turned up the hot water and sighed as the shower filled with steam. "As if I don't have enough drama in my life already."

The custody suit, her job situation...and now Brad's marriage proposal. She might have understood a proposal in the aftermath of lovemaking, as a reaction to their shared passion, but his proposal had nothing to do with desire—or love. It had to do with something much more simple—Evie's children.

Taken alone, the decision to marry him should have been easy. She'd vowed to do everything she could to keep the children, and there was no doubt that a husband would give her an advantage. A single working mother would have a hard road ahead, but add a partner with a job to the mix, and how could the judge find fault with her?

So why couldn't she bring herself to say yes? Was it

because she wanted a marriage between them to mean more? Dani moaned softly and covered her face with her hands. Marriage to Brad Cullen may have been an option if she truly loved him. And maybe she already did love him and didn't even know. But she'd had a serious shortage of that emotion in her lifetime and probably wouldn't recognize it if it bit her on the nose.

With a sharp yank on the shower tap, Dani turned off the water. This was crazy! She'd only known him for a few short weeks. People didn't fall in love that fast.

A loud knock sounded on the bathroom door. "Are you almost done in there?"

Dani sighed. She thought she'd be safe from Jack's morning routine if she started her shower at six-thirty. "I'll be out in a minute. While you're waiting, get some money from my purse for your lunch ticket. It's on the bed. I don't want you eating potato chips for lunch again."

She stepped out of the shower, then quickly dried herself with a thick towel before slipping into her robe. The mirror was covered with steam and she wiped it off with her fist, then examined her face shrewdly. She didn't look any different this morning. Women in love were supposed to be radiant, glowing. She just looked...tired. "I must not be in love."

When she opened the bathroom door, she expected Jack to be waiting impatiently on the other side. Instead, she found him sitting on the edge of her bed, her purse at his feet, a sheaf of papers clutched in his hand. He glanced up at her as she entered, and she saw fear in his expression.

"What are these?" he demanded.

He held the papers out to her and her heart immediately fell. She'd put a copy of the custody papers in her purse after her last visit with the lawyer, then forgotten they were there.

"The Wilsons are trying to take us away, aren't they."

Dani nodded. She'd wanted to keep it from the children as long as she could. Maybe that had been the wrong decision. Maybe she should have told them right away. She swallowed hard and forced a weak smile. "They are. I got the papers a few days ago."

"Why didn't you tell us? You should have told us. This is our life."

"I was going to tell you. But I didn't want you to worry. I'm doing everything I can to keep you with me, Jack. You have to believe that."

Tears swam in his eyes as he stared at her with an accusing glare. "What about us? Why don't we get to choose?"

She sat down beside him, then took his hand in hers. "Everything is going to be all right. I'm going to talk to the lawyer again today. She says things look good."

"What if it's not all right?" Jack demanded, snatching his hand away.

"There's no use thinking about that now. We have to keep a positive attitude. If we show that we're worried, it's only going to frighten Becca and Noah. And for now, we need to keep this between the two of us."

"I don't want to live with the Wilsons," he said.

"I don't either," Becca chimed in. Jack and Dani looked up to find Becca standing in the doorway.

"Sweetie, we don't need to think about that now," Dani said, hurrying over to the door to give her a hug. "You're going to stay right here with me."

"What do you even care?" Jack demanded. "You didn't want us in the first place."

"Don't say that!" Becca shouted.

"That's not true," Dani said.

"It is. I heard you talking to Brad. You told him you didn't want to be a mother. You told him it was too hard."

Dani thought back to all the conversations that Jack might have overheard. She probably had said something of the sort, but then her insecurities surfaced on a fairly regular basis. "I was upset," she explained. "I was probably tired and frustrated and things were going badly at my job. I was afraid I wouldn't be able to be a good mother to you. I didn't have a mother, Jack. At least I don't remember her very well. I'm just bumbling along here and I was worried that I was doing more harm than good."

Jack scrambled to his feet, throwing the papers on the floor. "Well, we don't care if you don't want us. I can take care of Becca and Noah. My mom left us money. We don't need you and we don't need the Wilsons." With that, the boy stormed out of the bedroom.

"I need you," Becca whispered, clinging to her waist.

Dani reached down and softly stroked her hair. "And I need you, sweetie. And Jack and Noah." They walked together to the children's room and found Noah out of his crib and playing with a small plastic dump truck. Dani bent down and picked him up, then gave him a kiss on the cheek. "Juice?" she asked.

Noah nodded and they all headed to the kitchen. Dani had the routine down by now. Get Noah his apple juice first thing, or he started whining impatiently. Line up the boxes of cereal on the counter so Becca could choose what she wanted. Pull out two toaster waffles for Jack and wait for him to put them in the toaster. Then put a handful of cereal in a bowl for Noah. Once she completed those steps, breakfast usually moved along at a nice pace.

Dani handed Noah his juice, then rubbed her hand on his head until he gave her a smile. "Becca, go get Jack. Tell him he has to eat breakfast before he starts on his hair or he'll run out of time.''

Becca slid off her chair and ran out of the kitchen. She returned a few seconds later. ''Jack's not here,'' she said, sliding back into her chair.

''What do you mean?''

''He's gone.''

Dani sighed. ''I'll find him. You pour a cup of milk for Noah and make sure you screw on the top nice and tight.''

She looked in the children's room, then in the bathroom and her bedroom. By the time she got back to the living room, she realized that Becca was right. Jack had left. His shoes and jacket were gone, along with his backpack.

Dani opened the front door and looked up and down the hall. He couldn't have been gone for long. And where would he go? He didn't know the city well and had never ridden the buses, and his school was nearly a mile away. She glanced over at the front door of Tom's apartment. He'd probably knocked on Brad's door.

Crossing the hall, she did the same. ''Brad?'' She knocked again.

The door swung open, and Brad, still sleepy, stood on the other side, dressed only in his boxer shorts. He frowned. ''What's wrong?''

''Is Jack here?''

''No. Is he supposed to be?''

''He's gone.''

''What do you mean, gone?''

''We had an argument and he left. I have to go find him. Can you watch Becca and Noah?''

''No,'' he said. ''I'll go find him. You go back inside with the kids.''

''He could have gone anywhere. He doesn't know this city. And who knows what kind of people are out there, waiting to take advantage of a boy like him. Maybe we should call the police.''

Brad reached out and placed his palm on her cheek, then gave her a quick kiss. ''Don't worry. I'll find him. I think I might know where he went. Now, go back to Becca and Noah.''

Dani stood in the hall until Brad finished dressing, then held the elevator for him. When she went back into the apartment, Becca was waiting for her, a worried look on her face. Dani smiled. ''It's all right. Brad is going to get him.''

After retrieving Noah from the kitchen, Dani sat down on the sofa and Becca sat next to her. The little girl reached out and grabbed Dani's hand, squeezing it hard. They sat there for a long time, nearly an hour, watching the door, watching Noah play with his dumptruck. The time to leave for school passed, and Dani knew she'd be late for her appointment with the lawyer. But she couldn't think about that right now. Maybe she should have found a family counselor, someone to help Jack deal with his anger. But then what effect might *that* have had on the custody suit?

If anything happened to Jack, she didn't deserve to be his mother. Horrible thoughts raced through her mind and she pinched her eyes shut and tried to think positively. But Seattle was a big city, a place where an angry young boy could get lost pretty fast.

When the door finally opened and Jack walked back inside, Dani was close to tears. She jumped up from the sofa and tried to go to him, but he brushed past her and strode to his room, slamming the door behind him. She looked at Brad and he smiled. ''He'll get over it,'' he said.

''Where was he?''

''Over in Kinnear Park. Louie saw him head in that direction. There are a few kids that hang out there with their skateboards.''

''Should I go talk to him?''

''Oh, we had a nice little talk. He won't be doing that again.'' He rubbed his eyes. ''I've got to catch a shower, then I'll take Becca and Noah to day care. You may want to take Jack to school. It will give you two a chance to talk.''

Dani followed him across the hall. ''Thanks.'' Her lower lip trembled and she fought back tears. Why was it that she felt compelled to cry every time Brad came to her rescue? This time she refused to give in to her emotions. ''I—I appreciate what you did.''

''He's all right. He didn't go far and I'm sure he would have come back before too long.''

''What am I doing?'' Dani asked, leaning back against the wall.

''It wasn't your fault he ran away,'' Brad said.

''It was. He found out about the custody suit and he was angry that I hadn't told him. He's smart enough to know that this might turn out badly.''

Brad pulled her into his arms and hugged her tightly. ''You did what you thought was right.''

''What about Becca? She'll think that the Wilsons are going to take her away and I don't know how to soothe those worries. I know exactly how they feel. I always knew when they were about to move me.''

''They?''

''The social workers. My foster parents. They'd avoid eye contact and they'd try hard to be nice, but I could tell it was only a matter of days.'' She drew a shaky breath. ''I don't ever want Evie's kids to feel that kind of fear and apprehension and rejection. A child shouldn't have to deal with that.''

"You do the best you can, Dani. That's all you can do."

She brushed an errant tear off her cheek and swallowed a sob. "I'm going to lose them. All this time, I've been thinking that maybe it would be best if I found real parents for them. And now that I'm faced with this custody suit, I can't stand the thought of them living anywhere but here. I know I can be a good mother to them."

"You are a good mother," Brad said.

"A single mother. A single mother who isn't a blood relative. A single working mother who makes a lot of mistakes who isn't a blood relative."

Brad stepped back and held tight to her shoulders. He hooked his finger under her chin and forced her gaze up to his. "Dani, this isn't going to help you or the children."

"I know," she murmured, resting her head against his shoulder. She closed her eyes. If only she could just stand here forever in his arms. Somehow, she knew if she could, then everything would be all right.

MUSIC PLAYED SOFTLY, an old Tony Bennett tune from one of Tom Hopson's compact discs. Brad lay stretched out on Dani's sofa, her body curled against his, her head resting on his shoulder. Since the children had gone to bed, they'd settled in. But unlike their other evenings together, silence took the place of conversation, each of them occupied with thoughts of their own.

Since they'd made love last night, Brad had sensed that something had changed between them. The passion they'd shared had been incredibly intense, like nothing he'd experienced before. He'd been certain it would change things between them, that Dani would realize how she felt about him. But the intimacy only seemed to push them apart, as if her feelings had frightened her rather than empowered her.

He closed his eyes and turned his face into her hair. Dani's scars ran deep and there were times when he almost forgot her past, the childhood that must have hardened her emotions. He'd fallen in love with a beautiful, sophisticated, confident woman. But there was a little girl beneath, a girl still nursing her wounds.

Maybe making love to her had been a mistake. Maybe he should have waited. But Dani wanted it as much as he did—he'd seen it in her eyes and in the way she touched him. And when their passion reached a peak, he knew the past had been stripped away and they were simply two people who needed each other, emotionally and physically.

"Are you asleep?" he murmured, his lips pressed to her hair.

She smoothed her hand over his chest. "No. I was just thinking."

"About what?"

"About what you said last night."

"I said a lot of things last night."

"About getting married." Dani paused, then shrugged. "When I talked to Elizabeth today, I mentioned it. Not anything specific, but I asked her how much difference it would make if the children would be going to a home with two parents. She said it all depends upon the judge. Some are more supportive of single-parent households, some have very strong feelings the other way."

His breath froze, and for a moment, he allowed himself to hope. He twisted and pushed up on an elbow so he could look into her eyes. "Are you considering my proposal?"

"I don't know. I guess I'd like to know why you made the offer."

"The truth, or the answer I think you want to hear?"

"How about the answer I want to hear first," Dani said.

"I want to help you and the children. I know what a good

mother you are to them and I don't want to see you lose them. They've been through enough already and they belong with you."

She nodded. "That's a good answer. What's the other answer?"

"I'm falling in love with you," Brad admitted, relieved to finally say what he'd been feeling for days.

She stared at him for a long moment, unblinking. "Oh."

It wasn't the response he was hoping for. He'd wanted her to return the words, to give him some clue as to her own feelings. "I know I shouldn't have said that."

"No," Dani protested. "If that's the way you feel, then you shouldn't have to keep it a secret."

"But that's not the way you feel?" Brad asked.

She sighed softly and laid her head back down against his chest. "I don't know how I feel." She distractedly rubbed his chest, her fingers slipping in and out of the opened buttons of his flannel shirt. "I've never been one to indulge in self-reflection. At least not until Evie died. Now I have enough feelings to keep a therapist in business for the next ten years."

"There's nothing wrong with that."

"But I don't know which ones are real and which are imagined." She paused. "How do you know you're falling in love with me? What does it feel like?"

Brad had never really put that particular emotion into words. He thought he'd loved Jo, but those feelings had grown so slowly and over such a long time. Maybe he'd mistaken familiarity with love. That hadn't happened with Dani. He knew he loved her as sure as he knew the sun would rise in the east every morning.

"It's like this dream I had when I was kid," Brad began. "I'm out riding, only I'm not on my horse. I'm on this huge beast that I'm barely able to control. And then something spooks him and we take off. And no matter how hard I haul back on the reins, this horse won't stop. We're flying along and I'm hanging on, knowing that I might fall off at any minute. And every time he slows down, I think maybe I should jump off and take my chances. But I don't. Because the ride is so damn exciting."

Dani cleared her throat. "So I'm the horse?"

He laughed and hugged her. "No. This wasn't a metaphor. I have the same dream about elevators and roller coasters."

"I have that dream about elevators! But I want to get off."

"Well, that's how I feel right now."

"Like you want to get off?"

"No. I feel like I'm on the ride, and it's exciting and exhilarating and I'm scared as hell that I'm going to get hurt, but I can't seem to stop myself. I guess that's what love is. Or the best I can explain it."

"I'll consider your proposal," Dani said.

"Good." Brad hugged her tight, then closed his eyes.

He wasn't sure how long they lay on the sofa listening to the CD. Brad drifted off until he felt her move beside him. A soft cry sounded from the guest room and Dani sat up. "Noah," she murmured, brushing her hair out of her eyes. "He's been having a lot of nightmares lately."

"I'll get him."

"No, I will," she said, her voice tinged with sleep. He waited for her to move, but instead she closed her eyes and curled back up against him. "He'll stop crying in just a minute. Just wait."

Brad did, and in that short time, Dani fell back asleep and Noah kept whining. If she'd gotten twice the sleep that he had last night, she was probably still exhausted. He carefully crawled over top of her and padded into the bedroom.

Noah was standing up in his crib, his face damp from tears. By the light from the hall, Brad could see Jack and Becca still sound asleep, Becca on the sofa bed and Jack in the sleeping bag Brad had bought him. He reached out and scooped Noah into his arms and the little boy clung to him, his sniffles shaking his whole body.

"What's wrong, buddy? You have a bad dream?"

Noah nodded, nestling his face in the curve of Brad's neck, his hair smelling like baby shampoo.

"Come on. Let's go get something to eat. When I can't sleep, graham crackers and milk always help."

He carried Noah into the kitchen and turned on the light, then grabbed the box of crackers from the cupboard. He sat Noah down on the edge of the counter, then reached into the fridge and got the milk. One of Noah's sippy cups was sitting in the dish rack and Brad filled it, then handed it to the little boy, along with a graham cracker.

With a smile, Brad smoothed his hand over Noah's pale blond hair, brushing the damp strands out of his eyes. "You need a haircut," he said. "Maybe you and I should go get one together. I'm getting a little shaggy, too."

Noah held up the graham cracker and Brad took a bite out of it, then made a goofy face. "Yum cah-cah," Noah said.

"Yummy cracker," Brad repeated.

Strange how these children had wormed their way into his heart. And how he'd slipped into the role of father without even thinking. When he thought about a future with Dani, as he had so many times over the past few days, the pictures in his mind always included the three Gregory children. He chuckled softly. Except, of course, the bedroom fantasies. They were strictly for the two of them.

"Feeling better now?"

Noah nodded. "Moh cah-cah."

"More crackers?" Brad handed him another. He'd never thought much about being a father. He'd assumed it would take a long time to settle into the job. The Gregory kids weren't his flesh and blood. He hadn't known them for long. Yet he cared deeply about their well-being.

"You'd like Montana," he told Noah. "There's lots of space to run. And the sky is so blue it hurts your eyes. And in the summer, there's this field of wildflowers near the west pasture that's so pretty you can't take your eyes off it. And I know you'd be good on a horse. I can tell. You like a little danger, don't you?"

Noah shook his head. Brad didn't think he understood the question, but it seemed like they were having a conversation, so he kept talking.

"I could teach you to ride. We'd start out on a pony until you got a little older. And then we'd find you a nice gentle mare, like Lily or Rosie." Brad grabbed another cracker and took a bite. "But if I were your daddy, I'd do a few things differently. I'd let you decide what you wanted to do with your life. I wouldn't try to push my choices on you."

"Daddy," Noah said.

Brad reached out and picked the little boy up, then gave him a fierce hug. "What you've been through. And I have the nerve to complain about my father. You'll never know yours, or your mother. You'll grow up wondering what it is about you that came from them."

Suddenly all his arguments with his father seemed so petty and childish. He loved the ranch and he loved his work with the horses. His father had spent a lifetime building a legacy for Brad and he'd just thrown it back in his face.

Brad wandered over to the breakfast nook and sat down, setting Noah on the table in front of him. He imagined a time years ago, when his father had looked at his new infant son. Walt Cullen must have had so many hopes and dreams for his firstborn. "It was all so easy back then," Brad said, staring at Noah. "I didn't talk back."

Split Rock was in his blood and in his soul—the majestic landscape, the wide skies and the clean air. If he left for good, a part of who he was would be gone forever. "I have to go back," he murmured. There were people in Montana who loved him. He wouldn't walk away from them or the place where he belonged—his legacy.

But Dani was still considering his proposal. If she accepted, would she be willing to move to Montana? A life there would be so unfamiliar to her, as strange as a life on the moon. Would she even consider marriage to him if she knew all his terms?

Brad sighed. First, he had to convince her that she loved him. If she accepted his proposal, then he had until the custody suit was settled to make her realize her true feelings. After that, the choice would be up to her—love him and live in Montana, or dissolve their business arrangement and go on with her life as if he had never stepped into it.

It would have to be that way. He couldn't stay in Seattle. Any attempt to build a place for himself here would pale in comparison with what he had at Split Rock. And loving a woman who didn't love him wasn't an option. He'd done that with Jo, and the end result had been public humiliation. If Dani didn't return the feelings, he'd walk.

"I guess that's a plan, then," Brad said, pressing his forehead to Noah's. "Either way, I'm going back to Montana."

"What are you two doing in here?" Dani stood at the kitchen door, her shoulder braced against the jamb.

"Mama!" Noah cried.

Dani stared at the little boy, stunned speechless. She opened her mouth, then covered it with her fingertips. Tears glistened in her eyes as Brad slowly stood and picked up Noah. He reached out and slipped his fingers through her hair, then kissed the top of Dani's head.

"Here, Mama," he said, putting Noah into her arms. "Why don't you put him back to bed?"

Dani nodded and walked back into the living room, chatting quietly to the little boy and hugging him tight. When she returned a few minutes later, she smiled, then stepped into Brad's embrace. "I'd better get to bed. It's been a pretty busy day."

"I'll see you in the morning," Brad said, ignoring the ache in his heart. He'd made his decision, but would he really be able to walk away? Somehow, he knew it wouldn't come easy.

She walked him to the door, her hand laced in his. As he stepped out into the hall, she pushed up on her toes and gave him a quick kiss, as if lingering might lead to something more passionate. "Thanks," she said.

"For what?"

"For whatever you said to Noah." She laughed softly. "He called me 'Mama.'"

"Sleep tight," Brad said, stepping through the door.

"You, too." Dani closed the door and Brad crossed the hall. But he didn't open the apartment door. Instead, he stood outside, thinking about how his life had changed in such a short time. When he'd come to Seattle, he'd been acting like a spoiled child, running away from all his problems, punishing his father for some imagined slight. But here, he'd been able to glimpse the man he truly was—a man who was ready to take on a wife and children, lifelong responsibility.

Unfortunately, he only wanted one woman as his wife. And without Dani, he'd never feel complete.

HANNAH RICHARDS rubbed her eyes, squinting at her computer. She'd been working on the same account for nearly an hour, trying to balance out teaching supplies before moving on to equipment depreciation. But somewhere in the string of numbers she'd lost $7.69.

She glanced at her watch. It was nearly nine and the day care had been quiet since six. After-hours was the best time to get work done. Besides, there were times when she needed something—anything—to occupy her thoughts. More and more of late, her mind shifted to the past, to the child she'd given up. He'd be nearly nine years old by now and she'd taken to looking for children his age on the street.

She'd even wandered by a schoolyard not too long ago and listened to the chatter, wondering what her son's voice sounded like, what favorite phrases he used. Hannah knew that her little obsession wasn't healthy, but she couldn't seem to stop herself.

With a sigh, she turned back to her work, but a strange sound drew her attention away again. Holding her breath, she listened. It sounded like someone was trying to get in the front door. Alex and Katherine had a key, so if either one of them were at the door, they'd surely announce their presence.

Hannah heard the door swing open and then whispered voices. With a soft cry, she reached for her desk lamp and flipped it off, then grabbed the phone and dialed 9-1-1. Someone had broken in to the day care! But just as the police dispatcher came on the line, Hannah recognized one of the voices and she quickly hung up.

Silently, she tiptoed to the door of her office and looked out into the hall. The light from the street filtered through the windows in the door, illuminating two figures. "Amy?"

Her voice split the silence, and for a moment, she thought they were going to run. But then the smaller figure took a step toward her. "Hannah?"

Hannah reached over and flipped on the hall light. Amy Tidwell stood in the hall with Will Tucker, her boyfriend. A tall, broad-shouldered young man, he wore a waterproof jacket and wellies, the kind of outfit that Hannah had seen on commercial fishermen. His blond hair was rumpled and damp from the rain that had been falling all evening.

"What are you doing here? How did you get in?"

Amy, her eyes red and puffy, held up her library card. "The front door lock doesn't always catch," she said, her voice trembling, "and if you jiggle the handle just right and slide the card in, it usually opens."

"Usually?" Hannah asked. "You've done this before?"

"Only when we're sure the place is empty," Amy explained. "Sometimes we come here to be alone. Not alone alone," she quickly added. "We just talk." Amy's gaze dropped to her shoes, her expression contrite, and her eyes filling with fresh tears. "You've met Will, haven't you, Hannah?"

Before Hannah could reply, Will leaned forward and offered her his hand. "Hi," he said as she took it. "It's nice to see you again."

Hannah forced a smile, then turned back to Amy. "Are you all right?"

Amy nodded, then quickly changed her mind and shook her head. "No."

"What happened?"

"She told her father," Will said.

"Oh, sweetie." Hannah opened her arms, and with a sob, Amy stepped into her embrace. "It's all right. You didn't expect him to jump for joy, did you? Tell me what happened."

"He—he was so angry. I've never seen him so mad. He

called me names and he kept telling me how ashamed he was, and then he started in on Will. And when I tried to explain to him what I wanted to do, he wouldn't listen. He told me that I couldn't go back to school and I wasn't allowed to see any of my friends and I'd have to quit my job here at the day care.'' Another ragged sob tore from her throat. ''And he said if I ever saw Will again that he'd call the police and have him arrested.''

''Arrested?'' Hannah said with a gasp.

Will nodded. ''I'm a few months older than Amy. He probably thinks he can get me for statutory rape. But we were both seventeen when Amy got pregnant, so I don't think he'll have much of a case.''

Hannah was amazed by the young man's composure. While his girlfriend was falling apart in Hannah's arms, he seemed to be in perfect control. ''I wouldn't think so. Besides, he's probably just using the police as a threat.''

Amy shook her head. ''No, he would do it. He hates Will so much, and now he has even more reason to want him out of my life.''

''Have you had anything to eat?'' Hannah asked, brushing a strand of hair off Amy's damp cheek. ''Why don't we go into the kitchen and get a soda and a snack. We can talk in there.''

When they were gathered around a low table in the dining area, Hannah set a can of soda and a granola bar in front of each of them. ''So what are you going to do?''

''I can't go home and we can't go to Will's house,'' Amy said. ''His mother doesn't know yet and I don't think she'd want me there anyway. We kind of figured we'd stay here tonight.''

Hannah shook her head. ''You can't sleep here.''

''Then we'll get a room,'' Will said. ''I've got a little bit of cash.''

"And what will you do after that?"

"I'll do what I have to," he said with a defensive edge in his voice. "I'll take care of Amy and our baby. I love her and she loves me."

"Couldn't we please sleep here?" Amy asked. "We wouldn't mess anything up. And we'd get out in the morning before Katherine or Alex showed up."

Will slipped his arm around Amy's shoulders and pressed a kiss to her forehead. "Don't worry. We'll find a place."

Hannah stared at them for a long minute. There wasn't much standing between them and the streets right now. And Seattle had enough street kids already. She didn't want to see Amy forced to panhandle for her next meal. "You don't have to worry about a place to stay. If worse comes to worse, Amy, you can stay with me."

"Really?" she asked, her face brightening with hope.

"As a last resort. And only if your father kicks you out, which I don't think he will. First, you need to try to talk to him again."

"I can't," Amy said.

"He won't listen," Will added. "He'd lock her in her bedroom before he'd let her see me again."

"Well, I don't think he's going to have much choice in the matter. You and Amy are eighteen. You're adults, and legally, you can make your own decisions. Either he's going to have to go along with what you want, or he's going to risk losing Amy and his grandchild. If he's too stubborn to see that, then maybe you should strike out on your own."

"That's what I think!" Amy cried. "But Will doesn't think we'll have enough money."

"I want to go to college," he said, "and so does Amy. And my job down at the fishing docks would barely cover my tuition and books, much less rent." He sighed deeply. "But I could take a job on one of the boats—I'd make enough to support Amy and the baby. She could go to college part-time and get her teaching degree, and when she's done, I could start.''

"No," Amy said. "I'll work and you'll go to college."

"Who's going to hire you when you're pregnant? You don't make enough here to send me through school and pay rent," Will said. "I have to be the one to work. Besides, I can make a lot of money working the boats, and we'll be able to save more."

"Maybe my dad was right," Amy said. "Maybe I should give the baby up for adoption."

"No!" Will's voice was hard and desperate. "No. We're not going to do that."

"What about your parents?" Hannah asked Will. "Can they help?"

"There's just my mom. And she jumps from job to job. I work now to help support her."

In Hannah's eyes, they didn't have many choices. Though she loathed the suggestion of adoption, she knew that it would have to be one of the options Will and Amy considered. "You two have a lot to think about. But you don't have to make any decisions tonight. Amy, I think you should go home and talk to your dad again."

Amy groaned, but Will took her hand and pressed it to her lips. "I'll come with you. We'll talk to him together. Or at least we'll try."

"Give him a week," Hannah said. "If things aren't better, you can come and stay with me." She stood up. "Come on, I'll drive you both home."

"That's all right," Will said. "We can take the bus."

Hannah was about to insist, but realized that Amy and Will needed to take care of themselves. The more she involved herself in their life, the more they might come to depend on her for help. She walked with them to the front door and let them out, making a mental note to have the lock fixed tomorrow. If Amy and Will could get in with a library card, any burglar with half a brain could get in as well.

Hannah walked back to her office and sat down at her desk, the light from the screen glowing green in the dark. She grabbed her mouse and closed the accounting program, then signed on to the Internet. When the search engine appeared on her screen, she typed in the words ''find adopted son'' and hit the search button. But when the results came up, she was stunned by the number of hits. Page after page of Web sites devoted to the subject of adoption—giving up a child for adoption, adopting a child into a family, finding birth parents, telling an adoptive child. The chance that her son was out there looking for her was next to nothing. He wasn't even nine years old!

Discouraged, Hannah turned the computer off. There had to be some way of putting her past behind her once and for all. She just needed to find it.

CHAPTER TEN

"COME ON, BECCA, eat your cereal. Brad will be here to take you and Noah to day care in a few minutes. You're going to be late." Dani turned just in time to see Noah pull the top off his cup. Orange juice went flying through the air, hitting her in the eye and staining the front of Becca's dress.

"No!" the little girl cried. She grabbed a handful of dry cereal and threw it at Noah. But the retaliation didn't have the desired effect. Noah just grinned and giggled, throwing the empty cup in the direction of his sister.

With a low growl, Dani grabbed Becca's bowl. "Enough! Go find something else to wear."

"What about my breakfast?"

"You can have a breakfast bar in the car." Dani grabbed a dish towel and started to wipe the juice from the walls and the table. When the phone rang, she called out for Becca to find it. It continued to ring and she shouted for Jack, but no one seemed to be listening. She grabbed Noah from his spot on top of the phone books and carried him to the living room. By the time she got there, Jack had the cordless phone in his hand. "It's your boss," he said.

Dani grabbed the phone, frowning as Jack slipped into the bathroom and closed the door. "I don't have a boss anymore. Hello?"

"Dani. Sam Bennett."

She wiped the sticky orange juice off Noah's face then

set him down. Even now, after her abrupt resignation, Sam's voice still had the power to command her immediate attention. "Hello, Sam."

"We need to talk. I'm downstairs in my car. Come down and I'll take you to breakfast."

"I have to get the children ready for school, Sam. I can't go to breakfast with you."

"Then buzz me up. I have to talk to you."

Dani sighed and tossed the dish towel over her shoulder. "Can't this wait?"

"No," he said.

With a silent curse, she walked to the front door, then waited for him to ring the security buzzer. This was the last thing she needed. They were already running late. She pushed the button that unlocked the front door when he rang, then stepped out into the hallway. When Sam appeared out of the elevator, she closed the apartment door behind her. "Couldn't this have waited? I have to drive Jack to school, and if we don't leave in the next fifteen minutes, we'll be late."

"Things are falling apart with Mo' Joe," Sam said, pacing back and forth in front of her. "I turned over the account to Kel Magnusson and he's made a royal mess out of it. You have to come back to work."

Dani stared at him. Though she knew things might fall apart with her accounts, she never expected Sam Bennett to ignore his considerable ego and beg her to return. He'd always acted as if he was the only one that mattered to the agency—everyone else was expendable.

Dani's mind raced, automatically switching to negotiating mode, the old business instincts coming right back to her. There was no denying that her job search wasn't going well. Though she'd had a few serious discussions, no one was willing to give her what she needed as far as salary and schedule. Now she held the power over Sam. "Why would I want to come back?"

"You haven't officially left," he said. "You never picked up your belongings. We can just pretend we never had that phone conversation. We'll call these last few days a vacation. You needed a vacation, right?"

A slow realization dawned. "Have you told anyone that I quit? Have you told the people at Mo' Joe?"

"No. I didn't think it was necessary. I thought once you cooled down, you'd regret your decision and want your job back. But I've given you enough time to cool down. I need you back at work. Today." He paused and drew a deep breath. "I'm ready to relax a bit on your schedule. There's no reason a mother can't be on the executive track at Bennett Marks. Besides, you're not really a mother. These kids aren't really yours."

A surge of anger shot through her. Nothing had changed. Sam Bennett was still the self-centered, avaricious ass he'd always been. "I think you better get out of here before I start kicking you," Dani said, sending him a tight smile and shoving him toward the elevator.

"We can make this work! Nine to four, five days a week. We'll hire you another assistant and I'll assign another junior account executive to Mo' Joe. No weekend travel. You can work from home on Friday afternoons. The agency will absorb whatever it costs to make this work."

"No," Dani said. "I know you, Sam. You'll act like you're fine with this for a week or two, and then everything will revert back to the way it was."

A door opened behind Dani, and a moment later, she heard Brad's voice. "Is everything all right out here?" he asked.

Dani glanced over her shoulder. "It's just fine."

"Hey, buddy, just mind your own business!" Sam shouted.

An instant later, Brad was at her side, his expression hard and unyielding. "If the lady needs my help, then I'm here to offer it. Whether you like it or not…buddy."

Dani pressed her palm against Brad's naked chest. "It's all right. I'll be fine. You can go back inside."

"Yeah," Sam said, "you can go back inside."

Brad sent Sam a look filled with unspoken warning, then returned to Tom's apartment and softly closed the door.

"What a hick," Sam muttered.

"Are you through? Because if you are, I'd like to get a cup of coffee and get on with my day."

Sam adjusted his silk tie. "Mo' Joe is going to walk if you're not on the account."

"Well, then you better get back to the office and figure out how *you're* going to keep that from happening. I've got to get *my* children ready for school." Dani walked back inside, then firmly shut the door behind her. A tiny smile touched her lips. At least she knew where to go for a job if she really got desperate. She made a mental note to call her lawyer and discuss this new development. And then she'd call the ad manager at Mo' Joe and find out how close they were to jumping ship. Maybe they could use her services.

A loud knock sounded on the door and Dani jumped. With a soft curse, she turned around and yanked the door open. "I told you I wasn't—" She stopped short when she saw Brad. He'd thrown on a flannel shirt, unbuttoned to the middle of his chest, the cuffs rolled at his wrists.

"Are you all right?" he asked, leaning forward and stealing a kiss.

Dani quickly turned away and walked into the apartment, hardly able to contain her delight. "My hero," she said with a wry smile. Dani sat down on the sofa and tugged her robe more tightly around her body, as if it might provide some protection from the thoughts that were racing through her mind, thoughts of how easy it would be to untie that robe and let it drop to the floor, to wrap her arms around him and kiss him silly. The children would be off to school before long, and then they'd have all day to turn her little fantasy into reality.

Brad sat down next to her and leaned forward, bracing his elbows on his knees. "Was that your old boss in the hall?"

Dani nodded. "He came to offer me my job back."

Brad blinked in surprise. "Did you take it?"

She shook her head. "Not yet. But if worse comes to worse, there's always that option. At least until after the custody suit. Sam said he's willing to be more flexible at work. I told him 'no,' but I'll let him stew a while." She grinned. "I guess things are looking up. And I'm going to call Mo' Joe this morning. If they're really serious about changing agencies, maybe we could talk. I mean, I could probably start my own agency. I'd make my own hours. I signed a non-compete with Bennett Marks. But there has to be a way to counter that. I'll have to call Elizabeth. Maybe she'd be able to refer me to a lawyer who would know." Dani giggled. "All of sudden, I feel like things are looking brighter."

"Sure," Brad said. "Right. That would probably work."

Dani reached out and took his hand. "I still haven't decided on the offer you made. But I'm not sure I'll be able to before the hearing. I don't want to get married out of desperation. That's not fair to either one of us. Or to the children. Maybe I'll just have to take my chances in court."

"Are you willing to take that risk?" he asked.

"I don't know," Dani said. "Maybe. Do you have to have an answer right now? We have time."

"Hey, it was a crazy idea anyway," Brad said, pushing up from the sofa. "I'm not ready to get married either. Not after what happened to me the last time I decided to walk down the aisle." He turned and strode back to the door, yanking it open. "I'm going to go catch a quick shower. Have Noah and Becca ready in ten minutes or we'll be late." He walked into the hall, slamming the door behind him.

Dani stared after him, stunned by the quick shift in his mood. What was that supposed to mean? Was he withdrawing his offer of marriage? She frowned. For a man who was so certain of his feelings for her, he'd beat a pretty quick retreat. And he ought to be happy that her job concerns had been eased.

She sighed. After she got the children off to school, she'd pick up a couple lattes and croissants and make a peace offering of them. They could spend some time together discussing all their options. And if talk didn't work, then she'd just have to resort to something more…persuasive.

BRAD PULLED HIS PICKUP to a stop in front of the day care, then glanced in the rearview mirror. Becca was already unbuckling her seat belt. "Stay in the truck until I open your door, Bec."

"Hurry!" she cried, kicking at the back of his seat. "I have to talk to Rachel. She's bringing her Ballerina Barbie. And I brought my Princess Barbie."

"Hold on, hold on." Brad glanced over his shoulder at the traffic, then hopped out of the cab. He popped the front seat forward and helped Becca out, then carried her to the curb. She didn't even bother to say goodbye. Instead, she raced up the steps, shouted her morning greeting to Katherine Kinard, who stood out front, then disappeared inside the door.

Brad circled around the truck and unfastened Noah from his car seat, then carried him up to the front. "Morning," he said.

"Hi, Brad," Katherine greeted him. "Say, Alexandra is looking for you. She said she needed to talk to you as soon as you dropped the kids off. I think she's upstairs."

In truth, Brad really didn't want to spend time chatting with Alex. He wanted to get back to the apartment and talk to Dani. He hadn't meant to get angry with her, but she'd so easily forgotten his proposal once she had a job offer. He wanted to know where he stood, and if it meant forcing her into a decision, then maybe that would be for the best.

Maybe he needed to remind her of the passion they'd shared just a few nights ago. They'd been perfect together and he knew she'd felt it. But for Dani, desire and passion didn't seem to be enough. She approached love so carefully, fearful of being burned.

His mind flashed an image of her, dressed in her silk robe, arguing with her boss in the hallway, her hands hitched on her hips, her color high. She was like no other woman he'd known. All he had to do was look at her and his mind drifted into fantasies of bare skin, warm flesh, and sweet curves.

He wanted a repeat of the passion they'd shared in his bed. When they were together like that, he knew she couldn't deny her feelings. Only in the light of day did her doubts creep in. Brad drew a ragged breath, an image of her, naked and straddling his hips, causing his blood to warm with desire. It would have been so easy had she accepted his marriage proposal the moment he'd made it. Marriage would throw them into the same bedroom every night—or at least the same apartment. It would have given him time to make it all work.

He glanced in the office as he passed, but Alex wasn't there, so he climbed the stairs to Noah's room and took the little boy inside. Noah's teacher, Rona Opitz, smiled as he set the boy down. Noah toddled toward her and she gave him a cheerful greeting. "How are you today?"

"Bye, buddy," Brad called.

"Bye-bye," Noah said, waving clumsily.

"Do you know where Alex is?" he asked Rona.

"The last time I saw her she was in the nurse's office. Across the hall."

Brad wandered back out into the hall and caught Alex just as she was stepping out of the office with an older, white-haired woman. She caught sight of him, but she didn't smile. Instead, she made her excuses to the woman, then hurried over to him. "I've been waiting for you to get here," she said.

"That anxious for our morning coffee? You've got to cut down on the caffeine."

"No," she muttered. "Come with me. We need to talk."

She started down the stairs and Brad had no choice but to follow her, now worried by her grim expression. Alex headed right for her office, waited until he stepped inside, then shut the door. Surely she wasn't angry because he'd kept Dani out late the night of their date? Or maybe she suspected what really had gone on that night and was upset that he hadn't filled her in on his relationship with Dani.

"I wanted to thank you for watching the kids the other night. Jack and Becca told me they had a great time with you. And I'm sorry if it got a little late but—"

"That's not what I need to talk to you about. Although I'm glad you had a good time. By the way Dani looked when she came in, I assumed you had a very nice time. But I didn't pry."

Brad nodded. "Very...very nice. So what is it that has you so upset?"

"I got a call from your mom this morning." She paused. "It's your father. He was thrown from a horse and broke his hip. He's having surgery this afternoon. She asked if I would let you know. I told her I would."

Brad frowned, his breath freezing in his throat. "How serious is it?"

Alex sat down on the edge of her desk. "Your mom tried to make it sound like he was fine, but I think she's really scared. I guess it's going to be a difficult surgery. If it's successful, he's going to be laid up for a long time."

"And if it's not?"

"She didn't say. You need to call her, Brad. You can't keep this up, running away from your problems. Your family needs you."

"You're right. But I'm not going to call." Brad ran a hand down the side of his jaw. "I've got to go home. What time is the surgery?"

"First thing in the morning, tomorrow."

"I've got a twelve-hour drive, and that's if the weather doesn't go to hell through the mountains. They've already had snow up there. What hospital?"

"St. Peter's in Helena," she said. "I'm going to fly out tonight. Why don't you come with me?"

Brad shook his head. "No, I'm going to leave now. I'll go crazy waiting around to find a flight." He bent over and gave Alex a quick kiss on the cheek. "Call my mom and tell her I'm on my way. And I guess I'll see you back home."

She nodded. "He'll be all right, Brad. It's Walt. He's tough as an old boot."

He nodded, then gave her a wave. She sent him an encouraging smile in return. As he jogged down the front steps, he tried to calculate how long it would take him to pack. And once he packed, how long it would take him to say goodbye to Dani.

Hell, this was no time to leave her. They'd finally broken down that last wall between them, and the only way to keep it down was to spend more time with her. If he left, she'd just build it back up again, convincing herself that she didn't need anyone, especially not him. And she'd have to deal with the custody suit all by herself.

Maybe he ought to see his father through the surgery, then come back. But with his father off his feet, who would run the ranch? Brad unlocked the truck and hopped inside. His brother Clint had a job teaching high school in Great Falls and a family to care for. Mac also had kids and worked long hours at his construction job, building log homes for west coast types. Vicki had her career as an occupational therapist. J.T. was the only sibling who worked full-time at Split Rock, but the twenty-five-year-old wasn't ready to take over the day-to-day operation.

He pulled the truck out into traffic and headed toward the Sound. Early morning rush hour was heavy and he tapped his fingers impatiently as he steered toward Western Avenue. It took him twice as long to reach Dani's building as it had to take the kids to day care, and by the time he got there he was about ready to jump out of his skin.

He grabbed Noah's car seat out of the back seat of the truck and tucked it under his arm. The lobby was empty when he entered, and he took the stairs instead of the elevator. He fought the impulse to go to Dani right away. He set the car seat down outside her door, then decided to pack first before he said goodbye. He'd need the time to figure out what he was going to say. As he entered the apartment, he found Mr. Whiskers waiting for his breakfast.

Brad swore. He'd have to ask Dani to take care of the cat and to water the plants. And Tom wouldn't be coming home to a completely clean apartment. Brad didn't have time to vacuum or clean out the leftovers from the fridge. He thought about calling Tom, then decided to wait until after he got back to Montana.

As he stuffed his backpack, he didn't bother folding anything, choosing instead to throw his clothing in haphazardly. He'd bought a number of things in Seattle, so the overflow went into a garbage bag, along with his shaving kit and his hiking boots. As he was carrying his pack and the bag to the door, he heard a knock and pulled it open. Dani stood on the other side.

"I thought I heard you come in. I was hoping you might—" Her gaze dropped to the backpack and she frowned. "Are you going camping again?"

Brad shook his head. "I'm leaving. I have to go home. My dad is having surgery tomorrow."

"What's wrong? Is he sick?"

"He was thrown from a horse and broke his hip. My mother called Alex because she didn't know where to find me. I suppose I should have called them. But I have to be there. He's going to need someone to run the ranch."

"Of course," Dani said. "Are you leaving right now? I'll take you to the airport. Let me just get my keys and purse."

"I'm driving back," he said. "If I go straight through, I'll be there in eleven or twelve hours."

Dani nodded and forced a smile. "All right." She paused. "So I guess this is goodbye. I always knew this day would come. I was getting used to having you around."

"I'll be back," Brad assured her, reaching out to take

her hand. "As soon as everything is all right with my father and I've got the ranch running smoothly, I'll be back."

"No," Dani replied, gazing up into his eyes. "Don't come back. It will only make things more difficult."

"What are you talking about? Dani, I'm in love with you. I'm not just going to walk away from you and the kids. You love me. I know you do."

"How do you know?" she demanded. "I don't even know. I've never loved anyone in my life. I don't know how it's supposed to feel."

"Like this," he said, cupping her face in his hands and kissing her. "And like this," he said, pressing her palm to his heart. "I know we can make this work. We just need a little more time."

"And I know it won't," she countered, her chin tilting up defensively. "Even if I knew I loved you, somehow it would get ruined. Sooner or later you'd leave. Everyone does."

"Damn it, I'm not everyone," Brad said. "Maybe you've forgotten, but I proposed to you."

"You never would have proposed if it hadn't been for the custody suit."

"How do you know?"

"How do *you?*" she said. "Besides, we can't get married. Where would we live?"

"Montana. You should see Montana. It's big and open and there's a lot of places for kids to run. We could raise them there, Dani. We'd be happy there."

"I called Mo' Joe a few minutes ago," she said. "They want to talk to me about setting up my own agency. They think it might be a good idea."

The revelation was like a punch to the stomach. With a job in Seattle—hell, her own business—she'd never consider moving to Montana. "I feel like we're leaving things unfinished. We have so much more to say."

Dani shrugged. "I didn't think you'd be leaving so soon."

"I have to go."

"And I have to stay. This is a great opportunity. And they know about the children and they're all right with that. Their offices are close by. I could find a bigger place, maybe even a house. We could get a dog. And the kids will be able to stay near their friends."

"I don't want to live without you," Brad said.

Dani shook her head. "You don't belong here any more than I belong in Montana."

Brad stared at her for a long moment. She'd already made up her mind and nothing he was going to say would change it. He was doing what everyone else except Evie's children had done. He was abandoning her. "So that's it then?"

Dani nodded. "I'd better get going," she said, putting on a brittle smile. "The furniture store is delivering the new beds for the children and I have to clean out the rest of the things from my office." She held out her hand, as if she expected him to shake it, then drew it back. "It was nice to know you, Brad Cullen. Thank you for all your help with the children. I know they'll miss you."

She turned and walked across the hall, then closed her apartment door behind her. He stared after her, unable to believe that it had all ended so quickly. For the first time since he met her, Brad felt truly sorry for Dani. For the past that had made her so distrustful. But even more for the present, for the woman who couldn't believe that he loved her—and that deep in her heart, she loved him.

DANI PULLED THE CAR up to the curb in front of the middle school and turned off the ignition. School wasn't out for another ten minutes, but the area in front of the school was often crowded with cars filled with parents waiting to pick their kids up and drive them to various after-school activities.

She'd closed her eyes and leaned back into the seat. Her mind spun with the events of the day. She'd gone from unbelievable elation about the prospect of starting her own agency to the depths of disbelief when Brad told her he was leaving Seattle.

Since they'd met, she'd always known this time would come, and she was certain she'd be able to handle it. After all, she was an expert at watching people walk in and out of her life. But Brad was different. He'd found a way into her heart, and now that he was gone, the spot he'd left felt empty and cold.

Pressing her hand to her chest, she fought back a surge of emotion. She'd come so close, so very close to finding something special with him. Was it there and had she just missed it? Had she found love and then let it go? Or had she simply been caught up in the passion and the romance and the fantasy of having a complete family?

She drew a ragged breath. It wouldn't do to dwell on her time with Brad Cullen. She'd do as she always had done— focus on the present, push the past aside, harden her heart and tell herself that she was the only person she could depend upon. She had her career to sort out and the custody suit to prepare for. And she had three wonderful children to raise.

A sliver of fear shot through her. Would they disappear from her life the same way Brad had? If she lost the custody suit, she'd be left with nothing, no one in the world who would need her. "Stop it," she said. "You're not going to lose the children."

She reached out and grabbed the steering wheel, wrapping her fingers around it. It was time to move on, time to focus on the children. She'd have to deal with Jack's anger and distrust. Maybe she'd talk to him about joining a soccer league or a swim team. Or maybe there was some kind of skateboard club he'd be interested in. Or maybe music lessons. She'd always wanted to take guitar lessons when she was younger. There must be something that he was interested in.

Camping, Dani mused. Jack had been interested in camping. But now that Brad was gone, there was every chance that interest would fade. She stared out the front window of her car, her gaze unfocused. He'd been gone for nearly six hours, but to Dani, it felt like a lifetime. She wondered where he was, how far he'd driven and how long it would take her to catch up with him. With effort, she fought the temptation to sink into depression over his absence.

Brad was gone. She'd managed on her own for twenty-four years. A passionate affair with a wonderful man was not going to change that. She'd always been able to convince herself that she didn't need anyone in the world to get along. But since the children had arrived, that had all changed. She needed Jack and Becca and Noah. So why was it so hard for her to need Brad?

"You'll forget him," Dani reassured herself. "Over time, the memory of him will fade."

She might be able to forget his chili recipe or his poker playing abilities. Or the tattered denim shirt he loved to wear. Or even the way his hair curled at the nape of his neck. But she would never be able to forget his smile or his voice...or the way he made love to her that night in Tom's apartment.

A horn behind her beeped and she glanced in the rear-view mirror, then moved the car up a few feet. A few seconds later, Jack appeared on the sidewalk, accompanied by two other boys, also dressed in baggy pants and oversized shirts. He waved goodbye to them and got in the front seat of Dani's car.

"Hi," he said.

"Were those your friends?" Dani asked. "Do they need a ride home?"

"Nah, they walk." He threw his backpack on the floor, then began to fiddle with the radio. "How do you set the stations on this thing?"

"Maybe your friends would like to come with us this weekend when we go to the skateboard shop," she offered.

"I told Charlie and Nathan about camping. Maybe Brad will take us camping this weekend."

Dani drew a slow breath. "Brad is gone. He had to go back to Montana this morning."

"Why?"

"His father had an accident. He needed to be with him."

"When is he coming back?"

Dani cleared her throat and tried to keep her voice indifferent, refusing to give way to the tears that threatened. "I don't think he is, Jack. He was only visiting here. He never intended to stay."

"But I thought you and him would…"

"No," Dani said. "We were very good friends and we liked each other a lot. I know you're going to miss him, and I'm sure if you wanted to write to him or call him, he'd be happy to hear from you. He cared for you and Becca and Noah, and I know he would have liked to say goodbye." She paused. "You know, Brad left the tent and your sleeping bags. Maybe we could go camping on our own. I think I could probably find that spot in the Cascades again. And Brad taught you how to start a campfire. I bet we could do it on our own."

"It was more fun with Brad," he muttered, slouching down in his seat and crossing his arms over his chest.

"It was fun," she quietly agreed.

They passed the rest of the drive in silence. Jack waited in the car when she went into the day care to get Becca and Noah. When they settled into the back seat, Dani knew they sensed something was wrong. Becca's gaze darted back and forth between the two of them and Noah started whining.

"How was school today?" Dani asked.

"I thought Brad was going to pick us up," Becca said.

"He's gone," Jack blurted out. "So just shut up."

Dani shot him a quieting glare. "Jack, there's no need to—"

"He died?"

Glancing in the rearview mirror, Dani could see Becca's eyes widen and fill with tears. She pulled the car over to the curb and twisted in her seat, reaching back to grab Becca's hand. "Oh, no, honey. Brad went home. To Montana. Remember when he told us about his ranch? That's where he went. His father had an accident and he had to go back and help on his ranch."

"When's he coming back?"

"I don't think he is. His vacation is over. He had a good time here in Seattle, but he has a home in Montana. But guess what? Pretty soon Tom is going to be back. He lives in the apartment across the hall and I'm sure he's looking forward to meeting you."

"But I like Brad better."

"I know, sweetie. But sometimes people will go in and out of your life. Just because they're gone doesn't mean we have to forget about them. Even though we don't see them, we can keep them in our hearts and in our memories."

"Like Mommy," Becca said. "And Daddy."

"That's different," Jack said. "They're dead. We're

never going to see Mom and Dad again, and I bet we're never going to see Brad again, either.''

Jack turned to Dani and waited for her reply. But Dani didn't have one. In Becca's eyes, Brad was gone. And whether he was dead or living in Montana, it didn't make a difference. The little girl would mourn his absence just the same.

"Maybe when we get home, we'll write Brad a nice long letter and thank him for everything he did for us. Then we'll ask Alexandra at the day care for his address and we'll put it in the mail.''

"Can I send him a picture of me?''

"You sure can, sweetie.''

Satisfied that she'd calmed Becca's upset, Dani turned her attention back to the road, concentrating on the traffic. She knew this was going to be difficult for them all. But Dani suspected that the temptation to call him would be the most difficult of all. What would she do after the children went to bed? Who would she talk to about the problems of the day?

She shook the thoughts out of her head and turned to more immediate matters. "So what are we going to have for supper tonight? How about hamburgers?''

She spent the rest of the ride home trying to engage Jack and Becca in conversation about school. But neither one of them seemed interested in talking about anything but Brad Cullen. They discussed the camping trip and their first outing to the Space Needle, and how Brad was so funny and so smart and so cool. By the time they got back to the apartment, Dani was seriously wondering why she hadn't accepted his marriage proposal since he seemed like the perfect man.

Louie was working in the lobby when they came in. "Hey, Miss O'Malley. Hey, kids.''

"Hi, Louie-Louie," Becca said, slapping his hand as she passed. "Did you know that Brad went home?"

"Yeah, he stopped by and gave me the keys. I was sorry to see him go. Now I've gotta take care of that darn cat."

"I'll feed the cat," Dani said. "I've got a key for Tom's place and maybe the kids would be interested in helping."

"Good," he said. "And Jack, I've got your skateboard fixed. It just needed a new screw on the wheel bracket. It's on my workbench downstairs. You can run down and get it."

"Thanks, Louie," Dani said as Jack took off down the stairs. "I don't know what we'd do without you."

"A messenger stopped by while you were gone. The envelope is in my apartment."

"Great." Dani set Noah down and let him run around the lobby with Becca. "I'm expecting something about a new job." She hadn't told Louie yet about her plan to find a bigger place. That all depended on what happened with the custody hearing.

Dani couldn't imagine going back to her old life, to a lonely apartment and a twenty-four-hour a-day career. She used to think that she had it all, but now, looking back, she knew that what she had was pretty superficial. There was more to life than luxury sedans and designer suits and first-class travel. There was the warmth and happiness of a real family.

"I think it's from your lawyer," Louie said

Apprehension shot through her. Why wouldn't her lawyer have called? Unless it was bad news. Dani chided herself for thinking the worst. She had to follow her own advice. Think positively, she repeated silently. "I'm going to take the children upstairs. Can you send Jack up after he gets his skateboard?"

"Sure thing."

Dani grabbed Noah's hand and led him to the elevator, then stepped inside. Becca followed and pushed the button. As soon as they got upstairs, Dani unlocked the door, set Noah down and went right to the sofa. She ripped open the envelope and pulled out a sheaf of papers, then scanned them quickly.

As she read, she held her breath, trying to keep her emotions under control. The custody hearing had been set for three weeks from tomorrow. A family court judge in Portland would decide whether she or the Wilsons would raise Evie Gregory's children. She reread the cover letter, then dropped the sheets on the floor in front of her. Tears filled her eyes, but this time she didn't try to contain her emotions. This time, she let the tears flow.

If Brad were here, he'd know how to calm her fears. He'd gather her into his arms and speak to her softly, reassuring her that everything would be just fine. But he wasn't here, and Dani would be forced to face her fears on her own.

CHAPTER ELEVEN

THE COURTROOM WAS SILENT, the shuffling of papers the only sound in the large, wood-paneled room. Dani held her breath, waiting for Judge Devoe to speak, wondering what was going through her mind.

"Deciding custody can sometimes be a very difficult task for me. I don't always have two decent and obviously qualified parties to choose from. It's clear that Ms. O'Malley cares deeply for these children, and though she is single, I don't believe that should affect her ability to love and raise these children. As for Mr. and Mrs. Wilson, their desire to raise her brother's children is certainly no less important. They are, after all, blood relatives. So, I am left to make a decision that will determine the future of three children who have already borne more sorrow and tragedy than any child deserves, and I'd like to be sure that I don't compound those tragedies by making a mistake. I'd like to hear from each of the parties and then I'll speak with the children in chambers."

Dani glanced over at her attorney and forced a smile. The custody hearing had started over an hour ago and she'd sat patiently as the two lawyers presented each side. There were times when it seemed as if no sane human being would take the children away from her. And then there had been other times when Dani had been certain she'd lose them. The judge had questioned her about her social life, her plans to start her own ad agency, her schedule with the children, anything and everything that might affect Jack, Becca and Noah. And now she had a chance to speak. "What should I say?"

Elizabeth reached out and patted her hand. "Just speak from the heart."

"Mr. and Mrs. Wilson, let's begin with you. Why do you believe I should award you custody of these children?"

Lucille Wilson squirmed in her seat, and when her husband started to speak, she gave him a jab with her elbow. "These children are my only blood relatives," she said. "My younger brother, John, married Evie Gregory against the family wishes. He rarely saw my parents after that, yet when they died, they left him an inheritance because he'd given them grandchildren. They didn't leave me anything. I hadn't given them grandchildren. It's only fair that they live with me. That's what Evie had planned from the start. She only changed her mind after that woman there paid her a visit and talked her into it."

Lucille's lawyer reached out and touched her elbow, then whispered something to her. Lucille nodded her head and continued. "We want to raise these children. We can give them a stable home with a mother *and* a father. They belong with us."

"Thank you, Mrs. Wilson. Ms. O'Malley, we'll hear from you now."

Dani pushed up from her seat and cleared her throat. She'd made hundreds of presentations before business associates without even a tiny flutter of nerves. But now the butterflies in her stomach had turned to bulldozers. She drew a deep breath and clutched her hands in front of her to keep them from shaking. "Evie Gregory was my best friend. From the very first time we met there was a…a bond between us. And even though we had been separated by time and distance, that bond was still there. I feel that very same bond with her children, more and more every day. For them, I can keep her memory alive. I can raise them the way that she would have raised them.''

For a moment Dani paused, trying to marshall the surge of emotion that brought tears to her eyes. ''I didn't have a very happy childhood. I never knew my father and my mother died when I was very young. I understand what these children are going through, the fear and the uncertainty. I think I can help them through this all, and maybe that's why Evie made me their guardian. I just want the chance to try.'' She forced a smile. ''I wasn't sure I'd be able to be a good mother, but I know now that I will. I love these children, Judge, and I'll do my very best to make them happy. That's all.''

She sat down and breathed a quiet sigh of relief. Her words had been honest and heartfelt, much more so than Lucille Wilson's almost bitter diatribe. And the judge seemed to have spent a lot of time on Evie's mental condition when she changed her will, citing affidavits from the hospice workers that attested to the fact that she was quite lucid until the last few days of her life. Dani felt a small measure of confidence, a sense that maybe things were going her way.

The judge grabbed up her papers, then stood. ''All right. I'd like to speak to the children. Ms. O'Malley, would you bring them to my chamber. Mr. and Mrs. Wilson, you and your attorney may be present, but I don't want either party putting any pressure on these children. You will not speak to them during our conversation or interrupt with comments of your own. Is that understood?''

''Yes, Your Honor,'' both lawyers said in tandem.

''Then let's go,'' the judge said.

Dani stood and hurried back down the center aisle of the courtroom. She found the children outside in the hall, sitting with Tom Hopson. All of them, including Tom, looked worried.

"Is it over?" Jack asked.

"No. The judge would like to see you now. She wants to talk to you and Becca."

Tom stood, reaching out to take her hand and give it a squeeze. Though Dani longed for Brad's strength and presence, Tom was trying to be a good substitute. "How did it go?"

"All right," Dani said. "I think it will be good. I hope."

Tom gathered her into his arms and gave her a fierce hug. She felt Becca's fingers tangled around hers and she looked down at the little girl and smiled.

"What should we say?" Becca whispered.

Dani drew away from Tom, then knelt in front of Becca and smoothed her hand over her hair. "Just say what you feel, honey. Tell the truth. She may ask you some questions, but you don't need to be scared. She's a very nice lady and she just wants what's best for you."

Five minutes later they were all gathered in the judge's chamber. The adults sat in the back of the room, with Jack and Becca in the leather-covered guest chairs near the desk. Noah toddled around the floor, picking up bits of fuzz from the carpet and handing them to Dani.

The judge glanced between Becca and Jack. "Well, I've certainly heard a lot of wonderful things about you two. I've heard how Dani feels and how your aunt and uncle feel. Now I want to hear from you. Becca, tell me about your time with Dani."

Becca clutched her hands in front of her and put on her most brilliant smile. "When we came to her house, we were sad. I was scared. Noah cried. Jack was mad. Then things got better. I went to school and now I have lots of friends."

She drew a quick breath, then glanced back at Dani. "Is that all right?"

Dani nodded, careful not to speak. Becca risked a look over at Lucille Wilson, only to find her aunt glaring at her coldly. She quickly turned back around.

"What do you do with Dani?"

"She reads me books and we play Barbies sometimes. And we went camping with Brad and her."

"Who's Brad?"

"He lived across the hall, but now he's gone. He was our friend. He took us to school and we played poker. And once, he even kissed Dani."

A rush of heat flooded Dani's cheeks. Jack poked Becca in the arm and gave her a silencing glare, and a look of confusion came over the little girl's face. "Now Tom lives there. Jack says he's gay, but I think he's funny. He buys us presents and tells Dani that she has to get her hair fixed. I think Dani looks pretty just the way she is."

A tiny smile quirked the judge's lips as she turned to Jack. "Why don't you tell me how you feel, Jack?"

Dani held her breath, wondering if Jack would express anger or frustration, if he'd accuse her of not being a good mother. But as he began to speak, Dani was taken by how carefully he measured his words. "When my mom died, I was mad. When we went to live with Dani, I was still mad. But she let me be that way. She didn't try to make me all happy. She knew it was all right to feel bad and that it was up to me to decide when I didn't want to feel bad, anymore."

"And how do you feel now?" the judge asked.

"A little better. I still miss my mom. But Dani found a bunch of pictures and we put them in an album. And we look at it a lot and talk about my mom. Aunt Lucille doesn't like my mom, and I don't think she'd want to talk about her.''

"That's not true!" Lucille shouted. "I just thought the children would get upset!''

Lucille's lawyer shushed her, warning her that the judge might ask them to leave. But Lucille continued to mutter to herself, angry at the perceived insult.

"Dani is a good mom. She takes care of us. Sometimes it's hard but she always tries her best. I know she loves us and we love her. We should live with her because it's the best place.''

A tear trickled down Dani's cheek and she brushed it away. She knew how difficult it was for Jack to express his feelings, and the true depth of them stunned her. Even though he acted as if she was the worst kind of mother, he felt differently, and that's all that mattered. Even if she did lose custody, maybe she'd managed to do some good in the time they'd spent with her.

"Thank you, Jack. You and your brother and sister can go now while I talk to the grown-ups.''

When they had rejoined Tom outside, the judge slowly closed the file folder on her desk. "Usually, I take time to think these cases through, but I know this will only cause more distress for these children. Eve Gregory appointed Danielle O'Malley as her children's guardian. There has been nothing presented here today that makes me believe she made a bad decision or that she wasn't completely in her right mind when she made it. Ms. O'Malley has given these children the space to grieve, and as a parent, that is the very best thing she could have done for them. Mr. Wilson, I'm not sure that you even care about becoming a father. From what I've seen, you're going along with this because your wife wants it. And Mrs. Wilson, I get the distinct feeling that this is not all about the welfare of these three children. I get the feeling that this might have more to do with some imagined slight that you feel over your parents' will. You have not given me any good reason to dispute Ms. O'Malley's guardianship.''

"But she's teaching those children to gamble. And she's got men in and out of her life. One of them is even gay!''

"And there is no evidence that this has caused any harm to these children. I'm ruling for Ms. O'Malley in this matter. Her custody of the Gregory children has been upheld. Ms. O'Malley, you may take the children home and get on with your lives with my best wishes.''

With a tiny cry of delight, Dani jumped up and gave Elizabeth a hug. "I have to tell the children.''

"Go,'' her lawyer said. "Take them home. We'll talk when you get back to Seattle.''

When she found them in the hall, Becca was sobbing softly and Tom was trying to console her. Jack sat with Noah on his lap, staring ahead silently. When they heard her footsteps, they all turned. "You're staying with me,'' Dani cried. "The judge decided that you can live with me!''

With a cry of delight, Becca jumped up and ran into Dani's outstretched arms. Jack smiled crookedly, then joined them in the embrace, holding Noah up in his arms. When they'd all been thoroughly hugged, Dani walked over to Tom and kissed him on the cheek. "Thanks for staying with us. Having you here was such a great help.''

"Now that it's decided, what are you going to do?'' Tom asked.

"I'm taking my children home,'' Dani replied with a laugh.

"That's not what I mean.''

She nodded. "I've been thinking about him, thinking about how much I wished he was here with me. How much I want to share this with him. If it hadn't been for Brad,

I'm not sure I would have ever realized that this was what I wanted or needed. He showed me that I could be a mother to these children. I owe him so much.''

"Then call him and tell him.''

Dani drew a deep breath and smiled. "Maybe I will. Just to say hi. But right now, I want to get back to the hotel, gather up our things and go home. If we leave right away, we can be home by dinner.''

Tom took Becca's hand and started down the hall, and Jack followed with Noah. Dani stood, watching them, thinking how the picture seemed somehow incomplete. Brad belonged here with them. Everything in her heart told her so. But then she was reminded that he had his life in Montana. He'd given her a choice and she'd made it. Now it was time to move on, to begin her life with her new family.

She followed her family to the parking lot and got in the car, allowing Tom to drive. She sat in the front seat, staring out the window, her mind still occupied with thoughts of Brad. Now that she had everything she'd ever wanted, Dani realized that it wasn't everything. She still wanted Brad.

"Tell me the story again,'' Becca said from the back seat. "About how the judge said we can stay with you forever.''

Dani laughed, then twisted around to smile at her. "The judge said you belong to me and I belong to you. And in a few months, we'll go to another judge and ask her if I can adopt you and you'll officially be my family.''

"And what will my name be?''

"Well, that's up to you. You can continue to be Rebecca Gregory, or you can be Becca Gregory O'Malley. Or you can be Becca O'Malley Gregory.''

"And I can call you Mommy?''

"Or you can call me Dani,'' she said. "We'll work that all out as we go along.''

"I'm so happy.''

"And so am I. What about you Jack? Are you happy?"

"Brad should be here," he said.

Dani hesitated, trying to come up with an appropriate response to his comment. "He'd probably like to know what happened. Maybe you could write him a letter."

"Or maybe we could go see him," Becca suggested. "I know where he lives. It's called Skip Rocks. And it's in some state that's two states that way," she said, pointing to her right. "He showed me on a map."

"Sweetie, Brad has lots of work at Split Rock. He probably wouldn't have time for us."

"Yes he would. He loves us. He said so."

"He did?" Dani asked.

Becca nodded. "Sometimes, when he'd drop me off at school, he'd say, 'Bye, Becca, love you,' and I would say, 'Love you, too.' Didn't he say it to you?"

"Yes," Dani replied. "He did say it to me."

"Then it must be true. Brad said, 'Never tell a lie.'" Becca glanced out of the car window. "Can we stop at McDonald's? I'm hungry."

"Sure. We'll pick up drive-thru and take it back to the hotel," Dani told her, thinking about what Becca had said. Brad had loved the children, and he'd loved her. He'd said the words, but even more important, he'd showed her his love in all that he'd done for her and the children. She'd been silly to dismiss his feelings, just because she wasn't sure of her own.

She'd doubted her own ability to love, but there was no doubt that she loved the children, with every ounce of her being. So why couldn't she…" "Stop the car," Dani said.

"What?"

"Do it. Stop the car!"

Tom pulled over to the curb and Dani hopped out. She hurried down the sidewalk, her breathing coming in short gasps. For a moment, she thought she was about to faint, and she bent over, bracing her hands on her knees. A few seconds later, Tom joined her.

"What's wrong?" he asked, bending down to peer at her face.

"Nothing. I—I can't breathe."

"Are you all right?"

Dani gulped in another breath. "I—I love him," she said, letting the realization sink in. "I do. I love him. I didn't realize it until just now, but I need him. He belongs in our life."

"Who?" Tom asked.

"Brad! I love him and I'm not going to stop. No matter how hard I try, it's not going to go away."

Now that she'd said it out loud, it wasn't frightening anymore. It was real and intense and so overwhelming that she felt dizzy. Though she'd tried to imagine a future without him, the effort had been half-hearted at best. Every time the phone rang, she expected it to be him. Every time there was a hang-up on her machine, Dani imagined that he'd called. And each morning, she'd waited for him to knock on the door and walk inside, ready to take the children to school.

Why was she waiting for him to make the first move? She'd never been one to sit back and wait passively for something she wanted. She went out and made it happen! And if she wanted Brad Cullen in their lives, then she'd have to take the initiative. And now was as good a time as any.

"We have to go," Dani said.

"Right." Tom agreed. "Back to Seattle. Home."

"No. We have to go to Montana. We're going back to the hotel and I'm going to pack our things and we're going to drive to Montana tonight."

"Are you sure?"

"Yes. And you're going to have to find another way home. We can drop you at the airport and you can rent a car." Dani hurried back to the car and got inside. "We're going on a little trip. When we get back to the hotel, I want you to pack all your things as fast as you can."

"Where are we going?" Jack asked.

"Camping," Dani replied. "In Montana."

"But we don't have our tent and our sleeping bags," Jack said. "Isn't Montana a long way away? What about school?"

"We may miss a little school. I'll call your teachers once we get there."

A grin slowly suffused Jack's expression. "No school. Cool."

Dani opened her purse and grabbed her day planner and her cell phone, searching through it for Alexandra Webber's phone number.

"Who are you calling?"

"Brad's cousin. I have to find out how to get to the ranch."

"I know how to get there," Tom said. "We used to go there all the time when we were in college. There's good climbing not too far from his parents' place. Hey, I could drive you."

"No, I have to do this on my own. How long will it take to get there?"

"I don't know," Tom said. "You have to drive all the way across Washington, across the top of Idaho and then through part of Montana. You'll probably get there sometime early tomorrow morning. Unless you stop along the way to sleep."

"I don't want to," Becca chimed in from the back seat. "I want to get there right away. I want to tell Brad our good news."

"Me, too, sweetie," Dani said. But that wasn't all she wanted to tell Brad Cullen. She was ready to tell him so much more—that she loved him, that she wanted him to be a part of her family, and that she wanted to spend the rest of her life with him, even if that life was in Montana. For wherever Brad was, that was home.

THE MORNING SUN was barely above the horizon, the low light illuminating the yard near the horse barns. "All right," Brad shouted. "Give it a try."

J.T. flipped the ignition of the pickup and the engine turned over but didn't catch. Brad leaned over the front fender and made another adjustment. "Again," he called. "Give it a little gas. But don't flood it."

"It's not going to start," J.T. said, leaning his head out the window.

"All right," Brad said to his brother. "Get out."

They stood in the dusty drive and stared at the fully-loaded horse trailer.

"So what do you think?" J.T. asked. "Can we move that thing without unloading the horses?"

"There are four horses in there," Brad said. "I think we're going to have to unload them."

J.T. groaned. The horses, unused to the trailer, had been hard enough to coax up the ramp. They'd be even more skittish backing down it. "Mac said he'd be stopping by," he said. "Maybe we should wait and get his help."

"This is our operation now, J.T. You and I are going to have to do this ourselves."

"Our operation," J.T. repeated. "That's a little hard to believe. I never thought I'd see the day that Walt Cullen walked away from Split Rock."

"I think it's gotten to be too much for him," Brad said. "That's why he was putting so much pressure on me. I can see him down in Arizona with a little spread of his own. He's always wanted to raise Arabians. Now maybe he'll have the chance.'' Brad pointed to the trailer. ''Come on, let's get them out of there. We don't get paid until these horses arrive in Colorado.''

''And I do want to get on the road,'' J.T. said. ''There's this pretty little thing that I met in Fort Collins the last time I was there.''

Brad strode to the back of the trailer and opened the doors, speaking softly to the horses as he did. ''Come on, come on.'' He grabbed a bridle and stood beside the bay, smoothing his palm over her chest as he pushed her back. ''That's right.''

When he had the horse out of the trailer, J.T. hooked a lead onto the bridle and led the mare over to the corral. But as Brad walked back inside the trailer, his little brother shouted to him, ''Are you expecting visitors?''

''No. Why?''

''There's a car comin' up the road. Black. Looks like a BMW. Who the hell has a car like that around these parts?''

Brad froze, his hand gripping the bridle. Dani had a black BMW. He shook his head. Wishful thinking. He'd love nothing more than for Dani to drive up to the house and jump out of the car. But fantasies had nothing to do with reality. She hadn't made any effort to contact him since he'd left Seattle, nor had he tried calling her.

On his long drive back to Montana, he'd decided that Dani would have to come to terms with her own feelings. He knew he loved her, and though he expected the feelings to fade with time and distance, they hadn't. But he couldn't spend a lifetime trying to convince her she felt the same. She would have to come to him.

He'd waited for nearly a month, satisfying himself with brief little bits of news from Alex and Tom. But neither one of them wanted to get in the middle of what they both saw as a finished relationship.

"It's a woman," J.T. said, carrying on a running commentary. "And it looks like she's got a few kids with her. She's stopping...now she's getting out of the car." He let out a low whistle. "Wow. She's a looker. What a babe."

Drawing a deep breath, Brad allowed himself a tiny bit of hope. He tugged off his work gloves and shoved them into his pocket. When he stepped out of the trailer, his breath caught in his throat. Dani stood in front of her car, the children gathered around her.

"Brad!" Becca shouted his name, then crossed the distance between them and threw herself into his arms. He picked her up and spun her around, causing her to squeal and giggle with glee.

"Hey, Bec. What are you doing here?"

Jack ventured forward, a hesitant smile brightening his expression. "We came to go camping. But we didn't bring our gear."

"I've got all the gear we need," Brad said, reaching out to clasp his shoulder. "There are some really great spots I want to show you. You're going to love Split Rock."

He slowly walked toward Dani, his gaze fixed on her face. Her image had drifted in and out of his mind since he'd left Seattle, and now that she was here, he realized his memories didn't do her justice. She took his breath away. Dressed in jeans and a canvas jacket, she almost looked like she fit in at Split Rock. Her sun-kissed hair was pulled into a haphazard ponytail, and Brad's fingers itched as he imagined removing the elastic and letting it fall to her shoulders. Though she smiled at him, he wasn't able to see her eyes behind her sunglasses.

"You're here," he said, unable to keep from smiling back. He was almost afraid to ask why, hoping that she'd come for all the right reasons, that she was here to begin their life together rather than put an end to it.

"I'm here," she replied, removing her sunglasses and looking up into his gaze.

"I'm glad," Brad said. He reached out and wove his fingers through the hair at her nape, then pulled her close to brush a kiss across her lips. "God, it's good to see you. I've missed you so much."

She reached up hesitantly and smoothed her hand along his cheek. "I—I've missed you, too."

"Tell Brad our news!" Becca cried. "Tell him, tell him."

Dani smiled. "You tell him, sweetie."

"We're a family. Dani is going to be our mom. Not our real mom but our adap—adot—"

"Adoptive mom," Dani said. She glanced up at Brad. "I won the custody suit. The children are staying with me."

Brad drew her into a hug. "I'm so glad. See? I told you everything would work out."

"You did," she said.

"Where are the horses?" Jack asked "How many horses do you have?"

"He's been asking about horses during the entire trip. I'm afraid I wasn't able to give him much information."

Brad tore his gaze from Dani. "J.T., come on over here." His brother jogged up, then pulled his hat from his head. "J.T., this is Dani O'Malley. And these are her children, Jack, Rebecca and Noah. Dani, my youngest brother, J.T."

J.T. yanked off his glove and held out his hand. "Nice to meet you, ma'am. I can't say I've heard a lot about you, but I'm sure I will. Brad plays his cards pretty close to the vest, although I can see why, considering how pretty you are."

"It's nice to meet you, too, J.T."

From the look in his younger brother's eyes, Brad could already tell that J.T. was smitten. "J.T., why don't you take the kids over to the stables and show them the horses. Answer all of Jack's questions and keep a close eye on the little ones. And then take them up to meet Mom. She'll make breakfast for them. Noah likes juice and toast, Jack likes waffles and Becca likes cereal."

"Come on, kids," J.T. said, scooping Noah up into his arms. "Let's go see the horses."

"I love horses!" Becca said. "I have My Pretty Pony."

"You have a horse?" J.T. asked.

"It's a not a horse, it's a pony," Becca explained. "A pony is like a horse, only smaller."

"It's a plastic toy with pink hair," Jack explained. "Can you ride these horses or are they just for looking at?"

"We ride 'em all the time," J.T. said. "Maybe later I can teach you to ride. You look like you could handle yourself pretty well on a horse."

"Cool," Jack said.

Brad and Dani watched as the children wandered away with J.T. Then Brad turned to her, grabbed her around the waist and pulled her into a fierce hug. When he was certain she was real, and not just some figment of his imagination, he stepped back, took her face between his hands and kissed her. His mouth covered hers and he drank in her taste like a man who had been caught in the desert for too long without water.

When he pulled back, he looked down into Dani's eyes. "I'm glad you're here."

"I wasn't sure if you would be. I didn't want to call in case you told me not to come. After the custody hearing I just decided to get in the car and drive."

"Come on," he said. "I want to take you somewhere." He grabbed her hand and pulled her toward the back porch where he'd tied Riot after his morning ride. Brad grabbed the horse's reins, then held out his hand to Dani.

"You want me to get up on that horse?" she asked.

"Don't worry. I'm going to sit right behind you. You won't fall."

"Camping was a stretch. I'm not sure I'm ready to ride a horse."

"Trust me," Brad said.

She wrapped her fingers around the saddle horn and slipped her foot into the stirrup. In one smooth motion, Brad helped her settle herself into the saddle, then quickly swung up behind her. With a click of Brad's tongue, Riot walked slowly out of the yard.

Brad steered the horse toward a rocky outcropping about a half mile west of the ranch house. He unbuttoned his jacket as they rode, wrapping it around Dani to keep her warm. She leaned back against him, her head resting on his shoulder.

"Where are we going?"

"Someplace where we can be alone," Brad said.

Dani laughed. "Somehow, when I thought about that very moment, I didn't imagine a horse and weather near freezing."

"What did you imagine? Silk bedcoverings and freshly laundered sheets?"

"Maybe," Dani said. "Or a nice restaurant with a good bottle of wine."

He kicked Riot into a slow gallop and Dani screamed as she bounced around in the saddle. But Brad held on to her and taught her how to move with the horse. Before long, she had become more comfortable in the saddle and he increased their speed.

When they reached the outcropping, Brad helped her off the horse, then grabbed her hand and pulled her along beside him. They climbed up through the rocks on a path that he'd cleared when he was a kid. And when they reached the top, he helped Dani to stand on a broad, flat table of stone, covered with carved letters.

From that spot, they could look in all four directions for miles and miles. Below them, the ranch house sat among a grove of trees. They could see the children walking back to the house with J.T. To the west were the mountains, to the east a wide vista of rolling hills.

"It's beautiful," Dani said.

"This is Split Rock. Legend says that the rock was split by lightning a couple hundred years ago. But I'm not sure that's even possible. All I know is that every person who has ever owned or worked this land has chiseled their initials into this rock at one time or another." He bent down and pointed to some letters. "W.C. and M.R.W. Walt Cullen and Mary Rose Williams. My parents put their name in the rock on their tenth wedding anniversary. And here's Ray Cullen and Delores Parker. They're my grandparents. They bought this ranch from Deke Anderson. His initials are over here."

Brad pointed to a spot near his left foot.

"D.O. plus B.C." Dani read the inscription carved into the stone inside a heart. "Did you do that?"

He nodded. "The first day I was back I came out here. I guess I chiseled our initials into the rock because I wanted to believe you'd come."

"And if I hadn't?"

"Then I would have turned them into a nice little carving of a horse, I guess."

She reached down and ran her fingers over the letters. "It must have taken you a while."

"It's going to be here for years. Probably long after we're gone." He took her hands and pressed them between his.

"Dani, I don't ever want to be apart from you again. The last month has been hell. I haven't been able to stop thinking about you and the children. I didn't sleep, I couldn't concentrate on work. All I wanted was to have you close again. You and the children. Nothing has changed. I still want you to marry me."

"I have custody of the children. We don't have to get married."

"Yes, we do," Brad said. "I love you and you love me, and with the kids, we can make a family together."

She paused, staring down at the letters he'd chiseled in the stone. "I do love you, Brad. I know that now. And I was hoping you'd ask me again."

"And why is that?"

"So that this time, I could say yes?" Her slow smile warmed Brad's heart and he tipped his head back and laughed, the sound echoing into the distance. Then he wrapped his arms around her and kissed her again, knowing full well that this wouldn't be the last time. It was only the first of many kisses…and many days…and years that they'd share together.

"So what do you think of Montana?" he asked.

Dani took a deep breath of the crisp, clean air. "I think it's beautiful. A good place for a new start. Jack would do so well here. And I'd never have to worry about Noah running across a busy street or being kidnapped at the shopping mall. And Becca would have plenty of handsome cowboys to choose from once she starts to date."

"This place is mine now," Brad said. "Mine and J.T.'s. My dad and mom are moving down to Arizona in a few months. I want it to be ours."

"I'd like that," Dani said.

"We have a big house, but if you don't like it, I was thinking maybe we'd build a house for ourselves right over that rise.'' He pointed to the west. ''My brother Mac builds log homes. I think he could build us a nice one in a pretty grove of aspens over there. A new house for our new life together.''

''I think that would be the perfect place for us,'' Dani said. She slipped her arms around his waist. ''You know, we really should ask the children if this is all right with them.'' She paused. ''I think it's important that we at least let them voice their opinion.''

''Then let's do it now. Are you ready to get back on that horse again?''

Dani nodded. ''I'm ready to go anywhere you want to take me.''

''There is one thing I worry about,'' he admitted, dropping a kiss on her lips. ''What will you find to do here in Montana?''

She sent him a sly grin. ''Well, since this really isn't the best spot for an advertising agency, I hear there's this horse rancher that doesn't like to do book work. I thought I might be able to help him out. I'm a really good businesswoman. I bet, with the proper marketing strategy, I could double his business in three years. I've got some charts in the car if you're interested,'' she teased.

''We'll have plenty of time to go over your charts,'' Brad said. He nuzzled her neck and growled playfully. ''Later. Much, much later.''

''YOU LOOK SO PRETTY,'' Becca said.

Dani stared at her reflection in the wide mirror over the sink, tucking a loose strand of hair into the casual French knot at the nape of her neck. Fresh rosebuds and baby's breath had been slipped into her hair in lieu of a veil, and Dani had to admit that Becca was right. She looked like a blushing bride.

Just three months ago, she had been a single woman with a busy career. Then the children had arrived and she'd learned to be a mother. And now, on New Year's Eve in a Seattle courthouse, she was about to become a bride.

She turned to Becca and bent down. "And you look pretty, too, honey. Do you like your new dress? Are you ready to be my maid of honor?"

Becca nodded. "When you hand me your flowers, I'm supposed to hold on to them. And when you ask for them back, then I'm supposed to give them to you."

"Good. And when the judge says, who gives this woman to marry this man, you say…"

"We do!" Becca jumped up and down, her curls bouncing along with her. "And what does the best man do?"

"Well, Jack has to hold on to the rings. And when the judge asks for them, he has to give them to us."

"And what about Noah?"

"Noah gets to throw the bird seed on the courthouse steps."

"He's going to throw bird seeds?"

"People used to throw rice at the bride and groom, but it was dangerous for the birds to eat. Now people throw bird seed, and afterward, all the little birds get a wedding feast."

"But they don't get to go on a honeymoon to Disney World like us."

"No, they don't." Dani smoothed her hands over her simple white suit then picked up her bouquet of pink roses from the edge of the sink. "I think I'm ready to get married. How about you?"

"Everybody's here. Brad's brothers and sister, his mommy and daddy and our new cousins. And Tom is here. And Alex and…" Becca frowned. "Who else?"

"That's all," Dani said. "Just the very most important people in our lives."

She opened the door and they left the courthouse bathroom and walked slowly through the marble-lined halls to the judge's chamber, their footsteps echoing through the quiet building. Brad had asked her if she wanted a traditional wedding, but Dani had never had dreams of a candlelit church and a fancy white dress. When she thought about her wedding to Brad, she thought about the children as well, and giving them something simple they could all share.

Brad, Jack and Noah, along with the rest of the guests, were waiting in the judge's chamber when she walked in. Tom came up and gave her a kiss on the cheek. "For once, I don't mind not being the prettiest person in the room," he teased.

Dani laughed, then slowly walked toward Brad. Her soon-to-be husband was in the midst of straightening Jack's tie, but when he saw her, he stopped and grinned, their gazes meeting. Dani's heart fluttered and she pressed her hand to her chest. She hoped the feeling would never stop, the excitement of seeing him again after a day apart.

Though they weren't having a traditional wedding, Brad had insisted on a few conventional ideas. He'd spent the previous night with Noah and Jack at Tom Hopson's apartment, away from his bride. He'd rented separate limousines to take them to and from the courthouse, so he hadn't seen her before the wedding. And after the wedding, they'd pack up her apartment before leaving for Disney World.

"Are we all here?" Judge Marlene Devoe stepped into the room, wearing her long robes and carrying a small black book.

Dani took her place beside Brad, motioning Becca to stand next to her. Jack held on to Noah's hand and looked as if he were taking his duties very seriously. Behind them, the judge's secretary and court clerk had joined the guests.

Brad took her hand and gave it a squeeze. "You look beautiful," he said.

She brushed her hand over the fine navy wool of his suit. "And you look very handsome."

The judge cleared her throat and they both turned to look at her.

"Before I begin, I'd like to say that performing this marriage ceremony gives me particular pleasure. It's not often I get to do two of my favorite things at the same time. First, I'd like to ask if anyone here has any objections to this marriage."

"No!" Jack and Becca cried in unison.

"No!" Noah added.

The Judge Devoe looked at Brad and then Dani. "I think we're clear to proceed," Dani said.

"Dearly beloved, we are gathered here today to unite this man and this woman in matrimony."

Dani always heard that brides and grooms barely remembered the wedding ceremony, that it passed by in a blur. But she was aware of every word. Her marriage was going to last a lifetime, and when she promised herself to Brad and when he promised himself to her, their vows would be kept.

"Do you, Danielle O'Malley, take this man, Brad Cullen, to be your husband?"

"I do," Dani said, gazing up into Brad's eyes. She remembered the very first time she'd looked into those eyes, that evening on the street in front of her apartment building. It had seemed like just yesterday, and yet her life had completely changed in that time. She'd experienced more love in these three months with Brad and the children than she had in all the rest of her life. And every day of the future would be filled with more of the same.

"And do you, Brad Cullen, take this woman, Danielle O'Malley, to be your wife?"

"I do," Brad said, his gaze like a caress to her face.

"May we have the rings, please."

Nervously, Jack fumbled in his pocket, then dropped Brad's ring on the floor. But Noah picked it up and handed it to Dani, a wide grin on his face. "My little ring-bearer," she said, ruffling his hair.

They exchanged rings, and before Dani knew it, the judge was pronouncing them husband and wife and demanding that Brad kiss his bride.

But before he did, Brad took her face between his hands and pressed his forehead to hers. "I love you, Dani. Now and forever."

"And I love you, Brad. Now and forever."

He covered her lips with his in a kiss so tender that Dani had to blink back her tears. And when he stepped away, Jack and Becca and Noah burst into applause, offering their hoots and screams as a substitute for good wishes. Brad's family gathered around them, and when she playfully tossed her bouquet, Tom pretended to fight for it before gallantly handing it to Brad's sister.

"And now, we have another ceremony that's just as important," the judge said in a serious tone. "And I need to ask each of you children an important question. Jack and Rebecca and Noah Gregory, I'm here today to preside over your adoption by Brad and Danielle Cullen. This is a very solemn occasion and one that I take very seriously. Do you promise to be good children, to respect your parents and to listen to what they say? Do you promise to go to them with your problems and to trust that they know what's best for you?"

"We do," Becca and Jack said.

"And so does Noah," Jack added.

"And Brad and Danielle Cullen, do you promise to be good parents, to respect your children and to listen to what they say? Do you promise to help them with their problems and always try to do what's best for them?"

"We do," Brad and Dani promised.

"Then, it is my honor to pronounce you…a family."

Dani bent down and gave Becca a hug. Then, while Brad scooped the little girl up in his arms, she gathered Noah and Jack into an embrace. Of all the things to happen to Dani O'Malley, she never in her life thought that she'd have a family to call her own. And now, with this perfect gift from Evie and the love that she shared with Brad, she'd finally found a place in the world. A place where she was loved for who she was.

"I know what my name is going to be!" Becca cried as they signed all the papers making the marriage and the adoption final. "I decided. My name is Rebecca Ann Gregory O'Malley Cullen. But everyone can just call me Becca."

Brad chuckled, then leaned over and gave Dani another kiss, Becca wriggling between them and Noah clinging to his leg. "Should we take our family home to Montana, Mrs. Cullen?"

"I think that would be a very good idea, Mr. Cullen."

As they walked out of the courthouse, Dani helped Noah open a small paper bag filled with birdseed, then passed it along to the other guests. Then she threw a handful up in the air, showing him what to do. Soon, Jack and Becca joined in the fun, and before long, the sparrows fluttered all around them. Dani smiled and stared up at the crystal-blue sky, wondering at the beauty of the day and knowing that, somewhere, Evie Gregory was watching them and laughing.

"I'll raise them well, Evie," she promised. "And I'll never let them forget you."

FORRESTER SQUARE,
a new Harlequin series,
continues in November 2003
with RING OF DECEPTION
by Sandra Marton...

*Detective Luke Sloan was out of his element working
undercover in Forrester Square Daycare. But it
gave him a perfect view of the jewelry exchange
where stolen goods were being fenced—and where
Abby Douglas worked. When Luke first encountered
her and her daughter, Abby's strange reaction had
immediately put her on his list of suspects. But
Luke's beginning to realize that her fear was over
something far more dangerous...*

Here's a preview

CHAPTER ONE

KATHERINE LOOKED PUZZLED, but only for a couple of seconds. Luke could tell the minute she figured out what he meant.

"You think one of our parents or teachers is involved in something criminal."

"I didn't say that."

"You didn't have to. The answer is still the same. No."

Luke wasn't really disappointed. He'd figured she'd turn him down...and she was right. He didn't have any legal grounds for gaining access to her records. Not yet, anyway.

Well, you couldn't blame a man for trying...and he was going to try one last time.

"That's that, then." He started to turn away, then swung toward Katherine. "One last thing," he said casually. "Is Abby Douglas the only parent here who works at Emerald City?"

Katherine smiled blandly. "Does Abby work there? I had no idea."

"You didn't, huh?"

"Is that all, Luke? If it is, I have some calls to make."

"How long has she had her child enrolled here?"

"Ask Ms. Douglas, why don't you?"

"Is she married?"

The words were out before he could call them back. Katherine looked surprised, but she couldn't be any more surprised than he was. He hadn't intended to ask that question. Abby Douglas's marital status had nothing to do with his investigation.

Still, he'd asked. Now he wanted an answer.

"Is she?"

Katherine puffed her cheeks with air, then blew it out.

"As far as I know, she's not."

"Never? Or is there a man—"

"Uh, uh, uh." Katherine wagged her finger at him. "The interview's over, Detective. And if I were you, I'd get as much work done as I could in the next few minutes because—" she looked at her watch, then flashed him a grin "—the next break is only twenty minutes away."

Luke groaned. "What did I do to deserve this?" he said, raising his eyes to the ceiling.

Katherine laughed as the undercover cop headed back to the corner he'd filled with tools, sawhorses and lumber. She didn't want him here, but she was a pretty good judge of character.

Try as he might to appear tough-skinned and hard-hearted, Luke Sloan seemed like a nice guy.

He had a job to do, though, and she hoped that job didn't include anything about Abby Douglas.

From the little she knew about Abby, Katherine had already concluded that Emily's mom had trouble buried somewhere in her past.

The last thing she needed was more.

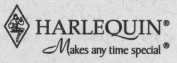

HARLEQUIN Presents

The world's bestselling romance series...
The series that brings you your favorite authors,
month after month:

Helen Bianchin...Emma Darcy
Lynne Graham...Penny Jordan
Miranda Lee...Sandra Marton
Anne Mather...Carole Mortimer
Susan Napier...Michelle Reid

and many more uniquely talented authors!

Wealthy, powerful, gorgeous men...
Women who have feelings just like your own...
The stories you love, set in exotic, glamorous locations...

HARLEQUIN Presents

Seduction and passion guaranteed!